I0831268

The Path of Fire

By Cameron R. E. Senek

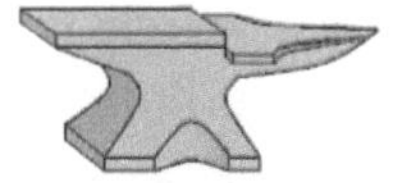

Drop Forge Publishing
Edmonton, Alberta
Canada

ISBN 978-0-9880242-4-3

Cover Graphics Designed by:
Jennifer Lee Graphics Design

Supporting Graphics Designed by:
Chandra Senek

Content Flow and Editing by:
Lonny Robison and Pam Nernberg

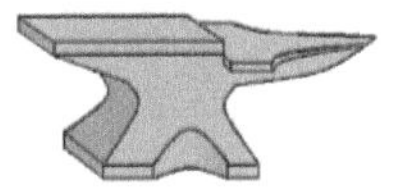

Drop Forge Publishing
Edmonton, Alberta
Canada

First Edition, 2014

Dedications

I would like to begin by dedicating this book to my Aunt Pam. Thank you Aunty Pam for editing both Andraya's Freedom and The Path of Fire. Thanks to your efforts both books are better in their presentation.

Secondly, I'd like to dedicate this book to my cousin Jennifer. I can't thank you enough for your designs adorning the covers of my books. You are an incredible artist.

But I would also like to dedicate this book to my friends. To my oldest friends, such as Dale and Derek, whom I never get to be with enough. To my newest friends Al and Todd for coming up with the idea's for the trials in this adventure. Once again to Lonny for your guidance in the creation of this book. And to my biggest fan, Matt, for encouraging me in everything I do.

But I don't want to forget my lost friends, to Danny and Pete whom we lost so long ago, and to my dear friend Brian, called Home far too early.

And finally my best friend, Chandra. You gave me my children, you comfort me when I'm afraid, and you bring laughter where I can't find any of my own.

But most importantly, I give my most humble thanks to God, for allowing these books to come to paper and for all my life's blessings. All of you give my life meaning and fill my days with joy.

Chapter 1

In the Age of the Eland Civil War

The storm raged as if all of creation was under attack. The winds howled and blew massive trees so hard their tops nearly swept the ground. It hammered against the walls of the small shack, its lone occupant huddled over letters and maps, sighing deeply in the din. His lamp flickered as the rain rolled off the roof and the wind whistled through the cracks in the walls. Austin Ironfist studied the maps before him, trying to determine where his enemies would move to next. The High General of Eland didn't know how, but somehow his enemy always seemed to know what he was going to do, even before he did sometimes.

Suddenly the door to his shelter flew open. As the rain and howling wind came flooding through the opening with abandon, Austin cursed under his breath. He scrambled to grab his papers as they flew across the room, getting pinned against the walls. Surrendering to the wind, he rushed to the door and throwing his weight against it, forced it closed. Latching it, he grabbed the bar and set it to stop it from bursting open again.

Panting, he stood with his face to the door, water dripping from his thick beard and forehead. Austin, a half Dwarf, wasn't as short as his forefathers, but he was twice as thick. His curly black beard and long black hair showed clear the signs of his heritage. The half Dwarf calmed his breathing, and suddenly his senses surged. Without turning he shifted his weight slightly, and as if spurred on by a sudden bolt of lightning, he grabbed his sword from its sheath and swung. The clash of steel on steel echoed in the night, rivaling the shock from the thunder outside.

He was about to swing again when he recognized the silhouette surrounded by shadows. Relaxing a bit he waited for his adversary to make the next move. Suddenly a lilting laughter filled the room as the figure, clothed in a brown cloak with a green hood, lowered and sheathed their sword. Austin followed suit and waited as the new arrival threw back their hood, showing the smiling face of a half Elf woman.

"Chloe," Austin yelled, "I almost took your head off!"

Chloe laughed again and shook the rain from her hair. "No you didn't, Austin. I could sense your stance shifting. I had my sword out before you finished making your mind up as to your next move. You're easy to read."

Chloe Duthain, Princess of the Kingdom of Andraya and sister of King William Duthain, smiled at her friend. The rain glimmered in her dark brown hair, as the shadows accented her delicate Elven features in her face.

"That's my problem these days," Austin sighed, "I seem to be following a battle plan, sent to me by my enemies."

"Don't worry about it Austin," Chloe calmly said. "you've been through battle before, as have both of your adversaries. You just need to think of what they will do, and then react in a way they won't expect."

"So you know the situation here?" he asked. Chloe smiled slightly and nodded. "I should have known. Well that's what I'm trying to do, but it's like they read my mind. Their movements are almost juvenile from a strategic stand point. To be honest, I'd expect this of Duke Wesset, but General Kiamet? The man has as much battle experience as I, but he is strategizing like a green recruit," Austin said, once again looking at the map and pawn pieces scattered across it.

"Well doesn't that work in your favor then?" Chloe asked.

"Sure against anyone else, heck even against Wesset it would make sense. That boy's an idiot, almost as bad as King Marcus. But when a seasoned warrior such as Kiamet makes these moves, it quite frankly makes no sense," Austin explained. "I mean his troop movements are so obvious. He either doesn't take me seriously, is coming at this from a direction I have yet to comprehend, or he has an ace in the hole and his confidence is betraying him."

"Ace in the hole? Do you think he has a secret?" Chloe asked as she grabbed a chair across the table from the General.

"We all do, or rather we all should. Wesset's ace is easy; he has money and some very influential backers in 'The Assembly'. Every aristocrat who wants to keep the status quo is backing him, and many of their wealthiest friends are funding his attempt at the throne.

"Kiamet, I don't know what he's got. But he HAS to have something; it's the only logical reason to behave like he has been. I just don't know what it is." The half Dwarf sighed deeply.

"And yours, Austin? What is your ace in the hole?" Chloe asked quietly, watching her friend struggle with what lay before him.

"Hmm, me? I don't have an ace in the hole. I'm on my own in this," he replied, the strain of the situation etched deeply in his face.

"You still have my brother's offer," Chloe reminded him.

"Of Andrayan forces at my command? Yeah, but like I explained to him when I left, I can't fight this war with Andrayans. No disrespect to your people, Chloe, but after the war between our kingdoms I would have failed before I started," he replied quietly.

"You know Will didn't have any choice but to do what he did," Chloe replied, her tone defensive.

"Of course not. That's not what I meant. My people owe him and your kingdom a debt of gratitude and they don't even know it yet. Life under Marcus would have been horrible for us. Could you imagine if he started acting like his father and began implementing slave villages here to feed his greed?" Austin violently shook his head. "No, Chloe. I am honored by your brother's faith in me, and thankful that he put me on this course to free my people from the monarchy. But the Eland people never suffered the rule of a Lianthus ruler, so they don't know how close to ruin we were. What they do know is that Andrayan soldiers marched in to Eland, took Lytton, and forced the end of the Porthanaclies family line. I need to limit the Andrayan influence in this war, just to help my people believe in themselves again. Our royal line is at an end, and if I win this war they will face a new form of government, elected by the people, and that is very new to all of us.

"No, this has to be fought by Elanders over the duration. I would have no problem with having help from your brother if things got messy. But if that should happen, then the Andrayans would have to leave almost immediately, and then how could I hold what I won?" General Austin explained. "I need to have the people behind me, have them fight for the freedom that they wish for. Just like you, Brody, Declan and William did to free Andraya."

"So we need to get you an ace in the hole then, don't we?" Chloe asked, a smile on her face. The glimmer in her eyes and the almost childlike confidence in her voice made the Half Dwarf smile.

"Yeah, that's all I need, is an ace in the hole," he chuckled.

"Well then, it's a good thing I took leave to join your efforts my friend. We'll figure it out together." She smiled back at him.

"Just like that, huh? I'm glad you're so confident. I haven't been this confused about tactics for decades." the General laughed. "Maybe I should have taken that Elf's offer for help more seriously," Austin said with a chuckle.

"Well my brother's offer is still on the table. If you meant that particular Elf," Chloe laughed.

"Oh, not that Elf. No, another one. A couple of weeks ago, an Elf in a long dark grey robe found me at a pub in Tyrene. He told me that if I was willing to give him free passage through Eland with his army, to march on the Mountain Kingdom of the Dwarves, he would help me in my bid for the throne," Austin replied, collecting some of the scattered papers from around the room.

The lightning flashed as the storm continued to batter the small wood hut.

"Do you remember the Elf's name, Austin?" Chloe asked. The sudden serious tone of her voice caught the Half Dwarf by surprise. He slowly turned around and was startled by the look on his friend's face. It had gone from happy and friendly, to angry, serious and even a little scared.

"Sure, it was… hmm, wait. I know it. It struck me at the time as ominous. I just can't. You know Chloe, it absolutely escapes me. I'm usually really good with names," the general said, taking his seat again, trying to grasp the name.

"Does Neamith the Dark Elf sound familiar?" she asked, again caution in her voice.

"Yes, that's it! Neamith. Now why couldn't I remember that?" he asked.

"You declined his offer I take it?" Chloe asked once again.

"Certainly. I have no love for the Dwarves, with the way they treated my parents, but they are my kin. Even if they won't have me, I wouldn't be the cause of their pain," Austin explained. "How do you know this Neamith?" he asked.

"That's not important right now. We can talk about it later. But I think now that you remember his name, you will find your luck might change a bit," she explained, a tense smile coming to her face as if forced.

"Sure Chloe. Whenever you want to talk about it, we can. As for luck, I sure can use as much as I can get right now," the large man chuckled, trying to lighten the mood.

"Well like I said, it's a good thing I came along when I did. Because I have an idea on how to do just that!" she replied, a genuine smile returning to her lips. As she smiled, it seemed the storm began to ease.

Miles away in the army encampment of General Kiamet, a scream echoed into the night. Bursting from his tent, the full human General rushed to the one next to his.

"What happened?" he shouted at the guards at the tent's entry way.

"We…don't know, General. No one's gone in or out. We haven't even entered to check yet," a nervous guard replied. Kiamet watched as the two men stared at the opening like terrified children. The tent's inhabitant had that effect on all his men, and if he was being honest with himself, the occupant had the same effect on him.

Setting aside his own fears, the general quickly threw open the tent door to find a crumpled figure lying on the floor.

“Neamith, what’s wrong?” Kiamet asked, rushing to the Elf’s side and rolling him over.

“My link with Ironfist has been broken, rather abruptly, and rather painfully,” the dark Elf panted in reply, his jet black skin almost glowing in the light from the brazier.

“How?” the general asked.

“There is a new player, milord. I don’t know who yet; their existence was veiled to me. But when I find out,” the Dark Elf said, malice in his eyes, “they will regret getting involved!”

Chapter 2

In the age of Quarath Porthanaclies

"Hurry up Ba'rel!" A call came from behind the stocky Dwarf. "This ore isn't going to move itself you know!"

Waking from his daydream the Dwarf grunted and put his weight behind his cart. "Sorry Le'stal. My mind was elsewhere," he replied.

"And where else would your mind rather be than here, pushing a loaded cart until your whole body aches?" his friend laughed, causing Ba'rel to join in.

"My mind was in a quiet corner, with a flagon of beer in my hand," the young Dwarf described as he continued to push his loaded rail car.

"Is it the flagon of beer that is on your mind, or the young maid serving it?" Le'stal chided his friend.

"What? Did you expect me to get it myself? If you're spry enough to get your own beer, perhaps we should load more onto your cart!" Ba'rel admonished, but joined in the laughter as the two trudged along.

Working in the mines of the Kingdom of Verengrath was all the two young adult Dwarves had ever known. They had spent their entire lives underground, learning, digging and smithing metal, as their fathers and grandfathers before them had done. As members of the Bronze Clan, they worked their area of the mountain, to produce enough metal to buy what their people needed to get by. As much as they hated to admit it, Dwarves needed the other races of Eland to provide them goods unavailable in the mountain. Since food didn't grow in the deep darkness, and the Dwarves weren't suited to life above ground, they needed trade to survive.

Verengrath was located in the Northern Divide, a long range of mountains that separated the Southern Kingdoms from the Northern Wastes. It was in the Northern Wastes, a barren and hard country, where Trolls, Ogres and the most barbaric Human tribes known in the world ruled.

But the wars between the Humans of Eland and the creatures of the Wastes didn't concern the Dwarves. Instead, they traded with the humans in the small village of Nord Byen and that was the extent of most of their dealings with those who lived in the open skies. But the relationship between the Dwarves and the villagers of Nord Byen was a good one. The Dwarves brought riches from the mountain deeps, and the humans brought food and supplies to the Dwarves.

It was a relationship that suited the Dwarves nicely, and it was a relationship that was the root of Le'stal's jokes. It didn't take a romantic to see that Ba'rel had begun paying a great deal of attention to a human woman, named Cassidy Berenhom. Cassidy was the owner of "The Wounded Hand" pub in Nord Byen. The two Dwarves would finish their days there once and a while. But since Cassidy moved to the small village and became the new owner of the pub, Le'stal couldn't help but notice that they did so more often now.

Relationships between Dwarves and humans didn't really cause a great concern in the mountain kingdom. It happened, men being men and women being women, but the two worlds could never merge properly. Humans had a need to be out in the open, and Dwarves never felt at peace unless they were deep underground. So it wasn't unheard of, but it usually amounted to nothing more than a phase for most young in the Jeweled Kingdom.

The two Dwarves chatted as they pushed their loads forward, shifting through the passageways with no concern of getting lost in the labyrinth of tunnels around them. Finally though, they walked out into a large open cavern and into a throng of noise and commotion all around them.

Verengrath, or the Jeweled Kingdom, as it was known to its occupants, was separated into five clans. Not so much families, but rather communities within the mountain itself. Ba'rel and Le'stal were from the Bronze Clan, owing allegiance to Ba'rel's father, Ba'toth.

Ba'toth was the leader of the Bronze Clan, and held the position of the Emerald Throne in the Chamber of the Kings. Each clan had a clan leader, and each leader held a throne in the assembled Chamber of Kings. Each throne represented a jewel that was readily found in the Dwarven mines. They were Emerald, Diamond, Ruby, Sapphire and finally the seat of the Emperor, the Jeweled Throne. Each throne was crafted using the jewels in its name. The Jeweled Throne was, as its name implied, a large gold throne, studded with the very rare and beautiful alexandrite gems. The color of alexandrite changed depending on where you stood, representing the unity of Verengrath.

Each throne was decided in a tournament, where the clan leaders would battle the others for their positions of power. It was decided based on who remained conscious at the end of the battle. The rules were simple, no weapons or intent to harm was allowed. You incapacitated an opponent by knocking them out, either by force or any way you could to cause them to lose consciousness. The first to fall would be given the Sapphire Throne by default. Next in line was the Ruby Throne, followed by the Diamond Throne, and the Emerald Throne. Finally to the victor of the tournament went the title of Emperor and with it, the Jeweled Throne.

The contest happened once a generation. As soon as one of the kings died of natural causes, then successors would be chosen by their clans and would once again battle for their place in the Chamber.

But none of this was on the minds of Le'stal and Ba'rel as they entered the main chamber of the Bronze Clan. Instead they directed their loads across the center of the chamber, waving at friends until they reached their destination, the bronze forges.

As the day ended the two friends once again met in the central cavern and decided to have supper in Nord Byen.

"Where in Nord Byen do you want to sup?" Le'stal asked as they walked towards the Verengrath Southern Gate, the huge gates that marked the southern entrance into the Jeweled Kingdom.

"The Wounded Hand. Tonight is roasted chicken with potatoes," Ba'rel replied, a grin twitching at the corners of his mouth.

"It's roasted chicken and potatoes EVERY night at The Hand, Ba'rel. What I would give for some good venison," Le'stal drooled.

"We could ask Cassidy if she has any. Perhaps she would prepare it for us tomorrow night?" Ba'rel said, his heart fluttering as he mentioned the bar maid's name.

"I suppose you think she'd make anything you asked, don't you, you great buffoon!" A voice came from behind them.

Sighing deeply, Ba'rel stopped and turned to face the Dwarf behind them. "Good evening to you, Ba'lain. How are you today brother?"

"Don't pretend you care how my day is going, *brother*," Ba'lain replied, sneering. "So you two fools are going to Nord Byen again. How quaint. My brother, champion of the Bronze Clan, in love with a human harlot."

Ba'rel grabbed his younger brother by his jet black beard and slammed him against the cavern wall. "Listen here, *brother*. You will never speak ill of Cassidy Berenhom again, do you understand me? We may share a father, but that is as far as my loyalty to you extends," he said, slamming his half-brother against the wall for emphasis. "My patience is shallow with you and your ignorance Ba'lain. Take your simpering, scheming self from my presence and don't return until you learn some humility and manners. That will be the day, when the opinion of one such as you, shall hold any real merit in this kingdom." Giving Ba'lain another shove, Ba'rel turned and rejoined Le'stal, who watched the exchange silently. The two young Dwarves then continued on their way.

"Yes *brother*," Ba'lain whispered to himself, "you will see the day, when my council bears listening to within the Chamber of the Kings. I assure you that day is quickly coming!"

Ba'rel and Le'stal sat in their booth enjoying the music being played by the minstrel, who had just drifted into the village that morning. With their bellies and their mugs full to the brim they enjoyed the entertainment provided.

But Ba'rel's attention kept wandering to the bar where Cassidy Berenhom stood at her post. Her smile was intoxicating. Long blonde hair, dancing blue eyes, it seemed to the young Dwarf that beauty itself had grown legs and walked amongst them.

Suddenly, as he stared, Cassidy's attention turned to him and before he could avert his love struck gaze, she smiled at him. Was his mind playing tricks on him? Did she really just return his smile? Dropping his gaze to his lap, he replayed the moment over and over in his mind, trying to make sense of it. His thoughts were interrupted as a sudden round of clapping erupted around him. He quickly joined in with the crowd, realizing the minstrel had just finished another tune, but quickly returned to his thoughts.

The young Dwarf couldn't be sure, but something tickled the back of his mind. Flashing a quick look back up in Cassidy's direction, he saw that her attention was back at the front of the room on the Minstrel. *'Could she really have taken notice of me?'* he asked himself. The possibility made his heart swoon in his chest.

Chapter 3

In the Age of the Eland Civil War

The sun rose over the shack, and beamed through the window and onto the opposite wall. Chloe opened her eyes to see it and smiled. But her smile quickly faded as the memory of last night flashed into her mind. Taking a deep breath she rolled over and looked across the room to see Austin, still asleep in his bed roll next to the opposite wall.

'It appears,' she thought to herself, *'that I arrived none too soon.'* Rolling on her back, she placed her hands behind her head and laid there, looking at the roof of the ramshackle hut above her.

She remembered the thoughts that had come to her the previous evening as she fought her way towards the hut in the driving rain. It was strange, that such an intense storm should occur out of season, and yet appear to be worse the closer she had struggled towards the hut. Austin had no clue she was coming to join his fight to free his people, but using her special abilities, she knew exactly where to find him.

Yet the closer she got to the location her senses told her to go, the worse the storm became. But after hearing the name Neamith, it all made sense. So her former friend was working for one of the others and had placed a tracer spell on Austin. She smiled thinking of the pain he must have endured when Austin broke the spell. By simply remembering his name, the magical tether that connected the two snapped like a spring, whipping back towards the person who cast it. That explained how such darkness could descend upon her friend. Again she looked across the room and watched as Austin's chest rose and fell with each breath, apparently in a deep and restful sleep.

She hadn't seen Neamith for a very long time, but she didn't doubt that he was up to no good. The last time she had been with him, he had been expelled from the Elvin village of Parinth for studying the Dark Arts too deeply. It saddened her to see him go. He was a very talented sorcerer, and the two had become friends, but his drive for power seemed to consume him. Finally when he was expelled, she had to admit she hardly knew him anymore.

The thought of his increased power startled her for a moment, but she quickly set it aside. She was certain that the only way he could have been able to not only monitor Austin's location, but to also read his thoughts, required the use of a Crow's Eye spell. It allowed you to plant your subconscious in another person, and to sense their thoughts. Not in a clear word by word reading of their mind, but as a pattern, allowing a skilled sorcerer to string it all together and come up with an understanding of what they were thinking.

But a trained sorcerer could reverse the flow of information and could plant highly suggestive thoughts into a receiver's mind. Again, the power required to accomplish this was immense, so she knew that if Neamith had been planting false thoughts in Austin's mind, her old classmate had grown very powerful indeed.

She sighed once again, this time in relief when she realized that her own identity would still be safe from the dark Elf. Because he couldn't really read Austin's mind while the spell was in place, he couldn't know who had helped free him. Her place in the large half Dwarf's mind would be a series of patterns, unrecognizable without an understanding of their relationship. As friends, it most likely came across to Neamith that Austin had met up with a pal in the storm.

That too, she realized, was controlled by the dark Elf. She smiled knowing that things definitely would change for Austin now that the spell had been broken. But she didn't for a moment think that her former colleague would give up that easily.

Austin awoke feeling better than he had in weeks. His mind didn't feel like it was working overtime while he slept and he felt alert and refreshed. Turning his head he looked across the room to where Chloe had slept. He noticed that she wasn't in her roll, so he got up and looked around. Still not seeing her, he strode out of the cabin only to find her tending a campfire with a hot pot of coffee brewing.

"Good morning, General." The half Elf smiled.

"Good morning, Princess." The general grinned back and walked over to the fire.

"You know I don't like being called that!" she said, poking a stick in his direction.

"Well I thought we were being formal, and you are a princess," General Austin reminded her.

"Yeah, well only because my brother is a king," she said, rolling her eyes, referring to her brother.

"If it wasn't for your brother I wouldn't be in this war at all. But I'm tired of serving a king who isn't accountable for his actions and dragging the people down whatever foolish road they choose," Austin said, staring into the fire. "When your brother won the throne in hand to hand combat and changed the government in Andraya, it freed your people. Not only were they freed from an oppressive ruler, but from any potential future oppression as well. He gave your people the ability to decide for themselves, freeing them for as long as they hold their freedom dear."

"Yes, and he bears the burden of that change too. I know Will; he's tired of ruling. He's been leading people since he was ten years old. It's wearing on him," she said, checking the coffee pot. "But he loves our people, and that is why Andraya has an opportunity.

"Eland is lucky to have you, Austin," she continued, looking up at her friend. "Duke Wesset would just be a continuation of his Uncle Yelantas Porthanaclies' family lineage. And granted that isn't as bad as the Lianthus line in Andraya; under King Porthanaclies' son in law, Marcus Lianthus, it would have gotten much worse. As for General Kiamet, I don't know him so I'm not sure what to expect from him."

"Kiamet is ambitious. He's always felt that a king should be a general, not a politician. Take what you think is yours by force if you have to. The man with the bigger stick wins," Austin replied.

"Do you know him well?" Chloe asked.

"Yeah I know him pretty well. We moved up the ranks together. He wasn't impressed when he was passed over as High General of Eland, and given the lesser role of High General of the Northern Command. It's an important position, but he wanted more," the Half Dwarf explained. "Did you know we almost came to blows when I was awarded the position?" Chloe shook her head. "Yeah, he had a problem with a 'half breed' being top dog in the Kingdom. It didn't matter that I was more skilled and a better tactician than him, it was all about blood lines.

"That's why I don't think life under him would be any better than a Porthanaclies or a Lianthus. If anyone questioned his authority, they would be silenced, brutally and publically. Chloe, I honestly believe this war is between the status quo, a thugocracy and freedom.

Or at least that's what I hope I offer my people. Shaping the future government of Eland along the lines of the elected monarchy of Andraya is my dream. What I can't figure out though is why William chose to remain a king? Why not another title?" he asked.

"Centuries ago during the last great upheaval between all the kingdoms, the ten Kings came together to bring an end to it. They signed an agreement, called the Law of the Ten Kings," she explained.

"Sure, everyone knows about The Law. But why is that important?" Austin asked.

"Because, those laws are held, and upheld by the kings of the nations. Generation by generation, the kings of the ten kingdoms have been bound by the blood oaths taken by our forefathers. But the magic within those oaths is only maintained by the *kings*," she said with emphasis. "If you are not a monarch, then the ancient magic is broken and your kingdom is not protected by law. It would open that kingdom to being attacked by the others, and divided amongst those on its borders."

"But we attacked you," Austin said with a shrug.

"Sure," Chloe replied, "but look what happened. You failed to take Czariana, your king ran from the battlefield in shame, and the bloodline of the current ruler has failed. I believe the magic did exactly what it was meant to."

Austin sighed again deeply. "It would have to go that way. I so desperately don't want people to call me "King". It's such a foreign title for me."

"It was for William, too. When he woke up after his battle with Corland, he had no understanding of what he had done. To be completely honest, he hadn't thought that far ahead. At least you are going into this knowing you work towards being King." Chloe laughed, "For all my brother's attention to detail, planning and preparations, he never thought it far enough ahead to actually becoming King. Although," she grumbled, "neither did I. When he became King, I became a princess. How's that for an exchange?"

Austin's belly laugh filled the clearing, and it was so infectious, that soon Chloe began to laugh along with him.

It was late morning when Chloe and Austin began to travel. Chloe had come without a horse, so Austin packed his with their belongings and they both walked.

"So, what do we do next?" Chloe asked.

"Well, my soldiers are out recruiting more people to our cause. The capitol city region is already favoring our position over either of the others. After the poor citizens were used by Marcus to defend Layton's gates, they don't have a desire to go back to a Porthanaclies." He shook his head, remembering the cowardice of his now dead ruler. "And with the war with Andraya, they don't want a War Lord in Kiamet. So the lands bordering Andraya, up to Lytton, are ripe with support.

"The problem is most of that land is wilderness, and all the strong, young people live in the North. So my troop numbers haven't been increased by much. But what my people lack in strength, they make up for in spirit. Do you remember Lyra and Artole?" he asked.

"Sure, they're the parents of that poor baby that was killed during the Andrayan siege of Lytton," Chloe replied, plucking a leaf from a tree as they walked. "What of them?"

"They are such strong supporters that I've made Artole my second in command. And Lyra, she is so passionate against the status quo that all who hear her can't help but take her position."

"It's sad that it took the death of her child to find that passion," Chloe said quietly.

"None of us blame the Andrayans, Chloe," Austin said gently. "We know that all you, William, Declan and Brody were doing was protecting Andraya from a power crazy animal. If the High King had silenced his son in law, this never would have happened to them. Instead your troops attacked the city, the coward Marcus used the poor in Lytton as human shields and fired upon them as your troops tried to protect them. It was only then that little Ethan died. William did his best to protect them all."

"War should never be our first choice, but freedom demands a high price of us. I know that all too well," Chloe replied remembering that it was her arrow that killed the former king of Andraya.

"It's a burden that I am taking very seriously. My life has changed since I met your brother, Chloe. I can't say it's changed for the better yet, but I hope upon hope that it will be in the end," Austin explained.

"My, aren't we a happy pair?" Chloe chuckled.

"That is too true, my dear lady. Let's lighten the mood a bit. Would you like to hear a song my father and mother used to sing? They told me that it was a song they heard sung by a minstrel before they were married!" Austin said with a smile. Chloe returned the smile and nodded prompting Austin to begin singing as they walked.

Chapter 4

In the Age of Quarath Porthanaclies

Ba'rel had just finished his shift in the mine when he started out to find Le'stal. The two friends had been assigned to different duties that day, and so far neither Dwarf's paths had crossed. He had just entered the central corridor when he heard a voice call his name.

"Ba'rel!" a young blonde haired, female Dwarf called running up to him.

"Hi Mar'di. What's the hurry?" he asked, smiling at his best friend's sister.

"It's Le'stal. There's been an accident!" she said, trying to catch her breath. A look of instant concern flashed across his face.

"What happened?" Ba'rel asked the young female.

"He was mining the old tunnels, and one of the supports came loose. He's trapped!" she said, panic edging her voice.

"Take me!" Ba'rel commanded and just as quickly as she came the two headed off towards the old tunnels.

Much of the underground mountain had been mined for centuries, as generation after generation of Dwarves continued to etch their existence out of the deep rocks and minerals. Each clan had an area that was first settled by their ancestors, and the Bronze Clan simply referred to their ancestral starting point as "The Old Tunnels". It was no secret that the old tunnels needed work. The roofs weren't cut to the same standards as newer generations, and the support beams were only made of timbers, and none reinforced with metal girders as became the practice. But that was being changed under the leadership of his father, Ba'toth. King Ba'toth had decided that those tunnels weren't safe enough, and that the timbers needed to be replaced. And so it was that every Dwarf worked in the old tunnels to repair, maintain and upgrade them.

But even though the tunnels were outdated and old, they were always steady. A cave in was unheard of in any of the old caverns.

Weaving through the crowds of people, most of whom had already heard word of the cave in, Ba'rel and Mar'di rushed onward. Finally they were able to get to the old tunnels, and following his guide, the two quickly made it to a massive wall of rock and rubble before them. Ba'rel stood amazed at the sheer rock wall in front of him. He couldn't believe what he was seeing. Nearly two tons of rock filled the tunnel before him, and somewhere behind or under it, was his best friend.

Desperately he looked around to see who was there and what was happening. So far no one from the Bronze clan council had arrived, including his father. Seeing that no one was taking an initiative he moved forward.

"What happened here Gar'dan?" he asked the chief engineer assigned to the tunnel that day

"I don't know Ba'rel. This tunnel was stable last I knew. All the reports show that it was in excellent condition to reinforce the supports. This doesn't make sense," Gar'dan replied.

"Perhaps you misread the drawings." A snide voice came from behind them. Ba'rel turned to see his half-brother, Ba'lain approaching.

"If you have nothing of import to add, then hold your tongue brother," Ba'rel commanded.

"You may be the next Bronze champion, *brother,* but you hold no station above me now," Ba'lain chided, loathing filling his voice.

Ba'rel was going to reply but he realized he had more important things to do. "Gar'dan, call in a team of excavators. I want emergency rails brought in right now. Mar'di, rush back to the main hall and get me forty stout Dwarves, and once you have them, arrange for as many more who will volunteer." Le'stals sister nodded and rushed away immediately. "I need someone to get to the supply room and bring back as many pick axes, shovels and cranes that you can," he yelled.

People all around him started to move when Ba'lain shouted, "On who's authority do you issue these orders, *brother*? Who are you to command us?"

"He gives them under my authority!" a loud voice shouted with rage. Everyone turned in hushed silence as King Ba'toth marched down the hall, pick ax in hand, followed by a troop of Dwarves behind him.

"Father! I'm glad you're here!" Ba'rel said, clasping his father's forearm.

"I heard of the accident, and when word reached me that it was Le'stal..." he said somberly. "But now all of you, you've heard what Ba'rel said; go do as he asked. We must make haste to free our people!" Then throwing a spare pick ax to his eldest son the king stepped forward and took the first swing at a huge boulder, smashing it in two.

Taking the king's lead everyone with a tool stepped forward and began breaking the rocks. Those who had yet to be issued one began hauling the rock away by hand until the temporary rails could be laid. Soon the chamber echoed with shouts, and tools bouncing off rocks. Everyone worked themselves to exhaustion, and soon replacements stepped forward to relieve the weary Dwarves at the front. But no matter how many picks changed hands, how many stepped back to rest, Ba'rel and his father worked at the Vanguard, breaking deep into the rock.

The night was long, and the work never ceased. As they went onward the work crews prayed that they would find their friends alive and safe.

Finally after hours of constant work, Ba'rel was convinced to move back and rest. Walking back with his weary father he found a place where he could catch his breath in the central chamber of his clan.

"Le'stal is an amazing miner, Ba'rel. He'll be alright," the king said to his son.

"A deep fear is within me, father. I love him like a brother." Seeing his step-brother across the way drinking at a pub, having never lifted a finger to help he whispered, "A real brother."

"Son, I know you and Ba'lain don't approve of one another. His envy of you is disheartening. But he is your brother. You must find a way to mend your differences," King Ba'rel said.

"His hatred of me goes beyond envy father. He loathes me, and everything I do. I'm so tired of patiently waiting for him to come around, and I've long since given up on any such hope. I fear it will only get worse for the two of us, never better," he explained rubbing his face wearily.

Looking up, he suddenly wasn't sure of his senses. He was certain that he saw Cassidy, being lead across the plaza to him. But the improbability of such a thing confounded him.

But reality quickly slapped him in the head when she called out, "Ba'rel. I heard about the cave in, and came as soon as I could. What can I do to help?" she asked.

"It's difficult in there right now, Cassidy," Ba'rel said, weariness winning out against his normal shyness in her presence.

"Who is this young lady, Ba'rel?" a voice spoke at his side. Suddenly Ba'rel remembered his father sitting next to him.

Jumping to his feet, Ba'rel turned to his father. "Father, this is Cassidy Berenhom. Cassidy, this is my father, King Ba'toth, ruler of the Bronze Clan, king of the Emerald Throne," he said bowing deep at his father's exalted title. As holder of the Emerald Throne, his father was second in command of the entire Dwarven kingdom.

"Oh your majesty!" she said. "Beg my pardon for not showing you proper respect when I arrived. Had I known Ba'rel was a prince, I would have minded myself more closely," she finished with a curtsy.

Ba'toth stood slowly, still weary from his efforts and bowed low. "Please pay no mind to titles, madam. I am indeed a king, but Dwarves have no princes. My son is like all sons, and daughters of Verengrath, citizens of our mountain kingdom. You consider my son and Le'stal friends enough to beseech entrance into the Mountain?" he asked.

"Yes, Majesty. They have been friends of the Wounded Hand and myself since I moved to Nord Byen," she explained.

"And you wish to help Le'stal?" the king asked.

"Yes Majesty, in any way I can," she replied.

"Good. We need any who will help. Come Ba'rel, we best get back to the front. Our people need us," the king commanded, and leading the way, lead Cassidy and his son back into the cavern to work again.

Chapter 5

In the Age of the Eland Civil War

Chloe sat quietly at the command table, overlooking the map that was laid out before those assembled. She glanced around the table and took in all of those who sat listening to the reports being delivered. First there was Artole, and his wife Lyra. Second was Cason and his twin sister Keira, both high commanders in the former Eland army and neither a fan of General Kiamet. The final person at the table was a quiet man, smoking a long stem pipe, who was clothed in a cloak, with his hood pulled down over his eyes.

"Commander Artole, what have you and Lyra to report?" Austin asked his second in command.

"We have been recruiting people in the Southwest of the kingdom, General," Artole replied. "We have added fifty two hundred more people to the cause."

"Unfortunately they are mostly farmers and trades people, but they have the heart to carry the day," Lyra added.

"I have no doubt the two of you have them all fired up. Your dedication to my bid to free our people has been incredible. Your spirit, more than anything, guides us in our cause," Austin said with a smile.

"I will never serve another self-appointed leader again, General," Lyra said, tears welling in her eyes. "We lost our newborn son because of the arrogance of *'kings'.* It won't happen again," she said, anger in her voice.

"Lyra," Chloe said quietly, "do you blame my brother as well for the death of your baby?" she asked.

A few years ago, the former ruler of Eland, King Yelantas Porthanaclies had given permission to his son in law, Marcus Lianthus to wage war against her home Kingdom of Andraya. Chloe's brother, King William, with the guidance of his advisors and best friends, Declan and Brody, repelled the attack and brought the conflict to an end. But many of the villages along the route of the attackers were destroyed. William then took the conflict to Eland and during the siege of Lytton, the capitol city of Eland, Lyra and many others were used as a human shield to protect the city.

It was during this stage in the battle that General Declan ordered the Andrayan troops forward and using their shields led the Eland civilians to safety. But while the soldiers and civilians were moving away from the city walls, King Marcus ordered his troops to open fire on Andrayan and Elander alike. Tragically, when a stray arrow found its way through the protective shell of the shields it struck and killed Lyra and Artole's baby, Ryn, shattering the existence of the two grief stricken parents.

"No, Princess, not your brother, nor any of your people," Lyra said, tears rolling down her cheeks. "King William cried for the death of our child. He dug Ryn's grave with his own bare hands. Although I wish I never had to meet your brother, I cannot blame him for trying to save me and our son," she explained.

"William still mourns over Ryn's death," Chloe said, her eyes welling with tears as well. "He doesn't show it, since he tries to be strong for his people, but it shook him to his core."

"I have no doubt that King William would mourn for our child," Artole replied. "He has honored us with his offer to live in Czariana. But our Kingdom needs us, and if we can place a good and genuine person, such as General Austin, on the throne, it is our duty. May he lead us to glory as your brother has led Andraya." Everyone nodded their agreement at the table, including the hooded figure in the corner.

"I have heard much of your brother," the figure said, his voice strong and distinct. "I have had the privilege of seeing him in your capitol city. It was," he paused, "uplifting."

"Indeed, and you have my thanks, Artole, for the compliment. I hope I can lead our people as King William has the Andrayan's. Yet we have a Civil War to win before that can happen," Austin said. "Commander Cason, what have you learned?"

"Keira and I have been going over General Kiamet's movements and something must have recently changed," the commander replied.

"Really? How?" Austin asked, leaning across the table.

"For months he has been brash, blatant and without fear," Keira began, "then around a week ago he altered his behavior."

"Now he has stopped all movement towards Lytton. His army hasn't moved an inch since and it appears he has been sending out scouts to get actual field data," Commander Cason added.

"Matt, what have you seen?" Austin asked.

"The same. I have been able to get close to the command center of the camp and it appears that something has spooked the general," Matt replied. "He was full of confidence, and then five or six days ago, nothing. It is as if he has lost all confidence in his plan and is trying to find a way to salvage what he thought was a perfect strategy."

"That's strange," the Half Dwarf General replied. "I wonder what has changed."

"Yes, indeed," Matt said, cocking an eyebrow in Chloe's direction, "I wonder what has changed."

Chloe noticed the look but said nothing, keeping what she knew secret. She would have to watch this spy. He knew a bit too much for her liking, about Austin, about her brother and apparently, about her.

"So what do you all suggest?" Austin asked.

"Do what you've been doing," Artole replied. "Continue to build our numbers, continue to watch the General, and prepare for battle. I don't think this is going to be a prolonged war. If what we have been hearing is true, then we are in for a battle of three factions that will end with a decided victor, most likely within a month of its start. It is the best our kingdom could hope for in the current environment."

"We agree," the twins said in unison.

"Until he starts to move again..." Cason began.

"...there isn't any rush to move to counter," Keira finished for him.

"I would suggest," Matt injected, "that we perhaps enlist the help of Ms.Duthain's rangers to keep an eye on Kiamet and Duke Wesset's scouts. It would be a wise decision to know what they are trying to find out."

"That is the other question that I have. What's been going on in Wesset's camp?" Austin asked.

"There is no camp, General," Matt replied. "He and his benefactors hang around his estate, dancing and plotting, but they don't do anything. I've been there for several 'high level' meetings comprised of a bunch of fools making plans like children. Their troops are made up of the current royalty and their castle guards, supplemented with the best merc's money can buy. Merc's won't die for a cause, so they aren't the threat."

"That's what we have concluded as well," Keira said. "But we believe that to disrupt him early on would be wise. Nothing that would motivate them to make a move, but something that would limit their effectiveness. We need to disrupt their monetary advantage," she finished.

"I'm open to suggestions folks. If you think of something, bring it forward. I agree that we don't need to make an aggressive move, but we have to do something so that we stay in the equation. We don't need to lose this war by inactivity," Austin said. "Now if you all could give me some time alone with Artole, I'd like to talk to him before I retire for the evening."

Everyone rose from the table and saluted, including Chloe and Lyra, and leaving the room, allowed Austin the privacy he asked for.

"You've done very well, Artole. I couldn't have chosen a better second than you my friend," he said.

"Thank you, General. Your support is appreciated," Artole said.

"Well you deserve it. To go from a field officer to the second in command of a growing army isn't anything to take lightly. And I couldn't have made a better choice.

"But I'm concerned about Lyra. She seems as if she is getting hard. Perhaps she should rest a while?" Austin suggested.

"She won't, General," Artole sighed. "She's driven by her hatred of the royals. General, can I be frank?"

"Certainly Artole, I need to know what you feel," Austin replied.

"General," Artole paused and then plunged onward, "if you don't implement a law such as the Andrayan's, where a ruler is chosen by the people, she will come after you, too. That is how violent her rage at the Lianthus and Porthanaclies type rulers is," the large soldier replied, afraid to look Austin in the eye.

The Half Dwarf General watched his friend and second in command and struggled with how to answer him. Unlike Chloe's brother, King William, Austin didn't know how to handle emotions. He pushed them down, and avoided them, being taught to do so by his father. But he could see the fear in his friend's face and knew he needed to act.

"Artole, if I don't implement such a government, I want both of you to depose of me. We don't need another man too full of self-importance to see the needs of the people aren't being met, no matter who he is. But I promise that I will make you both proud if I'm given the opportunity," he replied, trying to sound confident like he knew his Andrayan counterpart would if he were the one speaking.

"Thank you, Austin," Artole said, looking up at the general. "After the loss of our son, none of this would have any meaning if you did anything else."

Nodding his understanding, Austin digested the words as his second in command took his leave. Closing the door gently behind him, Artole walked out of the room. Austin stared at the door for a few minutes, thinking about the exchange. He knew when Marcus Lianthus was giving him orders during the siege of Czariana that what they were doing was wrong, but he never had the courage to stand up and make his thoughts known. He simply did as he was ordered. Seeing the strength and conviction in his friend, making it clear where he stood, made him feel shame. Hanging his head, he said a silent prayer to the Creator to guide him in freeing his people.

Chapter 6

In the Age of Quarath Porthanaclies

Ba'rel stopped working for a moment and wiped the thick sweat from his brow. He turned to see who still worked at his side. The army of Dwarves had fallen off. Many lay around him, sleeping after the mad pace that he himself set. But there, still working at his fevered pace, was his father, the king's personal guard and brother Al'bet, and Cassidy.

She never ceased. Her back must have been killing her from having to stoop down so far in the low ceilings of the old tunnels. But she never complained. Turning to look behind him once again, he caught sight of his brother, Ba'lain, staring at him from across the tunnel. Ba'lain never so much as moved a pebble in the search to free the trapped Dwarves. It was a transgression that Ba'rel could never forgive him for.

Turning back towards the pile to continue working he heard a shout from Cassidy. "Ba'rel," she called, "I found something!"

The Bronze Clan champion and his father rushed to her side to see what she had found. Hope flashed within him as he reached for the tattered piece of bright yellow cloth in her hands.

"We must be getting close to them!" Ba'toth exclaimed. Cassidy's shout and Ba'toth's deep voice woke several Dwarves around them. Quickly the work force tripled in size as once again everyone began to labor to reach those behind the wall of rock. No one comprehended what was waiting for them, but they knew now that they had to find out, either way.

Now that Cassidy found the yellow cloth, other objects were uncovered. A crushed lamp here, a broken pick there, a shovel head missing its handle. More and more items were found. At one point they came across the beam that appeared to be the cause of the cave in, but until they had time to look at it closer, they kept going.

All work halted for a moment, when the body of Ty'leen, a talented engineer was brought forth from the rubble. Laying him with respect, the King covered the dead Dwarf with his cloak and said a silent prayer on his behalf.

Then they continued digging. Rocks were carted out of the tunnel as fast as they could, and still the miners manning the carts couldn't keep up with the break neck pace. As they continued to dig, Ba'rel heard something. Shushing everyone around him, he was sure he heard the muffled sounds of shouts coming from the wall.

What was at one time an ordered dig became a mad scramble as Dwarves began to shift rock with little care for its placement. Soon a light broke through into the darkness as a small hole opened. Ba'rel scrambled to the top of the rock pile and looked inside. There he found sixteen miners, some in very bad condition, eagerly waiting for rescue. Continuing his scan he heart dropped as he saw his best friend lying with a blanket across his chest.

Tears rushed to his eyes, but he shifted his grief to rage and began to tear the wall apart in a mad surge. Rocks and rubble bounced down the pile as everyone stepped back to avoid getting hit by debris from the Dwarf's frenzied actions.

When the hole was big enough to squeeze through he did just that and rushed in to the cheers of those around him. Taking stock of everyone, he saw broken bones and deep cuts everywhere. Turning to the hole he began bellowing orders.

"We need gurneys to get these men out. Send for the medics to meet us at the central hall! Tell them to get boiling water, bandages and splints ready. We have a lot of wounded here!"

Hearing the urgency in his son's voice Ba'toth reissued the orders and once again they began clearing the pile from the opening to allow help in to see to the wounded.

Ba'rel turned to each Dwarf still awake and told them help was coming. The air in the tunnel had begun to run out, as the only refuge they had was within a small pocket, caught between two cave ins. Ba'rel was amazed at the carnage around him. Sure the old tunnels were indeed old, but they had always been reliable. His people had never dug a tunnel that wasn't. He couldn't understand how this could have happened, but that wasn't important. Rushing to his friend's side, he placed his head on his chest and listened. He heard the faint thumping of a heart beat and said a quiet prayer of thanks.

Looking at his friend, sadness crept over his face. His left leg appeared to be shattered; it would have to be severed to save him. Tears welled up in his eyes, knowing that he would never work side by side with his true brother ever again.

He felt a gentle hand on his shoulder, causing him to look up into the sweat streaked face of Cassidy standing at his side. Reaching up, he placed his hand on top of hers as his fatigue fueled grief took him and he openly wept.

Ba'toth gently took his son by his shoulders and moved him aside so that help could be given to the wounded Dwarf. Miner by miner was carried from the tunnel, but rather than just carry them out, their stiff, wooden gurneys were handed down the line, being carried by every Dwarf there to help until they were out of the tunnel. Ba'rel let his head fall into his hands as he cried. He was relieved that his friend was alive, but he feared that it might not be for much longer.

Cassidy pulled him to her chest and rocked him, shushing him gently, until he fell asleep.

Three weeks had passed, and Le'stal still hadn't woken. Ba'rel stayed at his friend's side, gently pouring water and soup broth into his lips, trying to give him what he could to help. Le'stal had indeed lost his leg, and although they were able to fashion another one for him, he would not be allowed to mine again.

Worse yet was the cave in report. Over the last few weeks, the old tunnel was completely excavated and reinforced. But when the engineering team checked the supports they found that they had been tampered with. The support ropes had been cut in some places, and in others the beams had been sawed. It was sabotage.

But who would do such a thing? Dwarves never turned their backs on one another. It was beyond high treason to murder another Dwarf, but this, this was something unheard of.

It was so serious that a council of kings was called. The treachery was incredible; none of them knew what to make of it. For two days they discussed it, and then issued a proclamation. The guilty party would be found, and for their treasonous act, they would be sent into the Path of Fire, never to return.

This was the harshest punishment a Dwarf could receive. It was worse than exile, since an exiled Dwarf could still survive. But the Path of Fire was a death sentence to all but a handful of the most prestigious amongst them.

Ancient lore spoke of great Dwarves who had entered the path to take the Trial of Fire. Mythology said that within the chamber the entrant would have to answer a riddle, or enter into combat. This choice was given by three "Judges". Who these judges were, it was unknown. But they were powerful in magic and strength, and all of them deceptive and cunning.

Only three Dwarves had ever completed the trials, and they were celebrated as the greatest generals of all time within the Dwarven community. But that didn't matter now. In this day and age, the Chamber was a death sentence, and no Dwarves ever returned who were given it.

Cassidy visited often. She was given the freedom to be treated as any Dwarf in the Bonze clan for her tireless efforts to free the trapped miners. She would sit with Ba'rel and ensure that he was taking care of himself, as well as his battered and bruised best friend. Ba'rel enjoyed her visits. She would tell stories of the places she had seen throughout her travels. She was the only one who could get him to smile through his pain and worry.

His father had freed him from his obligations in the tunnels and mines. If he felt his place was next to his friend, then so be it, that is where he would stay. Ba'lain had come around frequently, which darkened Ba'rel's days. He knew his half-brother didn't care about Le'stal and questioned him repeatedly as to his reason for being there. Yet the answer was always the same, he was concerned about the hurt Dwarf. Ba'rel refused to accept the answer. His brother was up to something, but he didn't have time to think about it now. Not with his friend so close to death's embrace.

Chapter 7

In the Age of the Eland Civil War

The storm was incredible, but this time Chloe was sure it wasn't the work of sorcery. Instead, everything about it seemed right. It was nearing the end of spring in the Ten Kingdoms, and Eland's location in relation to the mountains made it a very stormy time of year in this area. Chloe and Austin worked their way through town, its name unknown to Chloe, but it seemed a better option than sleeping in the storm.

Seeing the sign of a pub in the distance they quickly rushed inside and slammed the door shut behind them. The music that was previously playing before they entered stopped as all eyes turned towards the drenched pair. Austin pulled back his hood and nodded at the bar tender who nodded back prompting the music to begin again.

The two quickly found their way to an available booth in the corner, taking their drenched cloaks off. Austin reached above their table and dimmed the oil lantern hanging above them.

"Ooh, how romantic," Chloe joked.

"Not romantic, wise. We are currently in General Kiamet's region. I'd rather not be seen floating in the area," Austin informed her.

"Then what are we doing here?" Chloe asked.

"I don't know. I was drawn here. I've always been drawn here when things were at their darkest," Austin explained.

"Where is...here?" she asked, as she looked around taking note of the exits, windows and anything else that might help them in a jam.

"We're in Nord Byen. It's a small town in the North West area of Eland. It's a trading center with the Dwarves of Verengrath, but other than that, it just always seemed, comfortable." He stopped as a bar maid came around.

"Good evening." she welcomed. "What can I get you tonight?"

"I'll take a warm cider," Austin said.

"The same please," Chloe asked.

"For certain. Would you like me to bring you some supper? It's roast chicken and potatoes," she explained.

"Man what I'd give for some venison," Austin replied. "But, two plates of chicken and potatoes," he requested.

"Certainly," she said with a smile, and moved off to fill their order.

"The potatoes smell like the ones my mother used to make," Austin said, a smile forming on his lips.

"You've never told me anything about your parents. What was your family like?" Chloe asked.

"Nothing fancy. Mom was human and dad was a Dwarf. They never talked much about how they met, or why a Dwarf would marry a human. But it wasn't important. That and..." Austin said, his eyes clouding over.

"And what, Austin?" Chloe asked.

"And dad always seemed pained by his past. It didn't seem a topic he wanted to think about. But it was a good life. Being long lived as my father was, once my mother got sick when I was ten or so, that's when he urged me to join the army early recruits." He smiled. "It was then that I met Kiamet. We were friends, of sorts, back then, but time passed and things fell apart. I believe my rank bothered him."

"Speaking of rank, you're the Eland High General. Aren't you worried these folks will know you and report you?" his Elven friend asked.

"A bit, which is why I turned down the light. But to be honest, Nord Byen doesn't have a lot of long term inhabitants. The only folks who seem to be fixtures around here are the Dwarves. And something years ago caused them to close off from Nord Byen. They still trade, but the relationship has long been strained," he explained.

Almost as if on cue the door burst open, and again slammed as a Dwarf sought shelter from the rain. The Dwarf looked around the room and began limping to a nearby table.

"Well, if it isn't Le'stal!" a large man surrounded by a group of thugs shouted. "Come Le'stal, do a dance for us," he said to a loud chorus of laughter.

The Dwarf simply found a seat and sat down quietly, taking his rain drenched cloak off and hanging it on a nail by the table.

"I said dance you gimpy Dwarf!" the man shouted, this time rising menacingly from his table. Again laughter bellowed from the men around him.

"You leave him be, Nardok!" the bar maid shouted. "He's come to relax after a long day, like the rest of you." Quickly navigating the tables she came to the ragged Dwarf's side. Austin watched with anxious interest. He had caught the sight of a metal foot on the Dwarf's leg. He'd never met this Dwarf before, but his curiosity rose all the same.

"I'll do as I please!" Nardok roared. Tipping his chair over, he menacingly strode across the room towards the bar maid and the Dwarf.

"I think not!" Austin said loudly, and stepping out from behind his table, stepped between them all.

"And who are you to stop me?" Nardok sneered, standing at least a foot taller than the Half Dwarf General.

"More than you could guess," Austin replied.

"And what are you planning to do with us?" asked one of the men rising from Nardok's table, followed by the remaining seven.

Suddenly and arrow flew across the room, catching the new speaker's collar, and slamming him into the wall.

"You, my friend," Chloe said, "are for me!" Everyone turned and saw her, with another arrow already notched and aimed at the men around the table. "Sit down, NOW!" she shouted at the others.

Just as quickly as they rose, each man found his seat again. Chloe remained standing, bow in hand, but she eased the string forward. Now all that was left was Austin and Nardok.

"Well Nardok, what now?" Austin asked. "It's just the two of us. Do you think perhaps it would be wise for you to sit back with your friends and let it lie?"

"What I think," Nardok said quietly, "is that you should die!" he yelled. Taking a single stride he closed the distance between Austin and himself. Balling his fists tightly, the giant of a man swung as hard as he could, looking to smash his iron-like hand into the side of Austin's head. Austin stood calmly as the swing came towards him. Time seemed to slow for the general as he watched the attack come.

Before the large bar room brawler could make contact with his target though, the general lifted both of his arms and stopped the swing cold. As quick as a thought, he lifted his leg and slammed it into the front foot of Nardok with the heel of his boot. The giant man shouted in pain as he stumbled back, but now it was Austin's turn. Adeptly moving around his large opponent the Half Dwarf continued with a flurry of punches to Nardok's head. He moved so fast, that even when the giant tried to get a swing in he would only find air.

A shout came from across the room as one of Nardok's friends threw a club to his embattled comrade's hand. A cruel grin came across the giant's face as he swung the club with abandon at Austin's head. The young Half Dwarf was able to dodge it, and instead of it knocking his head off as was intended, he took the blow across his back, throwing him onto the floor. Nardok moved forward ominously. He paused for a split second, considering his next move when an arrow flew past his face, and instead of drilling into his neck, it left a razor thin line on his chin.

"You missed!" he shouted turning to Chloe.

The Half Elven archer smiled and shook her head no. The large man turned from her to see what she was looking at behind him. There pinned to the wall, next to the first man hung a second, his hand high above his head holding a knife.

"Carry on." She said with a devilish grin, as another arrow adorned her bow. Winking at Austin she motioned the other five who had gotten back to their feet to sit back down.

Smiling back at her, Austin waited until Nardok stood above him, then swinging his feet around he kicked the large man in the knee caps. Nardok shouted in pain, as he flung his arms backwards. Almost instantly, his club slipped from his grip and hurled across the room toward the barmaid. She stood there dazed as it launched in her direction. But the Dwarf, now standing beside her, was faster than he looked. He jumped, and grabbing the flying club he swung it quickly around him. Redirecting it towards the floor, it landed with a loud crash as he fell down next to it.

Jumping to his feet, Austin began to punch and beat the large man all around his head once again. Careful to shift his opponent around any furniture to avoid wrecking anything else, he continued to beat him mercilessly. Finally when he had driven the giant against the wall, Austin lifted his knee between the large man's legs, causing him to double over in pain. Then, sensing the fight was nearly over, the Eland High General delivered a stunning upper cut, blasting Nardok off his feet, causing the giant to land with a thud next to the fireplace.

The Half Dwarf stepped forward and grabbed the giant man by the hair. Lifting his head, he was just in time to see Nardok's eyes roll back as he fell unconscious. Austin stepped away from his fallen opponent, panting, and looked around the room. His damp hair, now slick with sweat as well as rain water, covered his eyes as he grinned threateningly at the men at Nardok's table.

"Anyone up for round two?" he asked. The remaining men sitting at the table turned away and quickly struck up a quiet conversation amongst themselves. Following suit, so too did everyone else in the room. "I didn't think so," Austin mumbled as he turned around. Seeing the Dwarf laying on the ground, he strode across the room and offered him his hand.

"My name is Austin Ironfist," he said quietly, so as to not give himself away to too many people in the room.

"Iron…fist?" the Dwarf asked. "How comes a human by a Dwarven surname, lad?"

"My father was a Dwarf," Austin said, helping the yellow haired Dwarf to his feet.

"He wouldn't have been, Ba'rel Ironfist, would he boy?" The question was almost a whisper, but the intensity of it rung in Austin's head.

"The same. How do you know my father's name?" Austin asked incredulous.

"He was my best friend, and was banished from Verengrath because of me," Le'stal replied, a look of shock etched into his face.

Chapter 8

In the Age of Quarath Porthanaclies

Soon all the Dwarves from the cave in who could be saved had recovered. The others were placed in tombs and were mourned by the entire Kingdom of Verengrath.

Two months passed and still Le'stal would not wake. Hope was lost by most of the people in the Kingdom; all that is, except for Ba'rel and Mar'di. When Ba'rel had to leave, she would stay. And so it was, that she relieved him after yet another uneventful night. The exhausted Dwarf got up and slowly left his wounded friend's side for another restless sleep.

He slowly stumbled back towards his home, with his head hung in grief. Too down trodden and exhausted to do much else, he just yearned for his bed. As he made his way across the central chamber of his clan, it too began to show signs of a new day. Vendors were opening their shops, people were meeting in small groups talking about the news of the day, and work crews were being issued orders. Each one stopped what they were doing as he walked by, and bowed their heads low in reverence and respect to the pain they knew he suffered.

Still moving slowly towards home, he was suddenly stopped by Ba'lain's hand on his shoulder. "Good morning, brother. How is our friend doing today?"

Rage instantly ignited within him. Grabbing his half-brother by the throat Ba'rel lifted him off his feet.

"*My* friend," he roared, "is in critical condition because some treacherous dog attempted to kill him. I wonder who would do such a thing!" he shouted with an accusatorial tone.

Seeing the commotion, a bunch of Dwarves ran to the scene and tried to get Ba'rel to let his choking half-brother down.

But Ba'rel's rage seethed within him. He had long ago suspected his brother was capable of such treachery against their people. But it wasn't until Ba'lain began to come around to check on Le'stal that suspicion set in.

Ba'lain hated Le'stal, if only for being Ba'rel's best friend. His half-brother had always hated the Bronze Clan champion for being first born, for his charisma and for being a natural leader to their people. It was no secret that Ba'lain yearned to be king. He wanted to rule, and thought he could do better than all the kings combined. Of that, Ba'lain was never silent. Yet there was Ba'rel, charming, hardworking, friendly and with a heart the people knew was meant to guide them all. Ba'lain would never be king, thanks to Ba'rel, and he hated him for it.

But it was years of enduring that hatred that caused it to seep into Ba'rel's heart and was reflected back towards his half-brother. The Dwarven champion knew his step mother was feeding the animosity, causing Ba'lain to continue to hate his brother and their father. But being hated by both of them didn't matter to Ba'rel. His own hatred fed off of it. The more division, the better he liked it.

So when the engineers found signs of tampering, it didn't take long for the hatred within him to find its target. Ba'lain was evil enough to do such a thing, and as an engineer, he had the knowledge of how to do it. Ba'rel was sure his brother was the cause, but he had no proof. But now, with his brother's neck tightly in his grasp, he didn't care. He began to squeeze his brother's throat tight in his hands, choking the life out of him.

"Ba'rel," a shout bellowed from across the hall, "what is the meaning of this?"

Again Ba'rel ignored it and focused his rage on his half-brother.

"Ba'rel, enough!" The voice again crept into his consciousness, but again he ignored it.

"Ba'rel. Let him down, son." There was the voice again, but this time it was gentler, softer and the hand on his shoulder made it real. Slowly turning his head, he saw his father, fear in his eyes, staring at him. Looking around he saw the four other Dwarves, still hanging on his arms as he held his half-brother, dangling above the ground.

Coming to his senses, he dropped Ba'lain. His brother drew a hard and ragged breath as he coughed on the floor.

"He tried to kill me!" Ba'lain shouted, pointing an accusatorial finger at his brother. "He tried to choke me to death!"

Ba'rel stood there, eyes on the ground, his rage filling his heart.

"Ba'rel, what do you have to say for yourself?" the king asked, this time louder and with a tone of command.

Ba'rel lifted his eyes and looked at his father as he spoke. "Ba'lain," he said, "is the traitor who cut the supports in the tunnel." Even though his response was a mere whisper everyone around him heard him clear as day.

"That is a grave accusation to make Ba'rel. Do you have any proof?" his father asked, shock etched on his face.

"No," Ba'rel said. He caught sight of his brother breathe a sigh of relief with his answer.

"Then how can you make such a charge?" his father asked angrily.

"Because I know." Again, his tone nothing more than a whisper as he replied.

"Well, unless you have proof, you have no place to lay such a charge at your brother's feet. And if you were correct, it would not be your place to pass judgment or sentence!" his father shouted.

Nodding gently, Ba'rel stood there, head hung in the torrent of emotions running through him. Silent he waited for his father's judgment.

"Al'bet, you and some of your men escort my son to his chambers and keep him under guard. He is only allowed to leave so long as one of your men are with him, do you understand?" the king commanded.

"Yes, my king. We will maintain him as you command," the commanding officer of the Bronze Clan guard replied.

Gently taking Ba'rel's arm in his hand, Al'bet and a group of his soldiers ushered him away from the crowd.

"He did it, Al'bet," Ba'rel said quietly.

"I believe you nephew," Al'bet replied. "But your father is right; you had no proof and no place to do what you did." Still walking together, Al'bet sighed. "Ba'rel, I've watched you grow since you were a child. You are smart, strong and a natural leader. Why would you let your brother's venom creep into you like this?" he asked.

"I don't know," Ba'rel replied, tears filling the corners of his eyes as he hung his head in shame. "I was tired, and he got in my way pretending to care about Le'stal. It was more than I could take. I just snapped. I…I don't know why I let it happen?"

"Be honest with everything they ask you Ba'rel. This isn't going to end quickly for you. Nor is it going to end well. You can be sure your half-brother will see to it," Al'bet explained softly.

Nodding his understanding, Ba'rel opened the door to his home and stepped inside. He turned back briefly to close it, and as he did he saw his uncle turn to stand watch before it. How could he let this happen?

The room was full of Bronze Clan Dwarves, and from the number of Dwarves in attendance, almost the entire kingdom came out to see the proceedings. Ba'rel stood before the Dwarven council of kings to face judgment. Al'bet was right, it didn't go away.

His step mother, Ba'lain's mother and his father's current wife, had demanded justice. When she was asked to be calm and be understanding by his father, she went over his head to the other kings and demanded they step in. So it was that a complete council was called to deal with his act of aggression towards his half-brother.

Ba'rel stood straight and proud before them. For weeks he was kept locked in his room, only to be let out at night to sit by his friend's bed. Ba'toth had seen to it that he be allowed that comfort, even in his imprisoned state. He had thought of what had happened, and now, more sure than ever, he was prepared to speak his mind.

"Ba'rel Ironfist," spoke Emperor Hou'tung of the Iron clan, current ruler of Verengrath, "you have been brought here, before this commission to answer for your crimes against your brother,"

“HALF-brother, milord,” Ba’rel injected.

Grunting at the intrusion the emperor continued, “Half or full, it makes no difference to us. He is of your blood young Dwarf. The distinction of percentage is not our concern.

“As I was saying, you have been brought before us to answer for your crime. You stand here accused of attempted murder of Ba’lain Ironfist. How do you plead?” Hou’tung asked.

“Guilty,” Ba’rel said, confident justice would rule the day.

“Guilty?” Hou’tung said incredulously. “You stand before your people and make no attempt at justification for your actions?”

“I can make no justification, for killing Ba’lain was indeed in my heart that day. My rulers, I have spent months at my best friend, Le’stal Strongarm’s side. He was one of the Dwarves who was trapped when the old tunnels of the Bronze Clan fell in the cave in.

“After freeing him and the others, it came to light that the supports in the tunnel were sabotaged. I believe my half-brother to be the culprit,” Ba’rel accused.

“What proof do you have of this?” Ga’lour, King of the Diamond throne and leader of the Silver clan asked.

“I have none but my instincts,” Ba’rel replied, looking at Ga’lour directly.

“It was explained to you,” Ba’rel’s father, Ba’toth injected from his seat in the Emerald throne, “that without proper evidence that no such charge could be leveled. Yet you continue to make that claim with nothing but your instinct. Ba’rel, I am ashamed.”

“I, too, am ashamed, Father,” Ba’rel replied. “I am ashamed that because my half-brother covered his tracks, he may never come to justice. That is a shame we all share.”

“Enough!” Ba’toth shouted rising from his seat.

"Indeed, enough," added Hou'tung, trying to get the council under control. "Ba'rel Ironfist, you have pleaded guilty to attempted murder of one of our own, and one of your own blood. This grievous crime has only one acceptable punishment, within these solid walls. It is that punishment that I am forced to mete out this day. For today, master Ironfist, you have been exiled from Verengrath. You shall be stripped of your honor, your belongings and your place amongst us, never to return.

"Pay heed to my words young Ironfist," Hou'tung said dangerously. "If you don't mind what I say, and return to our gates, you shall be executed on the spot, without trial. Are my words clear to you, young man?"

Shock ran through the Ruling Chamber. But Ba'rel knew it was the best he could hope for. Nodding his understanding he allowed the guards to take him and begin the long march to the Great Gates and his expulsion from his home. As they marched across the room, Ba'lain jumped out in front of his brother, standing a step above him.

"Oh how the mighty have fallen," his hated half-brother sneered.

Ba'rel stopped, his great strength causing the guards to stop with him, a gentle reminder that he went because he chose to, not because he was forced. Turning a half grin at Ba'lain he quickly spit at him in the eye. "True," Ba'rel said as Ba'lain cowered before him, "but at least I was mighty once. That is a claim you shall never be able to make!" And once again walking with the guards, he began climbing towards the exit of the hall.

Chapter 9

In the Age of the Eland Civil War

Austin stood, staring at the Dwarf before him. His tongue clung to the roof of his mouth, as it went instantly dry. He began to get light headed and looked like he was about to fall but Chloe stepped beside him and held him up.

"Easy Austin," she whispered, "we don't need a bar full of thugs to think you're vulnerable right now."

His warrior instincts cut in and, catching himself from falling, he sent his shocked mind into action.

"Thank you, Chloe. Once again you're here to save me from myself," he replied with a smile. "This nice lady called you Le'stal; may I call you the same?" He asked.

"Any son of Ba'rel Ironfist can do more than that; you can call me a friend," the blonde Dwarf replied with joy in his eyes.

"Is there somewhere we can talk Le'stal, that is less," looking around the room he noticed the remaining men at Nardok's table watching them, "open to prying eyes?" he asked.

"I live in a room in the back. Kierra here has been good enough to give me a home, after I left Verengrath," Le'stal replied. "Let's go to my room."

"Le'stal, take them to the private kitchens," Kierra replied. "There's more room in our home than just your room. I've told you that before, you silly Dwarf," she said with a wink.

“You have my thanks, lass. We’ll do just that. Step in whenever you wish. This is as much your story as it is mine,” Le’stal replied.

Following the hobbling Dwarf, they made their way back behind the bar and into Le’stal and Kierra’s private living quarters. Crossing through the main kitchen, they came to a quiet corner in the back where a small cozy table and chairs sat.

“So, Le’stal, when you said you are the cause of my father’s banishment, what did you mean?” Austin asked, his mind filling with questions.

“Although your grandfather” The word ‘grandfather’ struck Austin like an iron club. He had never thought about his extended family. The very idea of a grandfather seemed so out of place in his lonely life. “--would never admit it, nor would your father, Ba’rel was a prince of Verengrath.” Again shock ran through the Half Dwarf.

“A…prince?” Austin said in a near whisper. Chloe, seeing that her friend was going into shock, gently began to rub his back.

“Le’stal, forgive my friend’s continued surprise. He knows very little of his family history,” she explained.

The Dwarf before them nodded his understanding, “I have no doubt that Ba’rel didn’t speak of his past. My own self-imposed exile due to the actions of your Uncle, King Ba’lain, is difficult enough to live with. And I live at the foot of my old home. Your father…it must have been hell not being underground.”

“We did live underground!” Austin said, finally being able to be part of the conversation. “Well, partially. My father found a small hill, and even though we had rooms on top of the hill, he dug into it for most of our private rooms! It’s still there in Dayson, at the Golameed border!”

"That sounds like my old friend. Like the saying goes, 'You can take a Dwarf out of the mountain, but you can't take the mountain out of the Dwarf'," he said chuckling. "Yes lad, during that time your grandfather was King Ba'toth, ruler of the Emerald throne, second in command of Verengrath, and head of the Bronze clan. Ba'rel was our champion. He was to be the next to represent us in the Challenge of Kings. Your father would have been king if not for me."

"What do you mean, Le'stal? What happened?" Austin asked, wondering if he should trust the man before him.

"I don't know much, as I've only been told this second hand from my sister, but I was hurt in a cave in," he said reaching down and tapping his metal leg. "Your father, mother and grandfather, with many from our clan, worked tirelessly to free those of us who were trapped.

"I, apparently, was hurt the worst of all of our people involved and was unconscious for months. I would have died on the gurney if it wasn't for Mar'di and Ba'rel spooning chicken broth into my mouth each day," he said, his eyes looking somewhere deep in the past. "Shortly after the cave in, our engineers found that it didn't happen accidentally," he said with a frown.

"You mean the cave was sabotaged?" Chloe asked.

"Yes, darlin'. Well, tunnel actually, but yes all the same. Someone had weakened the supports to bring the entire roof of our old tunnels down on us," Le'stal replied.

"Who would do such a thing?" Austin asked incredulously.

"We don't know, but your father was sure he had the answer," Le'stal replied. "Ba'rel and your uncle Ba'lain hated one another. Your father in a moment of grief attacked your uncle, nearly killing him. Any fight between Dwarves is a grave affair. They happen, frequently these days, but we treat all Dwarves as family.

"But to actually attack your own blood is unheard of!" Le'stal explained. "Although your father would have received leniency for his grief from your grandfather, his wife, Ba'lain's mother, refused to let him.

"She called for a full council of kings, and they placed your father on trial. It was there that Ba'rel accused Ba'lain as the saboteur, and admitted his guilt in wanting to kill him. But making such a serious charge without proof damned him." Le'stal continued as Austin and Chloe listened. "Because he was a model citizen, in fact a role model for all Dwarves, he was banished and was forced to leave Verengrath as an example."

"That's where I come into this story," Kierra said, startling everyone in the room. They were so focused on one another, they hadn't heard her enter. "I've closed the pub now and sent everyone home," she explained. "Come sit around the fireplace, where there's more room." And again they moved back into the pub, to sit by the roaring fireplace.

"How do you play a role in this ma'am?" Austin asked.

"Well young man, you can start by calling me Cha-cha," she explained with a smile.

"What does Cha-cha mean?" Austin asked sheepishly.

"In our family, it means Aunt," she replied

"Ah, that's right!" Le'stal said, a smile creeping onto his face as well. "Austin meet Ms. Kiera Berenhom, your mother's sister."

"My mother's..." Again the new found family shocked Austin to his core. Kiera grabbed his hands, and although a quarter of his size pulled him to his feet and gave him a huge warm hug.

"I can see my sister in your face, Austin," she said. He felt her quiver a bit in his arms. Sensing her grief, he held her close to him, hugging her as he longed to hug his own mother again.

"I had no clue I had so much family," Austin said as they pulled apart.

"You have more, much more," Kiera said. "But we're getting ahead of ourselves."

"Why don't you take up the story from here Kiera?" Le'stal asked.

"Sure. I had come to visit my sister and see this pub that she had purchased, a lifelong dream of hers," she explained. "That's when we heard the news that something was going on at the Verengrath Great Gate.

"Rushing to the gate, we pushed our way through a crowd to see your father being led by a large contingent of Dwarven soldiers out of the gate. Your mother was terrified. She had been barred entrance to the kingdom for the weeks your father was incarcerated for attacking Ba'lain. This was the first time she had seen him since then," she explained.

"You'd have been proud of your father, son," Le'stal said. "It was explained to me that he stood head high and let them lead him where they may. That he only went because he chose to, and they knew it."

"Indeed, that's what I saw as well. The then-ruler of Verengrath came out and proclaimed your father's banishment. Then without so much as a goodbye, the Great gate was closed and your father stood all alone surrounded by humans, staring at his misfortune.

"Your mother went to him then, to see if he needed help, and that's when she offered him a room. It was the same room that Le'stal now resides in, to help him during his time of need," she explained.

"Aye, son, I have some things of his that he left behind if you'd like?" Le'stal said quietly.

"No, Le'stal. I have my own memories of my father. Keep them in good faith my friend.

"So," Austin continued, "that is how my parents came to be. I have often been asked why a human woman would marry a Dwarven man, but I can see now it was pity," he said sadly.

"Bite your tongue young man!" Kiera said, sternly. "It was quite the contrary. She loved him for months before this happened."

"And he her, Austin," Le'stal added.

"This tragedy just brought them together," Kiera said.

She softened when she saw the smile creep on Austin's face. She could see the layers of doubt begin to slip away about his beloved parents, the only family he knew.

"But, Ba'rel couldn't live here. We don't know who, most likely the saboteur, but someone began to send assassins after your parents," Le'stal said.

"After three failed attempts," Kierra jumped in, "your parents decided it was time to move on. That's when your mother gave me this pub, and they left together to start a new life."

"The last time I saw your father was the day before the cave in," Le'stal said sadly. "How are your parents doing?"

"They both died," Austin said sadly.

Kiera began to cry gently as Le'stal hung his head sadly. "He was so young, for a Dwarf that is."

"Yes. My mother died after I graduated from the academy. She had been sick for years by then, and he died shortly after," Austin said gently. Pain wracked his heart as old wounds reopened, and seeing the grief of his parent's closest loved ones.

"He died of a broken heart then?" Kierra said.

"That's what I always thought," Austin replied softly.

"What have I done to my best friend?" Le'stal said placing his face in his hands.

Chapter 10

In the Age of Quarath Porthanaclies

Cassidy sat in her kitchen, staring into a cup of coffee, worried about her Dwarven friends. She hadn't seen either Ba'rel or Le'stal since Ba'rel had been confined. King Ba'toth had suggested that she remain out of Verengrath until after Ba'rel's trial, for her safety. Regardless of who caused the cave in, someone had indeed done just that and there was a criminal on the loose in the Jeweled Kingdom.

Suddenly the door to her personal apartment in the back of the Wounded Hand burst open as her sister, Kierra, who was in Nord Byen to visit, rushed into the room. Startled, Cassidy jumped to her feet and quickly went to her.

"Something is happening at the gates to Verengrath!" Kiera said, panting at her sister's door.

Cassidy clutched her sister's hand, and the two of them raced across the village to see a throng of people at the giant gates to the Dwarven kingdom. The two of them pushed their way through the crowd of people gathered there to a site that made Cassidy gasp in apprehension. There, between his Uncle Al'bet and another guard stood Ba'rel, his hands in shackles. They were surrounded by a large contingent of Dwarven soldiers.

One of the Dwarven Kings stepped forward and carefully unrolled a scroll, its ink still wet, leaving marks on the back of the page.

“It is by decree,” the king began, “that Ba’rel Ironfist, son of the Bronze Clan, be stripped of his place in Verengrath. For threatening to do harm to his own blood, he has forsaken his people, and is from this day forth, exiled from the Jeweled Kingdom.”

A gasp and murmur spread through the crowd of humans watching. Many of them didn’t care to know the Dwarves, but those who came to know Ba’rel, knew him to be a friend. The shock rocked Cassidy, as tears ran down her face.

“Ba’rel Ironfist, you are no longer considered a citizen of Verengrath and any claims you have to your kinfolk are revoked,” the king continued. As he did, one of the guards came forward and unlocked the shackles on his hands and feet. “Furthermore, should you ever attempt to re-enter Verengrath, you shall be considered an enemy of the state and shall be executed on the spot.

“This decree is made to all whom now hear it,” the Herald shouted to the community surrounding them. “Any who would come forward to argue in Ba’rel Ironfist's defense before any member of Verengrath will be considered an accomplice, and they too shall be put to death. This is the word and decree of the Emperor of Verengrath, and as such, is the law of our people. Be warned.”

Then each Dwarf in attendance turned their backs on Ba’rel and began to walk towards the ornate Gold and Silver gilded doors of Verengrath. Ba’rel stood, head held high, staring forward yet seeing nothing. Suddenly he felt a hand on his shoulder. Turning his head he stared into his Uncle Al’bet's eyes. His face softened as he saw the sadness on his uncle’s face. Al’bet gently squeezed his nephew’s shoulder and nodded to him. Seeing his uncle’s tear rimmed eyes nearly broke Ba’rel’s stoicism, but he held strong and, nodding back, let out a deep sigh. Then, following the others, Al’bet entered the

Dwarven kingdom and bellowing a command had the doors slammed shut behind him.

Ba'rel wasn't really sure what had happened for the rest of that day. As far as he knew it was all a bad dream, as he awoke in a bed looking upwards. But he instantly knew it wasn't a dream, as the roof above him was made of wood, not the rock ceiling he was accustomed to. Swinging his legs off the edge of the bed he realized that this too was wrong. He sat there, legs dangling as if a child in their parent's room.

Taking in his surroundings he noticed that the room was very feminine. Flowers in vases and pots, lace trimming on the windows, and pink bedding surrounded him. Then he smelled the amazing odor of bacon grilling and the sizzle of eggs on a skillet. Gently jumping off his bed, he crept across the floor, and opened the door a crack to see where he was.

Surprise struck him as he looked across a kitchen to see Cassidy humming at the stove. Not wanting to scare her, he crept back to the bed, and stepped loudly across the room. Then coming to the door, he opened it slowly, making sure to cause it to squeak on its hinges to catch her attention.

She turned to him and smiled, as he walked out. "Good morning Ba'rel," she said. "I'm glad to see you up and about."

"Good morning to you too, Cassidy," he said, smiling back at her. "That smells very good," he said, not knowing what he should say.

"That's what I was hoping for," she replied, turning back to the stove and grabbing a plate from the shelf. "How do you like your eggs?" she asked.

"From a chicken," he joked.

Laughing, she scooped two eggs and some bacon from the pan and setting the plate before him said, "Well too bad, all I've got is dragon eggs."

"Those came from a pretty small dragon," he said, grinning at her.

She laughed again, her mirth filling a void in his chest causing him to feel at peace for the moment. The two ate silently, as Cassidy allowed Ba'rel to process everything that had occurred the day before. She caught his eyes darting around, taking in his surroundings and she could see his mind at work, trying to plan his unsure future.

Once breakfast was done, Cassidy pulled out a long stemmed pipe and a bag of tobacco and handed it to him. He felt like he was in a dream to have such an amazing start to his day. Without saying a word, she ushered him to the back door of the pub, and sitting next to him on a bench waited as he filled the pipe and lit it.

Enjoying the aroma from the tobacco, Ba'rel took a couple of deep pulls of the smoke and rested his head against the wall, looking at the massive mountain before him.

"Cassidy?" Ba'rel said after a few more moments of silence.

"Yes, Ba'rel?" she replied.

"What happened yesterday? What am I going to do now?" he asked, his fears and doubts coming to the surface.

"After the ceremony, you stood there, staring into the distance not moving. Kierra and I couldn't stand to see you there alone, so we came to you and gently coaxed you back to the Wounded Hand," she explained. "You sat at your table, unmoving. You wouldn't eat or drink, you just sat there in a daze.

"After spending the entire day without moving a muscle, staring into nothing, a few of my patrons and I moved you back into my room where you slept last night," she continued.

"I didn't put you out did I?" he asked, genuinely concerned that his behavior had affected her adversely.

"Certainly not, Ba'rel," she said. "I slept in one of the rooms above the pub. I haven't had need to use it as an inn since taking ownership, but they are still in good repair. I just slept there last night. I didn't want you to wake in a stark, empty room."

"The others will talk about me being in your bedroom," he said as color rushed to his cheeks.

"Let them. I'll not let old gossips turn me from helping my friend," she explained.

Ba'rel looked at her and smiled a weak smile at her. "You have my thanks, Cassidy. For this and for everything you did for Le'stal. I shall never again see my best friend, but thanks to you, I'm sure he will survive."

"I would have done much more for you and him, Ba'rel. You two have become much more to me than patrons," she explained. "And as for your second question," she said, moving on, "what will you do? That question can be answered with time, Ba'rel. There is no rush. You have a home, so long as I have a roof to offer you. Together we will find a future where you can be happy," sShe said with a smile. He reached over, tentatively and took her hand in his. She warmly squeezed it when he did and smiled at him. The two sat there, silently, deep in their own thoughts as they stared at the mountains. Never before had their sharp edges looked so uninviting to the young Dwarf. But now, they looked like a massive wall, warning him to never return.

Chapter 11

In the Age of the Eland Civil War

Austin awoke and looked out the window by his bed. The mountains rose high behind the quiet village. His mind was full of questions about his father and mother, questions that had never before seen the light of day. Where was his grandfather? What would have happened to his father if he remained in the Dwarven kingdom? Would he even have existed, should the exile never have happened? Sliding out of bed he dressed in a shirt and pants, and wandered down to his aunt's kitchen.

When he arrived he found his aunt at the stove cooking breakfast, talking with Chloe. Both women smiled as he entered the room, and as Kierra ushered him to a chair, Chloe poured him a cup of coffee.

"Did I interrupt you?" he asked, taking a sip of the black fluid, putting a smile on his lips. His aunt made it just like his mother.

"Not at all. We were talking about how time balances itself out," Chloe replied.

"What do you mean?" Austin asked, not really paying attention.

"Well before yesterday, you didn't know you had a family, and they didn't know they had you. Now, here you all are and you may have found the answer to your problems," Chloe explained.

"Answer to what problem?" Austin asked, suddenly devoting the half Elf his full attention.

"We travelled this way in search of troops, to help you free Eland," she explained, "and we find that there may be an army at your disposal."

"Who? The Dwarves? Yeah, like that is even a consideration," he snickered.

"Why not?" Kierra asked.

"Because I am the son of a Dwarf they consider a traitor, a criminal and an exile. They would just as soon execute me as listen to my pleas for help," he sighed.

"You're most likely right," Le'stal said, joining everyone at the table. "The decree was quite clear; I read it for myself. That's why I left. I would never live in a place that wouldn't have Ba'rel. I would rather never set foot in a rocky cavern ever again, than admit my friend was a criminal.

"But be that as it may, after I was exiled I studied a lot of our culture and history. Not being able to work in the mines or foundries gave me a lot of free time. What I found during that time, was that in the case of your father's particular crime, attempted murder and accusation without merit, you could find a way to clear him.

"The decree that said that no one could come to your father's defense was bogus, and was never made in Verengrath before. It was precedent setting, and as such could be challenged," Le'stal explained. "The problem is that no Dwarf would ever challenge the dictates of the Jeweled Throne. It had never happened in all of our history, and no one is strong enough politically to do so now. The closest person I knew who could have done it was Ba'rel."

"Well, I'm not here to clear my father's name anyway," Austin said. "I'm here to try to find troops to free Eland from a history of royal heredity. It's time our people were allowed to choose its king, rather than be stuck with one," he explained.

"Well, I still think it's worth a try," Chloe said, frowning at the direction the conversation was taking. She was getting tired of all the negativity around her. For all of her brothers flaws, being a defeatist wasn't one of them. "There is a dark Elf out there who has a goal to attack the Dwarven kingdom. That should be enough to garner some support."

"What's this about a dark Elf?" Le'stal asked.

"His name is Neamith the Dark," Austin explained, suddenly remembering the Elf again. "He petitioned me, several months ago, to work for my campaign if I would allow him to march on Verengrath once I was victorious. I denied him."

"Neamith the Dark?" Le'stal said, chewing the name in his mind. "I know of no such Elf, but," he said, still remembering details, "it seems to me that an Elf was implicated in the cave in."

"How do you mean?" Chloe asked. She hadn't seen the Elf for so long, but she could easily see him being a part in a murder attempt.

"We Dwarves know weapons. Well at least, we have specialists who do. During the investigation into my cave in, the investigators brought in a team of weapons specialists to look at the cuts made in the ties we use to hold up the support beams. The team found that the slices made to the ropes were done with a knife, forged in Verengrath, but used by an Elf. It confused everyone greatly at the time," Le'stal explained.

"How can you tell if a slice is made by an Elf, Dwarf or human?" Chloe asked, genuinely curious.

“Oh that’s easy,” Le’stal replied. “Come here and cut this rope Chloe,” he said, giving her a piece of rope to cut. Once she was done, he pulled his knife from his belt and cut a piece next to it. “Dwarves cut with force. Our blades are made so that with each slice, we dig deeper. It allows us to make fewer cuts to get through something.

“Elves on the other hand take lighter slices, requiring more of a saw like motion to cut through something. If you look closely at the cuts you and I made, you will see what looks like little steps cut into it. If you compare the number of steps in your rope to the steps in mine, you will notice that you have more, because you sawed back and forth more often than I did.”

Chloe looked closely at the two cuts, recognizing what he was describing. “But it’s so hard to tell the difference,” she said. “How do your people determine what race made the cuts with such assurance?”

“They are trained, first off, and secondly, when cutting a rope under extreme tension, they show up more prominently,” Le’stal explained.

“So your people had proof that the saboteur was not Ba’lain, but rather an Elf. So my father is twice damned,” Austin broke in.

“Not really,” Le’stal replied. “It’s one thing for a human to petition entry into Verengrath and to be quickly allowed entrance. But an Elf, even a half Elf,” he said, looking at Chloe, “would take some work. If an Elf got into Verengrath, someone should know about it.”

“Did anyone know of an Elf entering?” Kierra asked.

“No, no one. That means that they were smuggled in. Verengrath is a labyrinth of tunnels. To the casual observer, it is a confusing, complicated place. So for an outsider to sneak in undetected is unheard of,” Le’stal explained. “If an Elf did get in, it was with the help of a Dwarf, there is no doubt in my mind. Your uncle may not have committed the act, but he could have been the mastermind behind it."

"Well, it makes no difference anyway," Austin added. "I cannot free two kingdoms. I have enough trouble trying to find a way to free one."

"I think, though," Le'stal replied, "that someone should be told. I know a Dwarf whom I'd like to talk to about this. He committed himself to exile at the same time I did and he would be the best to discuss this new information with."

"Who is he, Le'stal?" Chloe asked.

"He's Austin's great uncle, Al'bet Ironfist," Le'stal explained. "He's the village blacksmith now, but back during your father's trial, he was the head of the Verengrath army, and head of the Bronze Clan's security forces."

"My uncle is a Dwarven General?" Austin asked, amazed.

"WAS a Dwarven General. He resigned his commission when your father's appeal was dropped. It was such a strange thing," Le'stal said, once again chewing a memory over in his mind. "Ba'rel was so well loved that an appeal was almost guaranteed. But for some reason, the majority of the council voted against such a thing. As if they were trying to hide something."

Austin's curiosity was suddenly piqued. "Are you saying," he asked, "that my father was forced out because he was getting too close to something?"

"That is exactly what I'm saying," Le'stal replied.

"Austin, what are you thinking?" Chloe asked, the corners of her mouth twitching as she tried to hide an excited smile.

"I'm thinking that even if she hates me for the rest of my life, Lyra and the others will have to carry on without me. I think it is now time to find out what really happened, and to clear my father's name," Austin replied, pounding his fist on the kitchen table.

Chapter 12

In the Age of Quarath Porthanaclies

As the months passed, Ba'rel and Cassidy began a new life together at the Wounded Hand. Not long after his exile, Ba'rel asked Cassidy to marry him, which she happily accepted. They were married in a temple of the Creator, by a priest of the Divine Order, who, although had never married a Dwarf and human before, couldn't deny the love the two had for one another.

But as their time together went on, a couple of recent accidents began to concern the newlywed couple. The first was when Ba'rel went into the basement of the Wounded Hand to get a bottle of wine for a patron. As he walked down the steps, he tripped on something and was nearly hung by a rope dangling from the ceiling. The second came as Cassidy was walking home from the market. She was nearly home when a rider bumped into her, causing her to fall, nearly impaling her on a sharp, jagged piece of steel lying on the side of the road.

Ba'rel wasn't normally a suspicious person, but something wasn't right here. So it was that he began to wonder if Nord Byen was the best place for the two of them to stay. More importantly, he began to wonder if he was a threat to his new bride.

As Ba'rel began to take the chairs down off the table to prepare for the supper rush he heard a knock on the front door. "We're not open yet," he shouted. But once again the knock echoed in the room.

“I said,” he yelled, louder this time, as he walked towards the door, “we’re not open yet.”

Again, the knock came, but this time it was harder and more violent. Thinking that the town drunk was causing the commotion, he made his way to the door, prepared to send him on his way in a less than peaceful manner. Turning the lock he opened the door and began to say, “I told you…” but his sentence was cut off. For as soon as the door swung open, the figure at the door threw itself onto him and drove a dagger into his rib cage.

The sting of the blade startled him into action as he swung as hard as he could. His fist connected with the intruder’s head, knocking it back with a loud roar. Ba’rel looked up to see the cloaked figure’s hood thrown back, and to his surprise he was face to face with a Lyren. The Lyren were a race of cat like people, who inhabited the mountains of the Northern Divide. Nearly as tall as the High Elves, their bodies were covered with colored hair and they were well known for their ferocity. Their savage power could rip a man to shreds with their fully extended claws, hidden in their fingertips.

Realizing his danger, Ba’rel went on the attack. Using the stunned state of his opponent to his advantage, he quickly darted under its claws and slammed his thick skull into its chest, driving it back against the wall. He was welcomed with the sound of bones breaking as the creature screamed in pain and dropped to its knees. Reaching to his side, he quickly pulled the knife from his ribs and raised it above his head. He was about to deliver a killing blow, when he noticed the handle.

Shock coursed through him as he recognized his own work. Somehow this beast had acquired one of his own knives to use against him. His suspicions were now made clear; someone was trying to kill him and Cassidy. He stood there staring at the knife, stunned at the tremendous realization he had just made.

A loud scream shattered his stupor, and as he came to his senses he looked up to see the Lyren, arms above its head, ready to strike. He stood, stoic as he faced his death, knowing he could not do anything to save himself now. As he watched the beast bunch its knees, preparing to launch, there was a sudden flash between him and it. Its eyes, once angry and vicious, now flared open with surprise and pain. It stood there frozen, unable to move from where it stood. Ba'rel slowly circled to the side of the beast, where he saw an old rusted sword, dripping with blood, sticking out of the front of its chest.

The beast fell with a thud, and made a sound as air escaped from its lungs and it began to twitch on the floor at his feet. The Dwarf, in a moment of shocked amazement that he was still alive, looked up into the face of his wife, panting with rage. Her hair had come undone, and panic was in her eyes, as he quickly ran to her to catch her from fainting.

"My warrior queen," he said softly, "I'd be dead many times over if not for you, my love."

"My life would have no meaning if you weren't here to share it with," she replied weakly.

Holding her head to his chest, the two of them sat and stared at the dead creature inside the doorway of their beloved pub, with the antique sword that normally hung beside the door through its chest. A crowd of people began to gather around, each one amazed at what lay on the floor before them.

It was no surprise to the people of Nord Byen when Cassidy's younger sister, Kierra, took over the pub. Cassidy and Ba'rel had decided after the Lyren's attack that they had to leave or face yet another assassination attempt. They had loaded their wagon with their belongings and after a final goodbye to their friends, they began their long journey away from Nord Byen to start a new life.

Weeks passed as the pair made their way through Eland, searching for a new home. They had heard rumors of barbarians raiding villages along the coast, so they decided to keep as far inland as they could. Finally, after trying to find a community they could call home, they settled in a little village called Dayson, in the southeastern corner of the kingdom.

Also, and much to their surprise and joy, Cassidy announced that she was with child and that they would be parents soon. None of the priests, who served as healers, knew what to expect from a Dwarf and human coupling. So unfortunately, it would happen when it would happen. Humans having a gestation of 9 months would have been the norm, but Dwarves carried their young for much longer, and the pregnancy could have gone as long as two years.

So it was that when the two found Dayson, they decided to stop and try to make Cassidy as comfortable as they could during this difficult time. The problem was, Ba'rel was a miner and Cassidy an Innkeeper, but Dayson already had an Inn.

Being new in the community, Cassidy was welcomed as a new barmaid at the River Nymph. But it was Ba'rel who didn't know what to do.

"I can't have my wife being the bread winner," Ba'rel said, as they sat around their small campfire outside of town.

"I know Ba'rel. So keep looking. What else did you used to do in Verengrath that could help?" Cassidy asked, trying support his bruised ego.

"Not much," He replied. "I was an entry level engineer, and a miner. In our culture, I'm still fairly young at 173. I was just moving along through life without thought to the future," he said blushing.

"As do all young people, my dear," Cassidy smiled at him. "Well you won't give up, and if you have to, you'll just have to learn something new. Remember, even a menial job is better than nothing at all. So even if you have to haul boxes by hand, it will keep us fed."

The Dwarf nodded, accepting her advice with an open mind.

The next day Ba'rel set out to do exactly that, get a job doing whatever he could. He moved from business to business, trying to lend a hand where he could, but no one really needed a laborer. Small towns are blessed with back breaking labor so unfortunately, all positions were full.

It wasn't until he made his way to the blacksmith that he found his big break. "Mr. Robison?" he said at the door.

The Blacksmith never looked up from his work but kept hammering as he answered, "Yup, I need a man who can work long hours and can keep at it until a critical job is done."

"How'd you know I needed work? Or for that matter, who I was at your door?" Ba'rel asked.

"I'm the blacksmith, son. I know everything that goes on in this town. I'm a bit surprised you didn't come to me sooner," he said, dipping the glowing metal in his tongs into a vat of oil.

"I never thought of working with metal. Besides dabbling in the smithy, I just always mined it," the Dwarf said with a chuckle.

"Well no bother. I'm glad to have you on. Now grab that apron and whichever hammer feels right in your hand and let's get to it," Mr. Robison said, winking at the Dwarf with a grin.

That night Ba'rel slowly dragged himself home. His hands were blistered, and his back was sore, but he did so with a smile on his face. As he rounded the bend to their little camp he was glad to see Cassidy, waiting there for him with soup on.

"Ba'rel!" Cassidy exclaimed and running to him she hugged him close. "I was beginning to worry about you."

"Sorry my love," the Dwarf replied. "I was working and needed to finish a project."

"Working? You found a job?" she said happily.

"Yes, with Mr. Robison, the blacksmith. As of today, I'm an apprentice blacksmith," He said with a tired smile.

"Oh Ba'rel, that's fantastic!" she said, hugging him again.

"It gets better. What time do you work tomorrow?" he asked.

"Not until midday. Why?" she replied.

"Because Mr. Robison has a single room shack available behind the smithy. It used to be his home, but he moved out when he was able to build his wife and himself a bigger one. He said we could use it until we could move to our own home," Ba'rel said with a smile.

"Thank God for this blessing," Cassidy exclaimed. "I was getting tired of sleeping on the ground."

"Well, we might have to sleep on the floor for a few weeks, until we get enough money together for a mattress and bed, but it will be dry and warm," Ba'rel replied.

"You've done well, my heart," Cassidy said, smiling at him. "You really came through for us."

The Dwarven male could only smile with pride at his wife's joy. "Yeah, I'm very happy with this too. Just a few months ago, I wasn't sure if I had a life left to live. Now I have a wife, a job, and a roof over our heads." His pride showed through his fatigue. "I don't just have a life, we have a future," he said as he gently rubbed Cassidy's already bulging belly.

Chapter 13

In the Age of the Eland Civil War

Le'stal, Austin and Chloe walked across the village towards the sound of steel on steel ringing in the air, the signature of a village blacksmith. They soon rounded a bend in the village road and came across the open doors as a Dwarf stood, swinging his hammer onto a piece of metal, held by tongs.

Austin was impressed by his size. For a Dwarf, he was quite tall, and his shirtless form showed the defined muscles of a seasoned smith. Once the Dwarven smith saw Le'stal, he stopped swinging his hammer, and walked to meet them, grasping the blonde Dwarf's forearm warmly.

"Le'stal, how good to see you," Al'bet said with a smile on his black bearded face.

"And you, Al'bet. My friend, I bring some visitors who might interest you," Le'stal said, indicating the pair beside him.

"Oh? Well, any friend of Le'stal is a friend of mine," the Dwarf said, beaming.

"Well more so family than a friend," Le'stal said. A look of confusion crossed Al'bet's face as Le'stal ushered him into the smithy and closed the door behind them. "Al'bet, this young lady is Chloe Duthain. Princess of Andraya, and commander of their notorious Rangers," he explained.

"Well met young lady. I have heard much of your Rangers. They carry with them the whispers of respect, even within the walls of Verengrath themselves," he said politely.

"You have my thanks, Al'bet," she said, bowing slightly in respect to the master smith.

"And this," Le'stal continued, pointing at Austin, "is Austin. Austin Ironfist." He stood silent, watching as the blacksmith were about to reply, then stop, and after a moment of contemplation a look of understanding crossed his face.

"You're Ba'rel's boy, aren't you son?" he said in a near whisper.

"Yes sir, I am," Austin said gently.

The Dwarf let out a loud bellow and rushing across the room, grabbed Austin around the middle of his torso and squeezed for all his worth. "Boy, I never thought I would see the son of my nephew! It gladdens my heart to see an Ironfist in such form!" he beamed.

Smiling at the young man before him, tears rimmed his eyes. He stepped back a couple of steps to take him in. "But boy, if you're here like this, then your father..."

"Is dead. Yes sir, I lost him many years ago," Austin explained.

A lone tear fell down the face of the Dwarven smith, who quickly wiped the rest away. "No more sir, son. I am your Uncle Al'bet, and I am as proud of a Half Dwarf, half human son of your father as I would be a full blooded Dwarf," he said, trying to be strong. "Now tell me, what brings you here after so many years?" he asked.

"I've been here a couple of times in the past. I even believe your smithy fixed a piece of armor for me once," Austin said. "But I never knew any of you were my family until yesterday. I came to Nord Byen to find troops to help me in my bid to free Eland, but we believe we may have uncovered a threat to Verengrath and so I'm here to see if you can help make sense of all this," he explained.

Al'bet ushered them to chairs and they explained everything that they knew, about the Elf and his possible role in the cave in, and about the threat to the Dwarven Kingdom.

After several hours passed, and the day began to wane, Al'bet finally spoke. He had sat nearly silent as everything was explained to him, taking it all in. Austin knew a seasoned veteran when he saw one, and his uncle was not to be taken lightly.

"Lad," Al'bet started, "you said you've been here before."

"Yes Uncle, once or twice on my way to the front," Austin replied.

"How is it your name never came to be known?" the Dwarven smith asked him.

"As a lesser officer," Austin explained, "I was trained to hold my tongue. To be honest, my superiors always spoke for me. Either that or their errand runners. It was like that for all of us."

The Dwarven smith nodded his understanding. "Yes, we do the same thing in Verengrath. Well, it appears that we have an enemy within," Al'bet said quietly.

"Indeed. But the problem is how do we explain it to the council without breaking the law?" Le'stal asked.

"That's simple enough," Al'bet replied, almost off handedly. "We just do it. There will be huffing and puffing, and shouts for our execution, but not before we can make our case."

"Oh that's all then. Just put our heads in the noose while we plead with them then?" Le'stal said with sigh.

"Le'stal, your foot wasn't all you lost in that cave in," Al'bet replied. "You've lost your stomach for battle. What kind of Dwarf would fear the noose?"

"A Dwarf with one foot, you giant block head," Le'stal said with a grin. The larger Dwarf looked at him for a moment and began laughing, clapping his friend on the back. "Ah Le'stal, it is always good when you come to visit!"

"Okay, but he does have a point, Uncle," Austin injected. "How patient will they be to see the son of an exile, a half Elf, and two self-exiled Dwarves telling them they're wrong?"

"Leave those details to me," Al'bet replied. "I'll deal with the dance with death. But we must act. I've heard rumors that the Kiamet armies are preparing to make their move. I expect that you shall see battle in a little over a month in the Lytton region of the kingdom, nephew."

"How do you know that?" Austin asked, suddenly worried about his lack of progress and troops.

"Kiamet had men here to get weapons a while back. They had loose lips. No son, you are in a lot of trouble on the war front. But that will not matter, should that Elf decide to bring war to Verengrath," he said, his eyes staring into the distance. "If that should happen, all of Eland shall ring. There is no way that the Dwarves would allow their mountain home to be invaded by an enemy. No, they would meet them out here on Eland soil if a threat came their way."

"But I have no troops to fight this war. Only a few thousand who trusted me during the protection of Andraya," Austin moaned.

"Let's cross one bridge at a time," Chloe said. "First, we must sort out this other problem."

"Perhaps we should come back to it?" Austin said, taking her aside.

"No Austin," she replied, "we must do this now. The Creator brought us here for a reason, we should follow this path."

Austin hated to agree with her. He had never put much faith in the Creator, but he had faith in his friend. Nodding his agreement they went back to discuss plans with Al'bet and Le'stal before heading back to the Pub and their beds for the night.

A Kingdom away, King William slept in his bed, with his wife Emma at his side. Suddenly a gentle blue glow formed at his bedside, causing him to stir and wake. Opening his eyes, the ruler of Andraya was startled to see a large blue lion glowing in his chamber.

The half Elf ruler took a long breath and sighed deeply, attempting to calm himself. After a moment he realized that the spectral creature wasn't there to attack him. Instead it was sitting there, patiently waiting for him to calm down. Then after waiting a moment longer, the glowing lion got up and began moving towards the door. It stopped for a moment to glance over its shoulder at the curious King, as if asking, "Are you coming?"

Understanding the silent question, William got to his feet, threw on his robe embroidered with the Andrayan Lion, and followed the large cat out of his home. They moved away from the Royal Household of the Czariana Ruling Court and back into the Private Royal Gardens.

As they walked, the lion led William back to a small secluded fountain that William immediately recognized as Chloe's favorite in all the gardens. They broke through the hedges only to be joined by a spectral wolf followed by Declan, and a glowing blue fox followed by Brody.

The three old friends nodded at each other as they turned their attentions back to their guides before them.

Then as the three glowing blue animals came to the fountain in the center of the clearing, they turned and, lifting their heads, they all looked to a fourth glowing blue creature. William, Declan and Brody hadn't noticed this fourth animal before, but now that they saw it, they knew what was happening. For there, sitting on the top of a carved tree that made up the fountain's center piece, sat a glowing blue falcon.

William stepped forward and as all four creatures calmly turned his way he said, "I understand," and bowed deeply to them.

The three guides turned to one another and slowly walked towards the trees, disappearing into the dew heavy mist. The falcon remained for a moment, a look of fear on its face. Then it too leapt from its perch, and flying passed the three men, disappeared into the night air.

"What would you have of us my king?" Brody asked.

"Chloe needs us. Prepare the troops. We march for Lytton at day break," he commanded. The two commanders saluted him with a fist to their chests and quickly rushed off to mobilize the Andrayan army.

As he watched them go, William gazed off in the direction his sister's spirit totem had flown, which was directly towards their neighboring kingdom of Eland. "We're coming Chloe!" William said loudly into the night air and was answered with a thunderous roar in the distance!

Chapter 14

In the Age of Quarath Porthanaclies

"Austin, come back here!" Cassidy yelled as she chased behind her son. He giggled as she rushed after him. "Austin, get some pants on!" she shouted.

The boy stopped, looked down and realized he was rushing out the door in nothing but his tunic. Quickly grabbing the front of his shirt, he pulled it down over his private area as some girls walked by, water buckets in hand, giggling.

"Golly mom, did you have to make such a scene?" he moaned, as his face turned red with embarrassment.

"It would have been a much bigger scene if you showed up at the smithy like that," she said with a grin. Handing him his pants, she smiled as he scurried back into the house.

They were able to build their own place, several years ago, shortly after Austin was born. The friendship and support of Lonny, the blacksmith and his wife, Mary Ann, had helped them from the moment they arrived in the village of Dayson. Lonny's patience, guidance and mentoring had not only given them hope, but it gave Ba'rel an outlet for his talents. None of them knew how exceptional a smith he truly was. Since taking him on, Lonny's business had more than doubled, and he shamelessly attributed it to his new apprentice.

"Come on mom. It's a big day today!" the seven year old Austin shouted, running out the door once again. "We don't want to be late."

Cassidy laughed as she followed her son. "It'll be fine Austin. We won't miss anything." Again she laughed as she saw him run on. But her laughter was cut off as a bout of coughing racked her body. She quickly lifted the handkerchief she always kept on hand to her lips to muffle the sound. She slowly took it away to once again see the blood staining its white fringes.

She had been coughing like this for a couple of months, but only in the last week had she began seeing blood. Ba'rel made enough money that she was able to consult several physicians, but none of them had a solution. Ba'rel knew, of course, but the decision to keep it from Austin was one she held strong on. A little boy didn't need to think about such things.

Composing herself, Cassidy once again followed her son across town to the blacksmith shop. She was right, of course, in her warnings to Austin. They were still very early for Ba'rel's exciting day. He had come so far in the last several years, and his apprenticeship had gone from an entry level apprentice, to an intermediate and on until they reached today. Today would be the day he received his own anvil, hammer and tongs as a sign of his mastery of the art.

Lonny had always been amazed at how fast Ba'rel learned. It had taken him nearly thirteen years to achieve his hammer and tongs, and as far as he was concerned, Ba'rel was ready for his years ago. But the Dwarf wouldn't hear of it then, saying it disrespected the art to be given such a prestigious title so quickly. Well today was the day, and it was a huge celebration for the entire village.

As she arrived, she heard the familiar clang as two hammers worked side by side in the smithy. That was how Ba'rel and Lonny did everything, working face to face, hammering the steel to its final shape and form. It didn't surprise her one bit, that even on this prestigious day, the two of them worked. Hammer to hammer, bringing another project to conclusion; one mind, two beings.

She and Austin watched as the two worked tirelessly, until they were interrupted by a gentle cough at the door. Everyone looked up to see the village mayor, Keith Talbreth, standing there surrounded by most of the people of the community.

"Mayor, it's good to see you," Lonny said, extending his hand. The mayor shook each smith's hand, and took the outstretched hand of young Austin in turn smiling at them all.

"Gentlemen, as much as I enjoy watching you work, if we don't start this ceremony soon, you'll end up with a whole cart before you're ready," he laughed, and was joined by the crowd around him.

"Sorry mayor," Ba'rel said, taking off his apron and putting a shirt on. "I guess we get lost in the rhythm sometimes," he explained.

"We all do, Ba'rel," the Mayor replied, and then turned to everyone assembled and shouted loudly, "Ba'rel, when you and Cassidy joined our family it was a new and exciting change for us. Never before, had any of the other races of people chosen to make Dayson their home, and yet here you were on our doorstep.

"It has been to the absolute betterment and blessing to our village that you both made that decision too, Ba'rel and Cassidy. The River Nymph runs as smooth as clock work with your ever steady hand behind the bar, Ms. Cassidy, and our smithy has been singing music to all of us for years. We are thankful that you have come to us, my friends, and that you have added this fine young man to our numbers as well." The Mayor winked at Austin as he stood in the front row.

"Ba'rel, would you and Lonny come forward please?" the Mayor asked.

Both men stepped forward as requested. “Lonny, it’s now up to you,” Keith said gently.

“Thank you, Keith,” the senior blacksmith said with a smile.

“Ba’rel, you have taken on all the knowledge I can give you. You have exceeded me in every way, as all students should, and you truly make me proud. I can gratefully call you my apprentice no more.”

The master smith turned around to where his wife, Mary Ann, stood with a wooden box in her hands. “You have gone beyond the role of student, to that of a friend and equal. It gladdens my heart, that although Mary Ann and I didn’t have children, that I can pass my art to someone such as you.” Reaching into the box, Lonny lifted out a thick, blue and white ribbon and hanging from it was three medals.

“Ba’rel, I give to you the sign of a master smith. Pay attention to each medal, because each of them bears an important symbolism,” the blacksmith said solemnly. “The tongs represent reaching for more than your hands alone can grasp. The hammer, a sign that force must always be applied in measure to properly shape all things. The anvil, that when all else fails, you must never yield in all things that you do. Ba’rel, you have become like a son to us and we love your family deeply.

“It is with that love, respect and friendship that I bestow upon you the title of Master Smith. Bear it proudly, with honor and dignity, and make your brothers of the forge proud of you,” he said with a smile, as he lowered the ribbon around the Dwarf’s neck.

Then turning to Cassidy and Austin, he ushered them forward and brought all three Ironfist’s into his grasp, where his wife joined them. “It is also, on this day that Mary Ann and I give you all one more gift.” Lonny’s voice cracked as he began to speak, causing him to stop to compose himself. “Sorry, my age betrays me. Today, Mary Ann and

I would like to give to you one more gift." He turned and took the ring of keys from his wife as she smiled lovingly at them all. "Today we give you the keys to the smithy. My children, we give you what we have built here, to carry on in good faith."

An awed silence hung around them, as no one dared to speak at such an incredible gift. Ba'rel stared at the keys, as if they were a viper about to bite him. He couldn't believe what he had just heard. He stood there, as if locked in stone, until he felt a gentle grip on his shoulder. Looking up, he saw the loving look of his wife. Her eyes, rimmed with tears, were full of pride.

Turning back to his best friend, Ba'rel looked once more at the keys, but instead of taking them he wrapped his arms around his friend's waist and hugged him hard. The crowd erupted in cheers as Lonny hugged his friend back. Abandoning all pretenses he began to laugh openly with joy at his young friend's happiness.

Everyone celebrated till late in the night. But when everything was over, the only ones who remained were Ba'rel, Lonny and the Mayor, Keith Talbreth.

"It was a good day, fellas," Keith said.

"It certainly was that," Ba'rel replied. "I haven't had that much fun since Le'stal's 64th birthday," he chuckled.

"You don't talk much about your past, Ba'rel. You speak of Le'stal as if an old friend," Lonny said, taking another pull of his ale.

"Aye, he was my best friend in Verengrath. I don't know if he lives or not, and I miss him, but I don't look to my past, only my future.

"Working with you have been some of the happiest days of my life, Lonny. The way you two have set out to give my family a home here, a Dwarf could never have expected better," Ba'rel said with a smile at his two friends.

"Well it is our honor to have your family with us," Keith said, winking at his friend. "Besides, without you two, Dayson wouldn't have prospered as it has. Let's not delude ourselves, this village has done as well as it has because you brought trade here. All of Eland flourishes because of your efforts."

"You're sounding like a politician again," Lonny said with a laugh, which was openly joined by the other two.

"And a darn fine politician at that," Ba'rel added, and once again the three men laughed.

"So what are you working on next?" Keith asked in hushed tones.

"Ba'rel has designed something interesting," Lonny said with a grin.

"Oh, what's that?" Keith asked.

"It's a weapon I've envisioned. It's a sword of sorts. I've heard the Prince of Andraya is coming through here, to fight in the border wars. I thought we could present him with something different for combat." Ba'rel walked back into the smithy and walked out with a rough piece of metal in a strange shape.

Keith took it and held it awkwardly in front of him and frowned. Ba'rel and Lonny laughed. "That's what I thought at first, but you're holding it wrong," Lonny said, and turning it sideways he allowed his friend to grip it properly.

"That's an interesting design Ba'rel. What do you call it?" Keith asked, impressed by the ingenuity.

"I call it a Natal. I think it's going to change history someday," Ba'rel said with a smile.

Chapter 15

In the Age of the Eland Civil War

"Are you sure about this Uncle Al'bet?" Austin asked as they stood before the gates of Verengrath. Austin had seen them before, but in passing. Now that he was about to enter the Dwarven kingdom, they looked huge, menacing, as if they were casting judgment upon him.

"Calm yourself, son," Al'bet said, his grey streaked beard covering a solemn face. "Now is the time to start acting like a General."

It had been so long since he had commanded troops that Austin had forgotten his title. He was at one time the supreme commander of all of Eland's troops, and now he was behaving like a green recruit. His uncle was right, he was a commander, a High General of the Eland Army, and it was time to act like one. The young Half Dwarf stood tall, chest out, with his thumbs tucked into his belt.

"Very nice m'boy," he heard his Uncle say beside him. The phrase caught him by surprise. His father said that to him once during his graduation from the Academy. Suddenly though his attention was brought back to the gates before them, as a loud clank signaled the lock being drawn, as the doors creaked open outwards.

All four of Austin's party stood still, as the doors slowly opened. After the giant doors stopped moving, a delegation from Verengrath stepped out to meet them.

"Al'bet. Le'stal. I'm glad to see you both doing well," the Dwarf before them replied. Austin had never before seen a Dwarf without any facial hair, as the guard that addressed them was cleanly shaven.

"Commander Ro'tan, it's good to see you as well," Al'bet replied with a nod.

"What brings you to Verengrath today?" the Commander asked.

"This is High General Austin, of the Eland Army and one of the three parties vying for the throne of Eland," Le'stal replied. "He comes with a warning to the high council."

"A warning? What kind of warning?" Ro'tan asked, giving a cautious glance over the general.

"He has information of an impending attack and we must see the Kings of the jeweled thrones as soon as we can," Al'bet explained.

"I see. And who is this with him?" he asked, tilting his head towards Chloe.

"My name is Chloe Duthain, Princess of Andraya, and Emissary of the Throne of Andraya," she replied with a slight nod.

"You're an Elf?" Ro'tan asked.

"A half Elf, yes. But I do not represent the people of any Elven community. I am here as a friend and ally of High General Austin," sShe explained.

"We don't normally grant entry to elves lightly, madam," the commander replied.

"And you wouldn't be today either. As I said, I'm a half Elf, and a full blooded Andrayan," she said with a smile.

The commander thought for a moment and softened his expression, returning the smile with a small one of his own.

"I think we can allow the distinction," he said, and turning, he began to walk back to his delegation and then back into the open gates, followed by Austin, Chloe, Le'stal and Al'bet.

Chloe and Austin both nearly stumbled as they walked into the giant cavern before them. It was rough and ragged, but the sheer size of it was incredible. The natural elements surrounding them were beautiful.

"Just wait, it gets better," Al'bet said softly with a wink. The two adventurers continued on, and were led across the great open chamber and into a hallway that could easily allow eight men to walk abreast within. Here the floor changed from roughhewn stone to a more flat surface. The further they walked, the more the floor began to shine until it appeared that they walked on glass. They were so enamored of the floor that neither noticed when they exited the hallway.

"Welcome to Verengrath," Ro'tan said proudly, causing both to look up in awe as they beheld the beauty of the Dwarven Kingdom.

"Incredible," Austin said under his breath. The chamber they had been led into was even larger than the last. Floor upon floor spiraled up, as a series of ramps, bridges and causeways criss-crossed above them. Each level teemed with life as Dwarves hurried along everywhere they looked.

Everything glimmered all around them. From jeweled statues, to gold, silver, bronze and copper ornaments glittering on the walls. Austin had never before seen so much wealth combined in one place before, and it was breath taking.

"This is amazing," he gasped. He could feel his Dwarven roots tugging within him.

"This?" Al'bet chuckled. This is just the central hall. You should see the treasure rooms. Now there are gems in those vaults that would turn you inside out."

Chloe had remained quiet the entire journey within the mountain from the moment they entered the great gates. She had vowed to follow Austin wherever he may lead, but her fear of enclosed spaces was itching at the back of her mind. Focusing her thoughts, she attempted to calm her racing heart and mind.

Al'bet continued to lead the group across the center of the great hall, towards a corner that was decorated with the four Jewels of Verengrath. There they found a large round door, studded with Rubies, Emeralds, Diamonds and Sapphires. Everyone stood silently before the entrance, as Ro'tan knocked forcefully upon it with his staff. A shout of "enter" echoed loudly from within. Ro'tan signaled for them to wait, as he entered the open door to speak to whoever was inside.

Several minutes passed before the Commander returned to the waiting group at the door. "I have passed your request for a meeting of the Kings. The message will go out to the clans, and then I will be informed when a decision has been made. You are welcome to stay and wait, but it will take a few hours, perhaps even the night before an answer will be given."

"Do you suggest a place to stay?" Austin asked, looking around for a motel.

"You'll stay with your family, boy," Al'bet said quietly. "We'll head to the Bronze Clan now Ro'tan. If you need us that is where you will find us," he said to the Dwarf before them.

"Very good. I'll let you know as soon as I hear word." And moving away from the group, he strode to a nearby barracks, striking up a conversation with some soldiers milling around the door. Once again the small group followed as Le'stal and Al'bet marched across the Central Cavern and on to the Chambers of the Bronze Clan. Chloe couldn't help but notice that as soon as they exited the main public spaces, the floors lost their shine and became simple smooth pathways once again. As they travelled onward, they passed large groups of Dwarves who were guiding carts pulled by strange looking creatures. The beasts reminded Chloe of a small rodent one of her friends had as a youth, in Czariana, when it was still an unnamed village. The creatures were a deep brown with giant teeth and large bulging eyes.

"What are those strange looking animals?" she asked Le'stal.

"Those are Gorkor's. They live in the depths of the mountain, but over the centuries," Le'stal explained, "we've been able to domesticate them to help us within Verengrath. They are gentle beasts usually, but once threatened, they can turn deathly violent."

"Don't suppose we could catch a ride on one?" Austin chuckled.

"You could, if it would let you onto its back," Al'bet laughed. "Darn things are great at pulling rock, but jump on one, or even on an empty cart and the darned things will bite your head off."

And so it was that they continued to walk through the mountain until they reached the Bronze clan cavern, and Austin's ancestral home. It wasn't as impressive as the Central Hall of Verengrath, but it was still a sight to behold.

Here, rather than being adorned with all the different types of metals, as the Great Hall was, the clans central cavern only had bronze embellishments. Busts of previous kings lined the walls, carved from granite, and each lamp that lit the room had a large bronze disk behind it to reflect the light throughout the chamber. This use of the orange tinted metal caused the chamber to glow with a slightly orange hue.

They quickly moved across the hall towards Le'stal's home within the clan. He didn't live there anymore, but he knew his sister Mar'di did. When they arrived, they found her sitting there, visiting with her best friend, Li'sa.

"Le'stal, you've come home!" Mar'di exclaimed.

"For a short while," he replied, giving her a hug. "Mar'di, Li'sa, I'd like to introduce you to Chloe Duthain and Austin Ironfist," he said quietly.

"Ironfist?" Li'sa said. "How... You're Ba'rel's son, aren't you?" she said in shock.

"Yes ma'am, I am," Austin replied holding his head high. He wasn't about to let anyone disrespect his parents.

"Ma'am nothing! I am your cousin, Austin. Welcome home!" she said and giving him a hug she pulled him tight against her.

Everyone sat within Mar'di's home visiting and waiting for Ro'tan to let them know when they could return to the Chamber of Kings.

"I can't believe how much of both your parents you have in your face," Li'sa said with a smile.

"Well lucky for me, my mother was a beautiful woman; otherwise I could have ended up looking like my father," he said with a chuckle that was joined by everyone in the room.

"So you are going to the council to say what, exactly?" Mar'di asked her brother.

"To be honest, I don't know," Le'stal replied. "We believe that Ba'rel was the target of several assassination attempts. We also have a link between a dark Elf that wants to attack Verengrath, and the Elf that caused the cave in."

"That's not much of an argument, Le'stal," Li'sa replied.

"No, it's so weak I expect to get thrown out of the kingdom. This time not of my own choice," Le'stal said quietly.

"Oh for goodness sakes, boy. We aren't here to try to change their minds!" Al'bet said shaking his head.

"Then what are we doing here?" Austin asked in amazement.

"We're here because you're going to challenge Ba'lain's right to the throne!" Al'bet said with a shrug.

"You've got to be kidding me!" Austin said incredulously.

"Well, I'm not. When we get in, we are going to deliver our evidence to the council. They are going to get all puffed up, make denouncements and you are going to demand that Ba'lain stand trial for his acts against Verengrath and your father," Al'bet explained.

"Why would they allow a challenge from a Half Dwarf?" Chloe asked, genuinely curious.

"That's simple. They'll do it because he's going to challenge the Path of Fire and will not only clear his father's name, but will have earned the right to sit as the champion of the Bronze Clan," Al'bet replied to her.

"The Path of Fire!" Le'stal shouted, jumping to his feet. "Are you out of your ever loving mind?"

Chapter 16

In the Age of Quarath Porthanaclies

Austin sat outside of his parents' room, with his head in his hands. He was a young man, and had watched for a decade as his mother fought off whatever evil had taken hold of her and slowly drained the life from the woman whom he adored with all his being. But now, it appeared that Cassidy could fight it no longer. His mother was slipping away.

He had received word of the turn in her health while he was at the academy. His father had become so successful in Eland, that even though he wasn't a noble, Austin had been accepted by the school that trained military commanders in Eland. Of course being of common birth made it hard enough, but the fact that he was a Half Dwarf made it nearly unbearable.

But it was because of his Dwarven heritage that he was able to persevere. One visit home after a particularly difficult term, Ba'rel sat with his son, worried it was too much for the boy.

"Dad, they're relentless. And when I retaliate, the Sergeants punish me for attacking another cadet. I hate it there," Austin said.

"Son," Ba'rel replied gently, "if you feel you have to quit, then I will stand by your decision. But you have to know, if you do, they win. They will have pushed you out and made you give up.

"Those pompous little know-nothings have never worked a hard day in their lives. They look down on you because you're stronger, harder working and you earned your place. They had theirs handed to them. You will work hard, and you will succeed, but only if you see it through." When the Dwarf finished his piece, he walked away to leave his son think it over. Austin left the next day to return to his training.

Now four years later, Austin had just graduated at the top of his class, and was given command of a sword and shield division when he received word about his mother. After obtaining permission from his superiors he rushed home so he could be with his parents during this terrifying time in their lives.

Soon a creaking sound came from the hinges, causing the young man to look up and, seeing his father, he stood. "How is she?" Austin asked.

"She won't beat it this time son," Ba'rel said with sadness etched deep in his face. Austin could see that a lifetime of hurt had fallen on his father, as if his mother was all that stood between him and some past grief that Ba'rel had never explained to his son.

"Is there no one who can help her?" Austin asked.

"No. I've called in the best healers from all of Eland and a few from neighboring kingdoms as well. But whatever has its hold on her lungs isn't letting go this time," the Dwarf said, and sat down. "The doctors needed a minute with her. We can go back in when they say."

Austin joined his father at the dinner table and hung his head in his grief. His parents were the only family he had ever had. Besides the Robison's and some close friends in Dayson, they were all he had ever cared about. Losing his mother was the most incredible pain he had ever felt.

Soon, though, the doctors emerged from the bedroom and softly spoke to his father. "She doesn't have much time left Ba'rel. She'd like you both to be with her now."

Ba'rel nodded and, leading the way, he and Austin walked into the bedroom. Austin felt a knot build in his chest as he saw the scene before him. Lying in his parents' bed, propped up on pillows, lay his weak and pale mother. The luster had left her hair and the radiance that was always there had dulled. Yet the moment she saw her son, new life surged into her and she reached for him to come to her.

The young man strode across the room with confidence, a confidence he hoped that could hide his mounting fear. "Austin, you've come," Cassidy said weakly.

"Nothing could have stopped me, mother," he said, sitting on the bed and taking her into his arms.

As they parted she reached up and grabbed his Captain's insignia on his chest. "I am so proud of you, Austin," she said with a smile. "You fought so hard for this, and we always knew you could do it."

"I did it thanks to you two," Austin replied, his voice soft in the silent room.

"No Austin, you did it thanks to you and who you are," Cassidy replied. She reached out for Ba'rel, who knelt down at the head of the bed next to her. Reaching up, she absent mindedly began to stroke his long salt and peppered hair. "My two men," Cassidy said with a smile. "God has blessed my life with you both, and even though He has called me home a little earlier than I would have liked, I am glad for the time I've had with you.

"I never could have had a better life with anyone else, and from the moment you walked into my tavern," she said, smiling at Ba'rel, "my life has been one beautiful sunrise after another." She began to cough and reached for a glass of water by the bed, which Ba'rel gave to her quickly. "I want the two of you to promise me that you will never give up on life. Know that everything I have lived for must live on in you. Austin, find love. Duty is incredible, but so too is love. Don't live this life alone, and always know I will be watching you until God calls you home to join me.

"And my Ba'rel," she said, turning him to face her. "I love you Ba'rel. Please don't mourn for long. Please know that I'm better where I go, and that I am waiting for you anxiously. But you mustn't hurry your trip; you must live until God calls upon you, or we will never be together again.

"You two are my light, and I will always be fulfilled because of you." Her voice grew very gentle and her eyes grew heavy. "You are my sunshine." And with that her last breath escaped her as she lay still in the bed.

Neither man cried. Austin wanted to, as his chest felt like his heart was about to explode, his grief was so great. But when he saw his father lean over his mother and kissed her on the mouth a final time, he decided he would remain strong for him.

The funeral was held a couple of days later and everyone in Dayson was there. The entire village shut down to mourn the loss of one of their brightest lights. Speeches were read, tears shed, and after, everyone wanted to give their condolences to both of the surviving members of the family. Lonny and Mary Ann never left them for a week, insisting that both Ba'rel and Austin stay at their home. Then the following week, Mary Ann stayed at the Ironfist home where she cooked, cleaned and did everything she could to help ease their pain.

Lonny thanked them for their patience with her as they sat at Ba'rel's kitchen table. "She deals with grief like this," he explained.

"She has to be busy, because if she slows down she will be overwhelmed and will have to face the sadness."

"It's okay, Lonny," Ba'rel said with a weak smile. "You are both family; having her with us does us some good."

"I'm glad. You two can come over any time you like you know," Lonny said with a gentle smile.

"Aye, we know. But it was our home for a long time, and it will be our home for as ever long as the Creator wishes it to be," Ba'rel said, to which Lonny could only nod.

"So, Austin, when do you return to the academy?" Lonny asked.

"I don't," Austin replied. The two men at his side gave him concerned looks. "Oh, no, it's not because of mother's death. She asked that I continue to live my life and I plan to, in her honor. But now that I've graduated and been given a command, I will lead them to the front lines and face the Northern Hordes with our troops," he explained.

"We are attacking the Wastes?" Ba'rel asked.

"No, they are making aggressive movements south. Things are rough up there. Food has been scarce since the cold has gotten worse, and the Humans, Trolls, Ogres and Polar's have joined forces and appear to be preparing for an attack. We expect it any week now," he explained.

"Polar's? Have you ever seen one in person?" Lonny asked the young man.

"Yes, once. We were training in the north to prepare us for combat there when we were attacked by one. Uncle Lonny, you have never seen a creature so huge! With the head and torso of a great white bear, with human arms and massive troll like legs; it was incredible," Austin explained, as his mind flashed back to the event.

"It came out of nowhere one afternoon. They are pure white, so trying to see them in the snow is very difficult when they are stalking. When it attacked it instantly killed two of my colleagues. We then attempted to fight it with swords, but that just put us too close within its long reach. We changed tactics and started to use spears, and although that gave us a reach advantage, we still couldn't get close enough to kill it.

"But then as we battled it, I noticed that its head could hardly turn from side to side. So I caught the attention of another cadet, named Kiamet, and told him to get its attention and to get it mad. If Kiamet can do anything, it's get you angry and so he started to poke and prod the giant beast with his spear. He ran side to side, trying to keep its attention focused on him, which in and of itself was terrifying to watch. The creature was huge, but fast! It could move like a cougar, and was vicious.

"Kiamet isn't like the others though, he's smart, agile and every time the beast would lunge at him, he would roll away, using the snow to cushion his tumble. But while he had lured the Polar away from the others, I snuck up behind it and when I was confident its attention was completely on Kiamet, I jumped onto its back.

"It thrashed and flailed madly about, trying to grab me off of its back. But I held on to its neck for dear life, knowing that if it got ahold of me, I was finished. It flung me around so violently that my legs flew off of its back, nearly throwing me from it, and in fact I would have fallen off if Kiamet hadn't stepped in and stabbed it in the chest with his spear. This caused it to redirect its attention back towards him, allowing me to compose myself.

“I then grabbed hold of it around its throat and began squeezing with all of my might. Its massive hands tried to rip my grip from its throat but it was unable to. I continued to choke the life out of it as best I could, desperately trying to avoid being grabbed and thrown off.

“At one point it threw a punch over its shoulder which rung my bell, but the adrenaline rushing through my body kept me awake. I continued to squeeze and when I felt it begin to weaken, I wrapped my legs around it and squeezed its chest while I choked it out. It was at this time, that it fell to a single knee and began to grunt rather than roar, so I continued to press its lungs with my legs and close its wind pipe with my arms,” Austin said, the excitement taking his mind from his grief.

“What happened then?” Lonny asked, amazed at the story.

“I leaned forward, causing the creature to fall face first into the snow, and I kept squeezing. It was then that Kiamet came to help, and drove his spear into its back, through its rib cage and into its lung. This of course caused the Polar to almost instantly lose all its strength and it dropped unconscious.

“I then eased off of it and watched as it labored for breath. It was amazing to see this massive creature, reduced to a weak and helpless animal. I then grabbed my sword and slammed it into the base of its skull, killing it instantly. The hide is a trophy in the cadet lounge back at the academy,” he said proudly.

“Incredible. Why is it that this is the first time I’ve heard of this?” Ba’rel asked.

“Because it happened just before graduation. Before…” and suddenly he was reminded of where he was and what had recently befallen them.

"Well, my boy," Lonny said, trying to lighten the suddenly somber mood, "that is an amazing story. But what do you do if you have to face an army of them?"

"I don't know, and I'll tell you this much, I would hate to find out!" Austin said with a shiver.

Chapter 17

In the Age of the Eland Civil War

"It's the only way we can set things right, and young Austin here is the only one who can do it," Al'bet said, remaining calm.

"What's the Path of Fire?" Austin asked, concern etched on his face.

"It's an ancient trial and the only route to salvation for some. When a crime is grievous enough, and a sentence too extreme for the Dwarf to accept, they can request the Path of Fire," Al'bet explained, staring into his nephew's face.

"Why didn't my father take this path then?" Austin asked.

"I don't know. Maybe he didn't think of it, or he felt his sentence was acceptable," Al'bet replied.

"Or he wasn't out of his mind! Al'bet, no one's successfully returned from the Path in over a thousand years!" Le'stal nearly shouted.

"Quiet yourself boy," Al'bet said with a growl. "This is the domain of Ba'lain. Or did you forget why you left with me all those years ago?"

Le'stal quickly calmed himself and checked around him as if he could see spies through the rock around them. "Right. I'm sorry for losing my temper. But Al'bet, this is insane! Austin could never survive the trial. We don't even know what beasts have taken the places of the ancients."

"He won't be going alone," Chloe said softly, laying her hand on Austin's arm. "Where Austin goes, I go."

Austin looked at her for the first time since entering the Dwarven Kingdom; saw the strain being in the mountain caused her, but also the strength of her conviction.

"You don't have to be in here, Chloe. I forgot your fear of closed spaces. We can take you back to Nord Byen, where you can breathe easier," he said gently.

"You don't listen too well, do you Austin?" she said with a smile. "My phobias can wait. You need me and I won't abandon you. No matter the outlook."

"Indeed son, and neither will I," Al'bet said, drawing everyone's attention to him. "I too shall go, as your Dwarven council."

"Then I should go as well," Le'stal said, in a less than eager tone.

"No Le'stal, you need to stay here and pay attention to what is going on in our absence. We have no idea what Ba'lain will do when we are gone. We need to prepare ourselves for whatever the outcome," Al'bet explained.

Suddenly there was a knock on the door that ended all conversation, as Ro'tan walked in. "The council will see you, Al'bet. Your name still holds a great deal of respect around here. Even if none of it comes from your own King. But be that as it may, the others will hear you."

Al'bet just chuckled at the title given his other nephew. "Will Ba'toth be there?"

"No, I'm afraid not. Ba'lain still denies his council as a living former ruler. The disrespect is incredible, but it is his right as a ruler," Ro'tan said shaking his head.

"He rules the weakest throne in the kingdom, because he is the weakest in the realm," Al'bet grumbled.

"Yes, well be that as it may, he is still a king and deserves the respect of one," Ro'tan emphasized.

"To you maybe. Well," Al'bet said, standing from the table with a grunt, "we better not leave our rulers waiting. Can we travel by the royal pathway to cut time, or do we take the regular?" he asked.

"The regular, Al'bet. You know the rules," Ro'tan chuckled.

"Well they wouldn't have to wait as long if we did. But none the less, let's go." And at that, everyone began the long walk back to the Central Cavern.

As they walked, everyone remained silent. Al'bet's warning about spies had made their tongues heavy, a blessing for which Austin was glad. Although he had never actually agreed to it, if he could clear his father's name, then he would take the risk. He knew that Eland couldn't wait for his return, since the days of the coming war were few, but he needed to do this for his family.

His father and mother gave up everything to be together, and they had raised him to be a part of something greater than himself, to be part of a family. This was his duty to his family, and not just his mother and father, but to his newly discovered extended family. He needed to clear his father's name, if for no other reason, than to bring honor back to the members of the Bronze Clan.

Deep in his thoughts, Austin didn't notice when they entered the massive central chamber and stood before the doors of the Royal

Council Room. But the hammering of Ro'tan's staff on the door brought him back to the reality around him.

Ro'tan waited for the door to open before them and when it did he led the group into the waiting chamber, where Mar'di, Li'sa and Le'stal all took a seat in the gallery to watch the proceedings below them.

Austin took in the massive chamber and was a bit disappointed in what he saw. Instead of a jeweled throne room, this was simply a massive amphitheater. From ceiling to floor, rows upon rows of seats, hewn from the living rock provided a place for any who wished to take part to sit. He also noticed how their footfalls seemed to echo around them and realized the acoustics of the room must be incredibly attuned. They slowly marched down hundreds of steps, making their way to the central dais below.

The central area now caught the young Half Dwarf's attention as they continued to walk down the steps. Here on a perfectly smooth floor stood five thrones, each one covered in so many finely cut pieces, it appeared that they were carved out of a single massive jewel. With two thrones covered with a single type of stone on either side, his gaze fell upon the throne in the middle. Covered in a strange jewel, it appeared to change color with each step he took forward. This jewel made it appear as though the throne was constructed of the other four colored jewels of the other thrones.

No one sat in these seats as of yet, but once they reached the floor and stood before them, Ro'tan raised his staff and knocked it on the floor three times and spoke. "All pay honor to the ruling council of Verengrath." And suddenly a large door at the back of the room opened, and out of it marched ten Dwarves in full armor, who lined up across from one another along the red carpet leading to the thrones.

Then coming out in twos, Dwarves clothed in royal robes, each in a different color, began to come forward. First entered the blue king, then the red king, followed by the white ruler and then the green king. Finally a Dwarf with a high crown came forth wearing all the colors, again in equal proportions.

Each Dwarf took their seats and waited in silence for the final Dwarf to begin.

"Ro'tan Sureswing, who is it that comes before the Ruling Council of Verengrath?" the central Dwarf asked.

"My Emperor of the Mountain Home, Di'an, I stand before you with Al'bet Ironfist of the Bronze Clan, High General Austin of the Eland Army, and Princess Chloe Duthain of the Kingdom of Andraya," Ro'tan said officially.

"We welcome you to our council. Princess Chloe, it isn't often that we have an Elf amongst us. Your beauty shows your race still flourishes," Emperor Di'an said with a smile.

Smiling back Chloe replied, "And the majesty of your Kingdom gladdens my heart to know the Dwarves do as well, ancient friend," he smiled, bowing. "But I am but a half Elf, milord and although I come from my brother's Kingdom and I carry the weight of his word, I am not here as a representative of Andraya today, but as a friend of General Austin."

"Ah, yes. High General Austin. We have heard the name before, High General. But rumor has reached my ears that you have a sire name as well, that we have yet to be introduced to," the Emperor said, turning his attention to Austin.

"Indeed your majesty. Few here in Verengrath know my surname, yet many of you speak it daily. For I am High General Austin Ironfist, son of Ba'rel Ironfist and Lady Cassidy Berenhom, and grandson of King Ba'toth Ironfist, as it has recently come to my attention," he said, his voice bouncing off the rocks around him.

"Silence your tongue, half breed!" shouted the Dwarf sitting in blue robes, upon the Sapphire throne. "You shall not speak the name of Ba'toth with familiarity!"

"Mind yourself, King Ba'lain," the Emperor said, rage simmering in the tone of his voice. "I hold court this day, not you. If you were so concerned of your father's place of honor you would not dishonor him as you continually choose to, by denying his place amongst us." A sudden hiss drew everyone's attention to the seats beside them, where a female Dwarf sat paying close attention to the proceedings.

It was then that Austin noticed the row of four Dwarves sitting behind the kings, in a private row. There sat three males and the female he first noticed. The Half Dwarf General realized that the four Dwarves were none other than the three surviving kings of the previous council and, whom he guessed, Ba'lain's mother.

Austin took in the seats before him. Of the six chairs available two of them, the green and the white, remained empty. Of the remaining four seats, it appeared that each of the previous generation of kings sat in the chair, marking their designation as advisors to the current rulers. The Half Dwarf General took in each of the occupants of those seated. First he saw the rainbow advisor, a solemn Dwarf with a long red braided beard. Next was the green chair, which was currently vacant, but beside it was a plain wood variation of the chairs upon which Ba'lain's mother sat. Austin guessed that this alternative advisor, was a point of contention with the other rulers of the Dwarven kingdom. The white seat, like the green, was also vacant. Again he guessed that his grandfather was still alive, since everyone used his name in the current context, which made it clear to him that the former Diamond King must be the ruler to previously have died. It would have been his death that would have triggered the Challenge of the Kings to be called and the current rulers to find their place of honor.

The red seat, whose occupant had a large ruby encrusted eye patch, was next. His thick bushy eyebrows were like large caterpillars upon his brow, matching his white beard and hair. Then finally the blue chair, where a Dwarf with a walking ax sat, his salt and pepper eyebrow cocked, looking at Ba'lain's mother with a smirk on his face. Austin instantly liked this Dwarf. He could see the mischief in the playful nature of his eyes.

"Austin Ironfist, we your half clan welcome you before us," Di'an continued, ignoring the woman. "Now what have you come to us about? Ro'tan said that you know of a threat to Verengrath?"

"Indeed Emperor. It has come to my attention that a Dark Elf has set his sights on attacking Verengrath, through the kingdom of Eland," Austin said, and again his booming voice echoed off the walls around them.

All the Dwarves looked visibly shaken by the news. War had not crept upon the Dwarves of Verengrath for centuries. To hear of it now shocked most of them, all that is, except for Ba'lain, Chloe noted.

"How do you know this?" Ba'lain sneered.

"I was approached by this Dark Elf some time ago, where he offered his services to me in my bid to free Eland during this time of civil war," Austin explained, turning to address his half uncle. "He said that all I would have to pay him, should I succeed in my efforts, is to allow him to move his army across Eland to attack you here in Verengrath."

"You saw his army? You can validate this *'threat'*?" Ba'lain replied quickly.

"No I did not. I sent him on his way. I have never been close to the Dwarves in the past, but I have no animus towards you. I had no desire to betray you," Austin said.

"My fellow rulers," Ba'lain said turning his attention from Austin to the council, "throw these miscreants out. This is a farce."

"I would rethink that King IRONFIST," Al'bet said, finally speaking up, and emphasizing Ba'lain's family name. He knew that by showing how openly disrespectful his nephew was being to his own blood he would create a rift between the Sapphire King and the rest of the council. The grizzled Dwarf was not new to Verengrath politics, and was playing the emotions in the room like a harp.

"And why would you do that, Al'bet?" the ruler from the Diamond throne asked.

"Because, King La'met, his services have been accepted by another Elander in this war of theirs," Al'bet explained.

"Why should that matter to us?" Ba'lain again jumped in.

"Because he obviously proved his worth to the other general. A man who is not without wisdom on the battlefield, and who wouldn't wager free passage through the kingdom on a whim," Austin replied for his uncle.

"We shall discuss this latest development and return with our decision on this rumored threat our people face. Please remain in Verengrath until our return." Emperor Di'an said, and with that he led the way out of the chamber, followed by the other kings and guards in the reverse order from which they entered.

Chapter 18

In the Age of Yelantas Porthanaclies

It was Austin's third tour of duty on the front lines in the North. The war was nearly a stalemate, as neither side had made any new ground in months and now that the snow was setting in, neither would. As the young Half Dwarf huddled by his campfire he heard a horse whinny and the crunch of fresh snow under hoof.

Looking up he saw a messenger rush to a command tent and jump off of his mount. Obviously an urgent message had just arrived for Lieutenant General Kiamet, Austin's colleague on the field. Returning his attention back to his fire, Austin continued to warm his hands while he waited for his coffee to perk before him.

Thoughts of a watched pot never boiling were echoing through his mind when a voice called out his name. "Lieutenant General Austin!" the voice called. Austin looked up to see the messenger searching around for him.

"Here soldier, and keep it down. I don't need a target painted on my forehead for the enemy," Austin said forcefully.

"I apologize sir," The soldier said, stopping before him and saluting. Austin returned the salute from his seat and pointed for the messenger to join him.

"What's all the excitement about, soldier?" Austin asked, once again turning his attention to his coffee pot.

"Sir, I come from command with an urgent message. High General Lethus has died," the messenger said.

"That's unfortunate," Austin replied. "I liked the High General. I hope he died well."

"I don't know if he did or not sir, but High King Yelantas Porthanaclies now has a command structure without a leader. He commands that you and Lieutenant General Kiamet return to Lytton immediately for consideration," the messenger replied.

The news struck Austin in the chest. He never thought he would rise as high as a Lieutenant General in the Eland ranks, never mind be considered for the highest position available.

"Well then, I had better prepare for the journey. I take it you have already informed General Kiamet?" Austin asked.

"Yes sir, he is preparing as well," the young soldier confirmed.

"Good. Find Captain Sulchin and send him to me," he commanded. The soldier nodded his understanding and began to walk away. "We haven't received command from Lytton in months. Why do we need a High Commander so badly that we have to pull two Lieutenant Generals from the line?" Austin asked himself out loud.

"Well sir, since the Princess married that noble from Andraya a couple of weeks ago, rumor has surfaced that there may be a campaign to retake his throne. A wedding present from High King Yelantas," the soldier replied.

"We don't have the troops for two campaigns," Austin said to the man.

"High King Yelantas is taking advice from King Marcus under advisement and is considering pulling the troops back from the line during the winter. They have noticed that nothing happens during the winter anyway, so they might as well make use of our troops elsewhere," the soldier again replied, relaying all the information he had available.

"Well, I can't fault them that logic. We should be able to leave a small contingent of men here to keep watch should the enemy make a move," Austin sighed.

"Yes General, and the pass is going to quickly fill with snow so only Polar's will be a threat then," the soldier said with confidence.

"Oh yeah, ONLY Polar's. Son, five Polar's are enough to give a Legion nightmares, let alone a contingent." The young man seemed stunned by the news, but Austin only signaled him to go and find the Captain while he entered his tent.

A couple of hours had passed and he was ready to go when he found Kiamet finishing up his preparations as well.

"Well Kiamet," Austin said, "shall we travel together?" Austin asked.

"Sure Austin, considering this is the last time we'll be equals, I don't see why not," Kiamet smirked.

"You figure you've got this one all wrapped up, don't you Kiamet?" Austin chuckled.

"And so do you Austin. We both know I was made for command. How you got this far is as much a mystery to you as it is to me," Kiamet said, his self-important, cocky attitude dripping in his tone.

Austin just chuckled. "Ah Kiamet. One day you are going to have your high hopes brought back to the ground."

"Most likely," Kiamet said as he mounted his horse, "but not today." And with a grin, he set his spurs to his mount's sides and the two began their long journey back to the Eland Capitol city.

After more than a week of hard riding the two men finally entered the city of Lytton. It had been a long time since either man had seen any such luxury as the city could provide. But they both knew that the High King and his new son-in-law awaited them.

Both men had learned as much as they could on their journey, hearing tales of how their new king, Marcus Lianthus, was the deposed prince of Andraya. They learned of his quest to retake his family throne, not just to regain the Lianthus family honor, but to expand the reach of Eland.

For nearly three hundred years, the Ten Kingdoms remained unchanged, thanks to the treaties of the First Kings. Long ago, when each city state attempted to claim all it could from their neighbors, a long and bloody war had erupted. Thousands of men, women and children died in a never ending series of attacks. But, it wasn't until the Gnomish Emperor Trian realized that they were destroying themselves that things began to change.

Emperor Trian was, like all gnomes, small in stature but as ambitious as the other kings assembled in the peace talks. His peoples love for all things that burn created some of the most terrifying weapons found on the battlefield. It was because of this lethal ingenuity, that regardless of their small stature, the Gnomes were terrifying to come against in combat. But Gnomes were also deep thinkers, philosophers and a people who could see the bigger picture. It was this foresight that caused him to call for a truce to bring them all together.

Sending emissaries to their neighboring King Rylan of Andrea and the Centaur ruler of Hadassah, Emir Xertang, he explained that based on the Gnomes' calculations the war would only last another hundred years before they would all be wiped out. Xertang and Rylan had long since learned to respect their Gnomish counterpart and agreed to meet with him to discuss his people's findings.

Each one had the ear of the other surrounding rulers and one by one the Council of the Ten Kings was called and the meeting to discuss the treaty began. They spent weeks arguing over the smallest things and it was quickly obvious, what couldn't be sorted on the battle field, might not be sorted at the bargaining table either.

Finally after nearly an entire month of bickering, when all ten kings were once again yelling at each other, Trian saw it all crashing down around him. Each day for a week, he would watch as the talks would follow a pattern. First everything would begin amicably. Then things would begin getting tense, until each ruler would begin hurling charges at one another, ranging from stolen property to murder, until you could hear nothing over the din of roaring voices.

He sat silent, watching them rage at one another and waited for his opening, knowing his next gambit could cost him his life. Because as the pattern has shown, he knew sooner or later, the death of King Wylat's brother, Feltyr would come up.

Feltyr was a general in the Agmora army. Unlike his brother Wylat, who looked completely human except for a small pair of horns, Feltyr had the hooved feet and pointy beard of their father. The general stood as tall as any human, unlike many Satyrs, who tended to be less than five feet tall and was a brilliant tactician. Neighboring Golameed on its southern border, Agmora was at war with the Gnomes longer than any other two kingdoms in the region. So when word reached Trian of Feltyr's attack, he wasn't about to wait for it to come to him. Instead, he set up an ambush in a gully on the path between Agmora's capitol city of Pianai and Nehine, the Gnomish capitol city. Here he lined the deep gully with fire throwers, and when enough of the Agmoran troops were within its confined space, he ordered the throwers into action. The flames and arrows of the Gnomes wounded many of the Agmoran soldiers in the gully and killed Feltyr almost immediately.

So Trian waited for his most despised enemy to once again charge him with his accusation of murder. Like clockwork, the Agmoran ruler began to rant about the Gnomish ambush that killed his brother, launching into a tirade about blood debts and family. Trian waited for the charge to be made clear and then stepped down from his seat and slowly walked across the room towards Wylat. Everyone silenced the moment he began walking, and the half Satyr King quickly dropped his hand to his sword, preparing to be attacked. The small ruler strode across to his nemesis and taking a deep breath fell to a knee and bowed his head to the man before him.

"King Wylat of Agmora. I, Emperor Trian, of the people of Golameed beseech your forgiveness for your loss. For ordering the attack on your people, which killed your beloved brother, I offer to you my life. I know it does nothing to assuage your loss, but I have nothing else to offer you." He spoke the words quietly, yet his voice moved across the room, clear to all those assembled.

For an instant, King Wylat's hand trembled on the hilt of his sword. He wanted to lash out, he wanted revenge, it was in fact the only reason he now commanded his troops to attack the Gnomes. But seeing the humbled form of his enemy, his heart lost its lust. Killing him in battle was his desire, not murdering him in cold blood. Tears rimmed his eyes as he thought of his brother, but more importantly his living children back home. The half Satyr stepped down from his seat and stood before the man who ordered the death of his brother.

“I’ve hated you for a long time Trian and spending each day staring across the room at you I wanted nothing more than to take my sword and run you through. But doing so now would condemn my people to a never ending war.” He slowly reached out to the Gnome before him, and gently lifted him to standing straight. “We will never be friends, Trian. I couldn’t bring myself to go that far, but for the sake of my children and my children’s children, I accept your apology and offer mine for the actions of my people as well. I pray, before the great spirits of the forest, that we can find a way to peace between our people.”

The hush was deafening, but as the two men clasped arms in a sign of peace the silence was broken by the sound of clapping. Everyone looked to see King Rylan of Andraya, clapping his support of the two rulers, and soon all the others joined in as well. This reaching out for peace was so critical to all those assembled, who allowed their pride to stop them from making the exact same gesture as the two individuals before them did, that almost instantly everyone began asking forgiveness from their fiercest rivals. This act between the Gnomes and the people of Agmora began the long path to peace they all wanted for their people. That one selfless moment of sacrifice signaled the last time any of the Ten Kingdoms went to war with one another.

That is, at least, until today.

Chapter 19

In the Age of the Eland Civil War

Austin and his companions sat in a Dwarven tavern, waiting for the rulers of Verengrath to call them back with their decision. But the look on Al'bet's face told Austin all he needed to know.

"They aren't going to do anything about this, are they?" he asked.

"Nope. I've seen that look before. They are all terrified..." Al'bet began.

"All except for Ba'lain," Chloe interrupted.

"You saw that too, did you?" Al'bet asked. "Seems he knows something no one else does. He wasn't at all surprised by the news."

"Do you think it's the same dark Elf that caused the cave in?" Le'stal asked.

"Most likely. How many dark elves do you know that would give that much attention to a kingdom of Dwarves? I just wonder why this Elf is so eager to attack us," he said quietly. "What did we ever do to him?"

"I think it's time I told you about Neamith, Austin," Chloe said, "about how he and I met in our youth."

"I forgot that you knew him. I didn't want to push you then, but if you're ready, it might help us to understand this clearer," Austin said, trying not to let his eagerness pressure her too hard.

"We studied together in Parinth. He wasn't always a dark Elf, but he was never satisfied with the more natural magics taught by the elves in Layeni." She explained. "He disappeared sometime in our fourth year of training, and no one knew where.

"Unlike Drugar, Elves aren't born with dark skin. The Drugar are a race of Dwarves, like the races of humans. And like the human races, their skin color is nothing more than a physical characteristic. But a dark Elf is born like all elves, and their skin color only turns black when they choose to go down a road filled with dark magic. It is a twisting of their souls that turn them dark, and the blacker their skin, the further from the light they have moved," she explained.

"So you knew he had cast a spell on me?" Austin asked, betrayal in his eyes.

"Not until I saw you. As I fought the storm to get to you, it felt unnatural," she explained. "Then when you said you seemed to have had your mind read, and the litany of bad luck, I paid closer attention to you.

"It was then that I sensed the spell upon you. It was also then that I sensed his… aura. When you spoke his name you broke the spell. Painfully, I might add, if that makes you feel any better," she said with a coy smile.

"Yeah, actually it does," he grinned.

"That's why things have shifted back in your favor, Austin," she explained. "Kiamet was using Neamith to spy on you. The spell isn't a perfect link, and it takes time deciphering the images that get transferred but with Kiamet's knowledge of you it would be easy to figure out," she explained.

"So this, Neamith," Le'stal said quietly, "does he have a reason to hate us?"

"Not that I know of. We all know that Elves and Dwarves aren't the best of friends, but still there have never been any serious disputes between Layeni and Verengrath. But that doesn't mean that when he found the enclave of the Dark Elves that he didn't take up their grievances with you," Chloe said with a shrug.

"But what grievance?" Le'stal asked. "We've never had dealings with Dark Elves in the past. It still doesn't make sense."

"There have been rumors for years," Li'sa said quietly, "that for the right amount of gold, the dark elves could be hired to take care of any underhanded needs a Dwarf might have. Maybe there is a Dwarf here that took it seriously."

"Ba'lain," Al'bet hissed. The name caught everyone off guard, causing them all to look up, as the Dwarven king marched towards them.

"You have been commanded to return to the chamber," Ba'lain angrily ordered. Then turning on his heel he marched away from them as quickly as his dignity would allow.

"What's that all about? Why did they send one of the kings?" Austin asked.

"The vote is in, and Ba'lain disrespected himself and the other kings during the discussion. He is being put in his place for his insolence," Al'bet explained, shaking his head.

They all got up and began following the Dwarven king back to the council room. When they arrived all the kings were already seated on their thrones. Once again, Le'stal, Mar'di and Li'sa all sat in the first row of seats watching, as Al'bet, Austin and Chloe approached the rulers of the Dwarven Kingdom.

When they stopped they all waited quietly for the council to address them. Emperor Di'an stood before speaking to them. This sign of respect was instantly recognized by Al'bet as he patiently stood with Chloe and Austin.

"High General Austin, Princess Chloe, and our own friend and brother Al'bet, we have discussed the warning you have placed before us. It is our belief at this time, that the threat you have come to us with isn't one of serious consequence." His tone betrayed his confidence, and each of those listening knew he was in turmoil. "Instead, we will increase our vigilance, and continue life as always within our sacred halls."

Austin shook his head in sadness, but Al'bet surprised them and stepped forward. "My leaders. It has been my greatest honor to have served most of you in my past. I even count some amongst you as my friends. But your desire to bury your heads in the sand is incredible. This young man, a man of our blood, has come to us with a warning and a hope and we choose to turn him away. Just as we chose to turn his father Ba'rel, away."

"Is there no end to the blasphemy this day?" Ba'lain screamed.

"Silence your feeble tongue, Ba'lain!" Al'bet shouted. His strong voice echoing off the walls. "The only reason you hold any throne is because you were guaranteed the blue one, just for being selected a champion! My brother must have been under a spell to choose you when Ba'rel was cast out!" The words he chose suddenly struck him. *'A spell!'* he thought to himself.

"My lords. Please, does it not seem strange that this particular Dwarf would be chosen, by his father, who was the first king during his reign?" Al'bet urged.

The title of "First King" was given to the ruler seated on the Emerald Throne. During combat, the last two Dwarves to battle each other for a throne knew one or the other would be Emperor. But the one who fell first would fill the role of second in command, and was given the title "the First King of Verengrath."

"My brother was second only to the Emperor himself. All of you know him, and know that he did not believe in the line of blood succession. He only chose Ba'rel as his successor because he was a champion among our people. Why then should he choose the weakest Dwarf in all of the Bronze clan?"

"I will not stand for this level of disrespect!" Ba'lain shouted, his face red with rage.

"Nor should you, as a ruler of Verengrath," Emperor Di'an added. "Al'bet, know that my tolerance of this is only because of your service to our people in the past."

"And I ask a little more tolerance, my Emperor," Al'bet asked bowing low before his ruler. "It has come to our attention that this dark Elf, of whom we warn you, is a sorcerer, as are all of his kind."

Sensing that the timing was right to help, Chloe stepped forward to stand next to Al'bet. "His name is Neamith the Dark. Have any of you heard that name before?" she asked all those assembled. She watched as each ruler mulled the name over quietly and smiled inside as each King spoke the name aloud. The inward smile found its way to her lips as she sensed a change in their auras. Her instincts were correct; Neamith had them all under a spell. Her grin grew at the thought of the tremendous pain and likely coma the Dark Elf would now be suffering through.

But the smile faded as she considered the power he must have amassed while in exile. To not only cast this spell on Austin, but also the rulers of Verengrath would have taken tremendous skill. Her former classmate was no novice in the dark arts. What she was dealing with was a powerful Sorcerer, well beyond anything she had yet to face.

"I don't know that name yet I feel as though I had heard it somewhere?" Di'an said. The other kings all echoed his sentiments as they began to awaken from their spell induced lethargy. "But it doesn't matter. Al'bet, you have come to the end of my leniency for you and now you had best leave. You chose to live apart from us when your nephew was exiled, it would be for the best if you continued that life it seems."

Knowing how his old friend would react to his next sentence Al'bet replied, "Is that a Royal Decree, my lord?" with a growl.

Seeing the Emperor's nostrils flare made the Dwarf grin behind his full beard. "It is!" Di'an replied.

"Then I demand the Trial by Fire!" Al'bet shouted.

The room hushed. "You would enter the Path of Fire?" King Shar'tal, ruler of the Ruby throne, said quietly.

"I would," Al'bet said with confidence.

"And I would go with him," Austin said, stepping beside his uncle.

"And I with them," Chloe said, placing her hands on her hips.

"You aren't Dwarves; you have no right to face the trials with him," Ba'lain said, the smile that was on his face from Al'bet's initial demand leaking away.

"Austin is a son of Verengrath," Al'bet said. "He is allowed the same respect as any of our blood."

"And," Chloe interrupted, "where Austin goes, I go." Austin glanced at her out of the corner of his eye, but he quickly turned his attention back to Dwarves before him.

"A demand to take the trial by fire is never denied to any exile," Emperor Di'an said loudly. "And it will not be denied here either. The gates to the Trail of Fire shall be opened at first bell tomorrow. Be prepared, for none who have entered have survived in our lifetimes."

With that he adjourned the council and led the kings from the room, his head hanging low at his hot headed response, and the inevitable death of one of his oldest friends.

Chapter 20

In the Age of Yelantas Porthanaclies

Austin sat in his private chamber inside the castle of Lytton, awaiting his King's command to join him. He had been allowed time to bathe, sleep and eat before being expected before the Eland Royals, a courtesy shown to Kiamet as well. But now that it was all done, the nervous anticipation in his stomach cried out for it all to be over, and quickly.

He hadn't been south of the Northern Mountain pass since his father died, and much had changed. The capitol city had grown and with it, unfortunately, so too did the slums within its massive walls. As always, Austin avoided condemning his ruler's decisions that created such disparity. There could be things going on that he had no clue of, and so slums and ghettos were probably a necessary evil of society.

But still, something about being either rich or poor bothered him. Even in his own life, he remembered going from being so poor that his family lived in Lonny's little house to being very wealthy. He thought back to that little house, no bigger than a shed and how they went from that to being major voices within the Dayson community. Not that he minded the shed. It was a roof over his head, and it was some of the happiest moments in his life. But still, you either had, or you didn't and that was always strange to him. Where was the middle ground?

Thoughts of his old home suddenly reminded him of both of his parents' deaths. Although it still saddened him, he had come to terms with his mother's death years ago. It was his father's passing that pained him now.

He had been deployed when the message came that his father had passed away. It struck him hard then, since he had no idea that Ba'rel was even sick at the time. Heck, for a Dwarf, he was still a young man, so it shouldn't have been age. Receiving his leave, he rushed home to be there as quickly as he could and found Mary Ann tending to his empty home. She embraced him the moment he arrived and cried into his chest, whispering her sympathies for his loss.

It was during a discussion with Lonny, his adopted Grandfather that he heard how it had happened.

"It was a strange disease," Lonny explained. "Your father was strong, and was still working in the forge, until the day he died. But all of a sudden, he just… died.

"One day I was walking in my garden, tending the flowers and deciding if we wanted to make a path to the garden shed. As usual, the ringing of steel echoed over the entire village, almost as if each rhythmic clang of your father's hammer set the tempo for everyone here. As it happens, the ringing stopped, a man can't swing his hammer forever after all, and I carried on my day not thinking anything of it," Lonny said, grief etched deep in his face, almost as if he should have known better.

"It wasn't until around supper time that I realized that the ringing hadn't started again all day. I decided to go visit your father when our dear friend Keith rushed to our home calling my name," the old blacksmith explained. "'*Lonny,*' he shouted, '*Lonny, come quick. Something has happened to Ba'rel!*' I rushed as quickly as my old bones would take me and when I arrived, a crowd had formed around the open doors of the smithy.

"I pushed my way through the crowd and entered the smithy, to find your father on the floor, with several of our friends around him." Austin's heart tightened as he listened. "He had died. The men had wondered why his hammer had gone silent about the same time I did, and came to check on him.

"They found him, crumpled over his anvil, his hammer on the ground by his limp hand," Lonny continued to explain. "His heart, it just, stopped."

The old man hung his head in defeat. He had lost his best friend and his grief, although over a month and a half old, was still raw within him. Austin's head hung, as he slowly rotated his empty coffee mug in his hand. Without even lifting his head, he reached out and put his hand on the man he called Grandfather's closed fist. The old man returned the gesture as the two of them just sat there in silence, their grief filling the room.

Austin left their house to Lonny and Mary Ann telling them to use it to give shelter to those who needed a start in life. As a soldier, he wouldn't need it any time soon. As for the belongings, he sold what he could and took the money with him, knowing he would one day need it again. He then left the village, not knowing if he would ever return.

It was at this moment, alone in his apartment awaiting the king's beckon, that he realized he'd like very much to see Lonny and Mary Ann again when this was all over. He now realized how important his friends and his adopted family were to him, and how much he wanted the people of Dayson to be kept safe.

But his thoughts were soon interrupted by a knock at the door. "Enter," he said loudly, getting up and walking towards the center of the room.

An elderly man wearing regal robes entered. "His Majesty, the High King Yelantas Porthanaclies commands your presence, Lieutenant General Austin." Austin nodded his understanding and, grabbing his formal coat from the back of the desk chair, he followed the herald out.

He wasn't surprised to see Kiamet already standing in the hallway waiting for him. "So we finally make this official then," he said with a self-confident grin.

"Yeah, we can get this confusion sorted and get back to fighting like we're meant to," Austin said, his own smile a cover for his emotions inside of him.

"Fighting is what you are meant to do, Austin. I'm meant to command," Kiamet chided, trying to goad Austin into a response. But the Half Dwarf simply huffed a forced chuckle and continued following their guide silently.

The two men entered the Lytton Throne room to find it full of every Royal they knew, as well as a handful they didn't. '*What was with the crowd?*' Austin thought to himself.

They continued to walk down the red carpet towards the throne when he noticed that slightly behind and to the left of the King was his daughter, Jasmine. Across from her, on the King's right hand side, stood a man that Austin could only imagine as the new King of Eland, Marcus Lianthus. He wondered if the new royal would improve things for the people of Eland. Hopefully some fresh blood would bring new ideas to their people.

Both men came to a stop before the royal trio and both took a knee, bowing before their sovereigns.

"Rise gentlemen," High King Porthanaclies commanded and both men followed his order immediately. "Lieutenant Generals Ironfist and Quileen, you have been called here because your names were left as possible successors by the former High General before his untimely death. You two have made quite an impression on your former commander, as well as upon me."

Both men shot curious looks at their king, seated before them. "Do you think this throne closes my eyes to the war on our Northern Border?" he asked with a chuckle. "No, for in my youth I too fought the creatures of the north, and although becoming a ruler, husband and father drew me home, I still yearn for the days of combat.

"But that makes no difference now, for it appears that war has come to us," he said, motioning for his new son-in-law to step forward. "Gentlemen, I present to you your king, Marcus Lianthus." Both men bowed low at the hip and rose again. "Marcus comes from a long line of royalty, that a couple of decades ago was deposed from their throne," he explained. "We are going to attempt to take that throne back, not only to restore the honor of the Lianthus family name, but also to expand the glory of Eland."

"Majesty, if I may?" Kiamet spoke to his king. The look on the High King's face warned Austin to keep his mouth shut.

"If you must," High King Yelantas replied.

"Your Excellency, as per the terms of the treaty of the Ten Kings, we aren't allowed to go to war with a neighbor. There must be emissaries and a diplomatic attempt at resolution," the head-strong general said, failing to catch the warning from his ruler.

"I'm very glad to see that you have paid attention to your lessons, Lieutenant General," the High King replied. "But in a time such as this, where a usurper sits upon the throne, then the laws controlling inter-kingdom conflict are not in play."

"I see my king. Then where are we going to draw our troops from to commit to this war?" Kiamet asked.

"From the Northern Front," the High King said simply. His refusal to elaborate was a clear indication that the wise course of action was to end this conversation where it was.

"But Milord, we could lose valuable ground in the North. We mustn't give up our position there." Austin squinted his eyes in pain as he listened to his colleague questioning the wisdom of the King. This wasn't going to go well; he could already see it in his King's posture.

"That's true, we cannot, and thanks to your determination and clear vision for the North I believe we have found our new High General of the Eland forces," High King Porthanaclies said with authority.

Austin quickly shot a glance at the man at his side, and caught Kiamet's look of confidence that his victory was at hand. He waited with a feeling of disappointment, for the answer he knew that was coming.

"General Kiamet Quileen, approach the throne," the High King said, his voice carrying clearly across the room. "General Kiamet, your dedication to the battles upon our northern border is both admirable and warming to my heart. It is because of this that I could not dream of taking you from your beloved post," Yelantas said. "So it is this day that I dub thee, General of the Northern Command. You shall return forthwith to the battlefield and command the troops during this, the Winter Season."

Austin watched the proceedings, completely confused. High General Lethus wasn't the General of the Northern Command. As far as Austin knew, that position didn't even exist. This made no sense. What was his King doing?

"You shall command all but two companies of our troops to return to Lytton upon your return," the King commanded. Austin's confusion deepened as he noted that even Kiamet was bewildered.

"My Lord, how can I command the troops of Eland to protect the Kingdom with only two companies?" Kiamet asked.

"You don't command the troops of Eland, General Kiamet. Lieutenant General Austin, step forward," the King commanded, and Austin joined his colleague at the foot of his king's throne. "Lieutenant General Austin, it is with great pleasure that I promote you to High General of Eland. You are now only second in command to my Royal Family in the defense and offense of our Kingdom. You, young man, are the official successor to High General Lethus' office."

Austin struggled to remain conscious, as all of the air was sucked out of his lungs, and the blood drained from his face. He hadn't thought this could actually happen to him. He wasn't a royal, he wasn't even from a family of affluence like Kiamet's. He was just the son of a blacksmith. This didn't make any sense to him, yet here he was, having the mark of the High General, the golden dagger, pinned to his chest.

The High King kissed him on both cheeks, a sign of his blessing, and continued. "High General Austin, you will have nearly a month to prepare for the troops to arrive. I suggest you use this time to visit any family and friends you may wish to see and to share this celebration with before that time. Because once they reach the Capitol city, you will have a lot of work to do."

He then turned to Kiamet, "As for you, General of the Northern command, you must leave this very day and make all haste back to your men. Prepare our troops to return immediately so that we might begin our campaign against Andraya, to free the throne for your new King." And with that he dismissed both men from his presence.

The two generals were almost out of the throne room when the High King's voice called out, "Oh and High General Austin please don't leave the capitol for a few days. We the people would like to celebrate your promotion with you before you go." Austin quickly turned and bowed low to his High King and then quickly retreated from the throne room.

When they were back at their apartments Kiamet quickly turned and faced Austin, red with rage. "You didn't deserve this post, I did! I come from the blood line of Queen Ianie, the original royal family. I had the upbringing and am the superior officer!" he shouted.

Austin's cool demeanor quickly faded. Years of taunts, of being picked on and being dismissed exploded within him. But he wasn't a stupid man, and controlling his rage he used his enemy's weaknesses against him. "General of the *Northern* command," he said, loathing thick in his words, "you will watch how you address me. I am your commanding officer, a post given to me by our High King. You will collect your belongings and head back to the North immediately! I will expect an official confirmation from you, once you reach our men, by carrier pigeon within a week and a half indicating you have returned to your post. Any delay, and I will assume you have abdicated your position, and will mark you as a deserter. I will then place a price so high on your head, even your own parents would give you up to me," he seethed.

"A week and a half! That only gives me a week to get there!" Kiamet shouted in exasperation.

"Then I suggest you get moving now. Sleep might be in short supply over the next several days, so get some extra coffee from the supply stores," Austin said, and turning he walked into his apartment and slammed the door behind him.

'Man,' he thought, *'that felt good.'*

Chapter 21

In the Age of the Eland Civil War

Austin and the others left the rulers of Verengrath after they had been dismissed. They could see word spreading before them as they walked, as the amazing story was passed from Dwarf to Dwarf. You could literally see where it moved from one group to another as if it were a tidal wave, gaining momentum. Austin looked at his Great Uncle to see if he could read anything on his face. But the stoic Dwarf was once again smiling and light hearted.

"Uncle," Austin said quietly.

"Don't worry about it son. Everything will be okay. But we have to prepare for the journey. We had better head back to my home. We will stay there tonight and can get the supplies that we will need," Al'bet said softly.

"Al'bet, I want to come too," Le'stal replied as he limped beside the aged Dwarf.

"I know Le'stal, but I need you out here to protect our people. Ba'lain now knows that we realize he has been using the Dark Elf to control the council. He is no doubt already attempting to contact him through whatever dark art they have been using," Al'bet replied.

"Oh, he won't be getting a reply for a few days," Chloe replied.

"Why's that?" Li'sa asked.

"Because the spell he placed on the leaders required a great deal of energy to perform. But it also created a link between him and them. When they each spoke his name it severed the link, forcibly, and will put his body into shock. When Austin broke the link, it would have caused a great deal of pain and agony. His head would have rung for hours. But with five links severed, all at once, I'd be surprised if he woke within the next week," she said, a grin forming on her face.

"Have you ever used such a spell?" Austin asked.

"Yes, during my training. I also had to endure the pain of having the link severed. Elves take their training in the magical realm very seriously. If you intend to delve there, you have to know the risks as well as the rewards to continue," she replied, her mind going back to her own childhood. "If you can't handle the risk, you aren't allowed the reward."

"Good, it will give us a couple of days head start then," Li'sa replied, grinning up at her. "Ba'lain is dumber than a sack of ore, without a real brain behind his mechanicians he'll be stalled."

"What about his mother?" Austin asked.

"That old witch?" Le'stal replied spitting on the floor. "Don't worry about her. She's meaner and nastier than Ba'lain, but she's just as stupid. Thinks she is some queen because of her marriage to your grandfather."

"Speaking of him. Shouldn't I make an effort to see him?" Austin asked, his cheeks flushing behind his beard.

"He'd like that son, he certainly would. But he is difficult to reach these days. He has taken to living in the high reaches of the kingdom. When Ba'lain refused to grant him the right of a successor's advisor, my brother took the hurt very deeply within himself," Al'bet replied sadly. "It was then that he knew that he had lost both of his sons."

"Well, I'd like to meet him one day, if I could," Austin said looking way up into the endless bridges, spirals and stairways above them.

They had made it to Al'bet's former home and after the Dwarf unlocked the pad lock on the doors they entered the dusty main room.

"I apologize for the mess. I've not been here for many years. But besides some dust, it should be comfortable and secure. As a former general, I was required to secure my home from all sorts of unwanted attention," Al'bet explained. "So no one should hear us speak while we're here."

The men cleaned up as Chloe, Mar'di and Li'sa started to prepare supper. When they were done, Al'bet took Austin and Le'stal with him to the very back of his cave-like home.

"This used to be my private smithy," Al'bet said, opening the door and ushering them into the room as he lit the lamps. "It was here that I came to clear my mind. Nothing is as calming to a Dwarf than the sound of ringing steel and the hiss of hot metal in some fluid or another."

"It looks like my father's," Austin said fondly as the memories of his father's forge came to his mind.

"I wouldn't doubt it. Your father spent hours here with me, although he never worked the metal. He was focusing his time on learning the ore, before taking up the hammer," Al'bet replied.

"I remember all those long nights we used to watch you work," Le'stal said with a grin. "You see Austin, since Dwarves have such long lives; we focus on one lesson of metal at a time. Your father and I chose to learn ore first, and then prepared to move on to smithing later." The smile faded from his lips when he thought of his long dead friend. "I'm glad he got to work the metal before he went home to the Creator."

"Aye lad, as am I," Al'bet replied. "But we can't allow that sadness in just yet boys." It was the first time Austin had seen such pain creep on to his uncle's face. Not even the first time he told him the story, did it show. But now the young general could see how the loss of his father affected everyone around him. "Austin, I'd like to give you something. It's something I created many years ago, intending to give it to your father. But since he can't take it up, and you have a more pressing need, I'd like you to have it instead," the Dwarf said, walking to a locked chest in the back corner of the room.

Austin and Le'stal watched as Al'bet reached into his tunic and pulled out a strange looking key. It appeared more like three keys, with a single handle. Austin looked at it in amazement, noticing it was made of gold, with many little gears connecting the handle to the three keys.

"This is a very special lock son," Al'bet explained. "I created it myself. Not only must you unlock three sets of tumblers, but you must do all three at the same time, and each lock must turn at its own speed. If any of those three requirements aren't met, then the traps that are set will go off and we will all be in a heap of trouble."

They watched as Al'bet slowly inserted the keys into the lock with a single movement. Then, as he turned the crank like handle, they watched as each key rotated at different speeds. The large central key hardly moved at all, while the smallest key, located on the left spun around and around as if it would never unlock its latch. They all held their breath as Al'bet continued turning until he heard the sound of three locks releasing at the same time. Taking a deep sigh, the dark haired Dwarf was about to open the lid, when he thought better of it and grabbing a broken chair leg on the floor beside the chest, held it up in front of his face and gently lifted the lid.

The lid swung open slowly until it rested against the back wall with a thud. Al'bet was about to set down the chair leg when he heard the twang of a spring releasing. His reflexes instantly reacted, as he flipped the board back in front of his large Dwarven nose, just in time to catch a long, feathered dart in it. It hit the board with a snap; right between his eyes.

"Whew. I was wondering if that spring would have lasted this long," Al'bet said with a chuckle, flipping the board over and looking at the dart embedded in it. "That's a nasty poison there too. You'd be going alone tomorrow if I caught that between the eyes!"

Putting it down, he reached inside the chest and started pulling out crowns, scepters and all sorts of amazing creations. But to Austin's amazement he just casually dropped them on the floor as if they were nothing of interest to the Dwarf. It wasn't until the chest was empty that Austin cleared his throat, trying to get his uncle's attention.

"Um, Uncle Al'bet," Austin said. "Was it stolen?"

"What?" Al'bet asked bent in half, his feet dangling off the floor. "Oh, this? No I put this stuff in there to make it look like these were what I was hiding. No the real treasure is under here." He said, and pressing several jewels within the chest walls he caused a hidden floor in it to slide open.

There, gently glowing green with its own light, nestled on top of a bed of silk, sat an incredible war hammer. Al'bet smiled proudly as he grabbed its handle and pulled it out. He jumped back down to the floor and held it before him with pride.

"This," he said in a near whisper, "is Eksils Torden."

Austin and Le'stal were spell bound by the amazing weapon. It was as much a work of art, as it was a work of war. The large hammer was shaped like a regular carpenters hammer, but instead of a claw on the back it formed into a large pick. Then as Al'bet rotated it in his hand, they noticed that the head wasn't round, but had eight sides, forming a large octagon, each one gleaming in the lamplight.

"One evening in my youth I was outside the mountain, with a lady whom I was interested in at the time. We were getting... well that part isn't important," he said as a red flush ran up his face and into his scalp. Clearing his throat he continued, "We weren't paying attention to the sky or anything, but suddenly the darkness lit up as a loud scream filled our ears. We turned our attention towards the heavens, covering our ears from the sheer magnitude of the sound and watched as a light shot down from the stars, and slammed in the valley below where we sat.

"I urged her to join me, but she was too frightened to follow. So I left her to find her way home and rushed down, while I could still see the glow in the distance.

"I travelled for hours, searching to see what had hit the ground, but I couldn't find anything in the wilderness. Still I searched, as the smell of burning wood began to fill the air. It was then that I came across a small forest fire, beginning to build up momentum. Before it could grow too large though, I simply pulled out my ax and started cutting down trees to try to slow its progress." Al'bet explained.

"Wait, you took an ax on a date?" Le'stal asked his jaw dropping.

"Sure, I never go anywhere without an ax," Al'bet said, a frown forming on his brow. "Anyhoo, I cleared an area and was lucky that whatever had fallen had actually created a huge furrow in the ground and pretty much killed most of what the fire could use as fuel. So it was that I was able to get through the flames to the most incredible sight I have ever seen. For there, at the end of a long gouge in the soil and rock sat something glowing in the deep darkness. I walked towards it, slowly, afraid of what God had sent to us, when I noticed it looked like a huge, glowing green nugget. I mean it was the size of my head!"

"That's not a nugget," Le'stal said quietly, "that's a boulder," causing Austin to burst out laughing.

"As I said," Al'bet carried on, frowning at the blond haired Dwarf's comment, "I stood there looking at it, I knew I wanted to learn more about it, and so I decided to take it back to Verengrath with me. But the problem was it looked too heavy for me to carry alone! And the girl had long since run home, none too happy with me I later found out," he said, lost in memory.

"I wonder why?" Le'stal whispered to Austin.

The large general attempted to contain his laughter and shushed his father's best friend, chuckling.

"But I was also afraid I'd never find it again, so I walked over to it and attempted to pick it up. I was amazed at how light it was. I could carry this small boulder with hardly any effort at all. And so it was that I brought the rock home to my shop.

"I was able to break off small pieces and found the ideal temperature with which to melt it, bend it and mold it. But what I found was that the most incredible nature of this metal was, once it was hardened in olive oil, I could never again bring it to its melting or breaking point. It became invincible to everything I could throw at it. And so it was that I took my remaining sample, which I purposely left largely unworked, and began to smith a new weapon with it.

"The metal knew what it wanted to be, and although I pictured a mighty battle ax, it wouldn't allow it. Instead it formed into a hammer and pick that you see before you now. I found that so long as I didn't dip it in olive oil, I could keep working on it, almost as if working a piece of gold. I carved it, shaped it and molded it into the greatest piece of functioning art I had ever created. But I left the portion here," he said pointing at an area where the head met the handle, "where I engraved its name until I could give it a proper one."

"So how did you choose Eksils Torden?" Austin asked in awe of his uncle's creation.

"It was after your father's farce of a trial," Al'bet explained sadly. "Your father was like a son to me, both he and Le'stal. But when he left, it tore the heart out of me. I knew one day he would come home, I just knew it. And when he did, all hell would break loose within our kingdom. So I named it Eksils Torden, the Exile's Thunder."

"But he never came home though." Austin said sadly.

"Yes son, he did," Al'bet said and grabbing his nephew by the beard he gave it a tug and a little wink, causing the young man to smile fondly back at the old Dwarf before him. "This hammer is yours, son. It has been heated and hardened in olive oil. It will not fail you in battle, and when things look darkest, it will light the way," he said, as he handed it to his nephew.

Austin swung the hammer around him, amazed at how light it was. It almost felt as if it wasn't there at all, and yet when he slammed it into the anvil by the long dark forge, it hit it with incredible force! He gently ran his finger along the spiked rear half, forming the pick-ax portion of the weapon.

"But what is this writing?" He asked his uncle.

"Those are Runes. We dwarves don't write in them much any longer, but we use them to imbue power to our work. Artists will write words of beauty into their art work. Tool smiths will forge words of strength and reliability into their tools.

"But for Eksils Torden, it commanded something different. You read them from right to left, and these ones speak to its nature. It begins with strength, reliability and trustworthiness. Then moves to internal focus, a search for clarity. Next is defense against evil, and finally freedom, courage, strength and wisdom."

Austin was in awe and truly touched by the gift.

"Thank you uncle. I won't fail you in this quest," he said, bowing his head deep in respect.

"I know you won't Austin. You're your father's son; and I know you will be anything but a failure in your life," Al'bet said with a proud smile.

Chapter 22

In the Age of Yelantas Porthanaclies

It was pitch black outside as Austin looked up from the maps and field reports that lay scattered before him. He could barely make out the silhouette of the castle, as the dark, new moon crept across the heavens. Leaning back, he stretched as his body screamed to be released from the cramped prone position he had been in for hours. He had been paying close attention to the reports coming in on the target of his new king's aggression, the Andrayan city of Czariana.

The city itself was historic in its design; massive walls that from all reports were pure stone and steel through and through. Even his best spy had nothing more than rumors that the walls were built upon the remains of defeated armies. Well he knew that part was pure fear mongering. King Marcus had explained how the new king, a King William Duthain, had stolen the kingdom from his family.

Austin never concerned himself with the laws of the land, preferring to do as he was instructed by his commanders instead. But now that he was the commander, he had spent considerable time reading the edicts of the Ten Kingdoms and he wasn't really sure how the Andrayan ruler had stolen anything. Besides an apparent loophole that was utilized by King Duthain, where he challenged for the throne based upon a force made up of nearly as many women and children as men, everything seemed in order. In fact, if King Marcus' father had been at all measured in his considering of the facts, he'd have realized that loophole really didn't apply. King Duthain wasn't the commander of a foreign army, and so he really didn't hold a right to use the challenge that way.

But once King Lianthus accepted, the loop hole was shut and from there forward all the rights of challenge were handled properly. The only truly remarkable point in the battle was their choice of weapon. Austin had recognized it instantly when King Marcus told him of the tale.

The Natal. Even now he couldn't believe it. He remembered when his father created the weapon. He was a young child, but he recalled the pride his father felt when he presented it to the then Prince of Andraya, Corland Lianthus. What was truly incredible to him was that this weapon that his father had envisioned and created had shaped the current kingdom of Andraya. It was truly incredible.

Turning his attention back to the desk before him, he froze for a moment, and then calmly continued working. He had sensed a shifting behind him, and noticed the candle flame pull, as if drawn by a sudden movement. The High General stretched his hands high above his head and arcing them back he quickly spun around and flung his dagger across the room.

The knife spun quietly through the air, and landed with a thud against a tapestry directly behind him, handle end first. The knife fell to the ground with a clank, followed by a loud thud as whomever was hiding behind the tapestry fell to the ground, unconscious. Austin quickly strode across the room, and pulled back the blue cloth emblazoned with the Porthanaclies family crest to see the body of a man lying there.

Acting quickly, Austin grabbed a rope that lashed the curtains by the window and tied the man's hands securely behind his back. With another he bound the unconscious man's feet to restrain him further. The High General then calmly grabbed his chair and a pitcher of water from the table. Then spinning the chair so he straddled it with his chest to the back rest, he splashed water in the face of the unconscious man on the floor before him.

The man instantly awoke, sputtering and flailing as he attempted to extricate himself from his current predicament. Realizing the futility of what he was attempting, he finally gave up, and resting his head against the wall watched his captor, waiting for the High General to make his move.

"Good morning cupcake," Austin said with a grin. The man remained silent. "Not in a talkative mood? I'm not surprised. I wouldn't be chatty either if I had just been caught breaking into a man's bed chamber. It could be the start to rumors that could ruin a fellow's reputation with the ladies."

"This isn't a bed chamber," the man replied, still a bit stunned.

"Ah, so you do talk. Good. This will go much quicker that way. What is your name stranger?" Austin asked.

"What difference does it make?" the man replied.

"I like to know the names of the men I kill. It helps make things more personal," Austin said. "So what is your name?"

"Matthew. Matthew Longblade," he replied.

"Well I doubt the Longblade, but Matthew seems reasonable enough. May I call you Matt, Matthew?" Austin asked.

"I don't care. Why don't you just kill me and be done with it?" the man asked.

"Because I want to know more about you, before I do anything. Such as, what, in all that is Holy, compelled you to break into a lit room at this time of night in a tower of the royal castle? That wasn't very bright of you, you know?" Austin questioned.

"I had no choice. I was trying to get into the room next to yours, but your window required that I come inside to move across the room and back out again," Matthew replied.

"The window next…wait that's the Queen's hand maiden's quarters. What's her name? Bernadette, isn't it?" Austin asked.

"Yes, Bernadette. Let's just say she caught my eye today and I wanted to leave her something," Matt said, his cheeks flushing crimson.

"So you steal hearts as well as other people's belongings?" Austin chuckled.

"A man's gotta do milord," the thief winked back.

This caused Austin to burst out laughing. "Thief Matt, I've decided not to kill you. I'll release you but I want you to stay and talk with me a while," Austin said.

"What comfort could you take from a conversation with a thief?" Matt asked.

"It has been a long week for me in my new post. I could use the diversion," Austin replied with a stretch.

"So you're the new High General. Well, I suppose it would merit me to spend some time in your company, so sure," Matt replied.

Austin gave the man one more look and grinning, released the bonds holding his hands and feet. Matt rubbed his raw wrists and sat up, his back against the wall.

"Well High General. What is it you wish to know of me?" Matt asked.

"I'd like to know, why is it that you have taken to this kind of life? The skills you have could benefit you in a more honorable way. Why aren't you a soldier?" Austin asked.

Matt laughed. "No thank you, sir. I'm not a military man." And again laughed.

"So why do you steal then?" Austin continued questioning.

"Because it's exciting, and I'm good at it," the thief replied. "Oh I don't steal from everyone. The odd maiden's heart, sure, and yeah the fat purse or two from a wealthy merchant. But I'd never steal from a poor person."

"What difference does it make? Does the rich man not deserve his wealth just as much as the poor man?" Austin asked.

"Of course he does, and there's a huge difference between the two. I'll not steal bread from a man's table, nor will I take what is in short supply," he explained. "A poor man works hard for his money, saves it, and spends it on what he needs most, food and clothing, for him and his family if he has one. A rich man, although he may have worked just as hard, won't miss a meal because of few silver pieces, or a gold pouch goes missing."

"But stealing is stealing. Both men worked for that money," Austin said, measuring the man before him.

"Certainly. I make no excuses. I am a thief. I steal from one person to enrich myself. I am no nobleman, I'm just... me," Matt shrugged. "And I ask no man for forgiveness either."

Suddenly there was a bang at the door, and instantly six castle guardsman burst into the room.

"High General. The watch saw a man enter this room by the window! We're searching... that's him! Get him men!" the leader of the watch commanded, and rushed at the thief with his sword high in the air. Suddenly the man swung his weapon down and would have driven his blade into Matthew's forehead if it wasn't stopped by Austin's own sword.

"Hold guardsmen. This man works for me. He was under instructions to get word to me in private and came through the window in secret," Austin lied. "He mistook my command and won't enter the castle that way again. Good work to you and your men in securing the castle, though. Your responses to the intrusion were excellent, but hold your swords this night and go back to your duties. This man is one of ours."

"I apologize High General! I never knew," the watch leader said humbling himself.

"You couldn't know. The nature of this man's employment is to have as few people as possible knowing of his existence. You've done well. But please go, we have much work to do before we move towards Andraya," Austin commanded.

Bowing, the men backed out of the room, again apologizing to both Matt and Austin.

"Why did you save me, High General?" Matt asked when the men were gone.

"Something about you makes me think I can trust you," Austin said.

"You know I like the ladies, right?" Matt said awkwardly.

This caused Austin to burst out with a full belly laugh. "Good, then we can find some later! But for now I have work to do."

"High General," Matt said.

"Yes Master Thief?" Austin replied returning his chair to his desk.

“I owe you my life, sir. That’s a debt I don’t take lightly,” Matt said seriously.

“It’s not a debt I can accept. But if you feel compelled then I ask this of you. Hire into my service. Work for me and me alone. I won’t conscript you into the army, but I could use a man of your… talents,” he said, and reaching into his desk he pulled out a large bag filled with gold. “Take this as a retainer. From now on you will no longer take belongings from anyone, rich or poor. Instead I want you to gather information for me.

“Our armies sit on the Northern Front, protecting us from the Hordes in the frozen waste. Go there and keep an eye on the High General of the Northern Command, Kiamet Quileen,” Austin commanded. “I don’t trust him, and I know he hates me deeply. My history with him, and our last meeting are enough to satisfy me that he isn’t happy with his new rank. I fear he is up to something more devious, and I wish to know what it is.”

“You have my word High General; I will ensure you know what he is thinking before he does,” Matt replied eagerly.

“Excellent. Now Master Thief, I believe you are one window away from your goal for this evening,” Austin said, sitting at his desk.

“That is very true, High General. But methinks this window was the more interesting,” the thief-turned-spy said with a grin, and bound out the window.

‘As do I,’ Austin thought to himself with a smile. *‘As do I!’*

Chapter 23

In the Age of the Eland Civil War

The morning bells tolled within the mountain kingdom of Verengrath. Like all things the Dwarves did, the bells were an engineering marvel. Long lines connected different series of bells, so that all the separate clans received the same warning at the same time spread across the entire Dwarven city. But each clan's bell chimed a different tone, so they were all as unique as the people within their separate halls. Yet if you stood in the center of the entire kingdom, which was the great Castle of the Emperor himself, you would hear how each hall's chime played a wondrous melody with each other. It was a symbol of how unique the Dwarves were within Verengrath, yet how as a united people they created a perfect harmony.

But this morning the chimes were different. "Hmm," Al'bet said quietly as he listened, "they are calling everyone to the Royal Chamber. This isn't going to be a quiet event."

"Well it has been several hundred years since anyone took the Quest," Mar'di said softly, listening to the tones for any other messages she could pick up.

"So we're being sent off with a crowd," Austin said, trying to sound confident. "Good. That means more people to witness the beginning of a new age here."

"That's it boy; steel yourself for what is coming. Because I assure you, it won't be easy," Al'bet replied.

"Nothing," Austin said with a glint of determination in his eye, "has ever been easy in my life. I see no reason why it should start now."

It was with that sentiment that everyone stood and began to file out of Al'bet's house. The small group once again made their way to the Royal Hall and joined the lines as Dwarves surged into the massive cavern. Austin couldn't help but wonder if the vast majority already knew exactly what was happening. The air was electric with the excitement of what was coming. Inch by inch they all moved to take their seats, and step by step, Austin, Chloe, Al'bet, Le'stal, Mar'di and Li'sa moved down to the main floor below them all.

Chloe was amazed at the sea of Dwarves as they surged to fill the room. There were entryways all over the cavern, at different levels and different directions, no two the same and all of them had what appeared to be a ceaseless line of Dwarves attempting to enter. Bearded faces had already filled much of the room, and as Dwarves pushed their way past those already seated, calling out good mornings to friends as they found their own seats, more continued to pour into the cavern.

The small party of friends finally found their place in the first row, where a small area had been roped off for them. And so it was that they sat down and waited for the tide of Dwarves to cease. It took three quarters of an hour before the loud clanking of doors echoed around the chamber, as each of the doorways was closed to better allow sound to travel unhindered to the masses.

A few minutes more passed until a large Dwarven Symphony stepped onto the central floor and began to play a beautiful and proud melody. From the first note, every Dwarf, followed by Austin and Chloe out of respect, stood and began singing the Verengrath anthem. Goosebumps covered Chloe's arms, and the hair stood on end behind her neck as the incredible anthem was sung. Men and women shared a common voice, each singing their piece to perfection, as the ground shook with the strength of their voices. '*If this is how they sing,*' Chloe said to herself, '*can you imagine if they chose to fight?*'

As the song carried on, the doors to the Royal chambers opened, and out walked the five kings. As they entered, each one stood beside their thrones, lifting their hands to their hearts and joining with the crowd added their unique voices to the throng. But the design of the room somehow enhanced their voices so that as they sang, theirs was heard the loudest.

Finally the anthem was sung and everyone stood silently, watching their rulers until the five took their seats, which signaled everyone else to do the same.

Once the silent signal to order was given and everyone sat waiting anxiously as to why they were called, Emperor Di'an stood and walked down to the open dais before the thrones. "Brothers and sisters of the clans," he spoke. His tone was gentle, only slightly raised, and yet Chloe was certain that everyone in the room heard him clearly. "We come together because a challenge has been made to the law of Verengrath."

A sound of wonder filled the room as everyone listened. No one ever challenged the laws within the Dwarven kingdom. "Would the challengers please rise?" Di'an asked. Austin, Chloe and Al'bet all rose from their seats and waited. "These three do not agree with the findings of our royal fathers, that Ba'rel Ironfist, son of Ba'toth Ironfist, former champion of the Bronze clan should have been exiled. Further, they challenge the cave in of the old tunnels that led to Ba'rel's exile was an act of sabotage. An act that was done in league with a Dark Elf, who now, they say wishes to bring war to our borders.

"It is the decision of the Royal Council, that if war should come, then we shall face it. The majority of us also doubted that such a rumor of war was true. That is until recently." His statement shocked Austin, as the young general stood with every eye upon him and his friends. "Something has changed in the minds of the Rulers, a fog lifted and although we believe the rumor to indeed ring true, we still see no reason to act.

"But, these good people, Princess Chloe of the Kingdom of Andraya, our own Master Al'bet Ironfist, and High General Austin Ironfist, son of Ba'rel Ironfist, choose to challenge the law none the less. The option of leaving Verengrath was given to them, but the honor of Ba'rel has been deemed more important than a self-imposed exile. Instead these good people have decided to take the Challenge of the Path of Fire," he said, his voice saying the last with a sound of reverence.

A wave of shock and awe rolled through the crowded room as all of the Dwarves began to comprehend what was happening. "So it is, Challengers of Fire," the Dwarven Emperor continued, "that you shall never be allowed to set foot in Verengrath again, should you not complete the Path of Fire. We know very little of what you shall encounter inside, but we do know that you shall experience three trials. One, a trial of the body, two, a trial of the spirit, and three, a trial of the heart. We don't know the order, or how the trials take place. What we do know is that should you be successful, you will receive a token that we, the Ruling Council shall be able to verify. Return with this sign, and you shall be given anything you ask of us.

"But be warned, for although no Dwarf in recent history has attempted this trial, and fewer yet have succeeded, we believe with confidence that if you fail you shall not survive. Do you still wish to take this challenge?" the Emperor asked. His beard filled with the woven jewels of all the kingdoms jingled slightly as he moved.

"We do, your Majesty," Austin said, his voice strong and clear in the large room.

"So be it. You shall follow us out of this room and we shall lead you to the gates of the Path of Fire!" Di'an commanded and as he turned the orchestra began to play a loud tribute, or as Al'bet knew it, the Hymn of Fire.

Chapter 24

In the Age of Yelantas Porthanaclies

"Get some more men to that edge of the camp!" Austin yelled, directing the men around him. "They'll try to make a break from the quarry out that side. We need to defend it!"

"General!" Artole called across the camp.

"Yes commander," Austin said, taking a moment to stop setting up the defenses to address the man running to him now. It had been nearly four weeks since they started their service to the Andrayans after they were forced to yield by King William Duthain.

The mercenaries who had been causing dissention in his ranks were dead, but to his shame many of his troops still wanted to attack the city of Czariana. Over half of the men he commanded had decided to disregard his orders, and nearly a third of those left, refused to take a side. So it was that Austin, with a little over a quarter of his men, fought day and night to keep the raging horde at bay.

Artole was one of his most steadfast supporters, and had quickly become his friend. To his shame, Austin had never even noticed Artole in the past. Certainly, commanding a massive army meant that there was no way to focus on individuals, but Artole should have caught his eye. The young man was an Elander through and through, and wanted nothing more than to create a safe home for his wife and young child, both of whom were living in the Eland capitol city of Lytton.

But it wasn't just his patriotism that caught Austin's eye, but the man's intelligence and his ability to visualize the battlefield that interested him.

"General Austin," Artole said, slowing down next to his leader, "I have been going over the reports of the enemies' movement." The enemy. Austin never would have dreamed in a million years, he would hear that term applied to his own countrymen. "They appear to be amassing for a forward strike," Artole explained.

"We've been able to keep them under control with our archers," Austin replied. "What makes you think they'll press on?"

"I've been monitoring their attack patterns and it looks like they've found a weakness in our defenses," Artole said, rolling out the map in his hand on the ground before them. "You are strengthening our forces on the Eastern side of the base, but I think they are purposely trying to get you to commit that action.

"Look here. They have been going at this point for days now, but nothing serious. It appears that they are trying to find a weak point on our Eastern flank. But the main of their force remains on the Western side of the quarry. If they were seriously looking to make a move, they should be preparing for it already," the soldier explained.

"Perhaps they aren't ready to make a move yet?" Austin questioned.

"Oh, they're ready." A voice came from behind them. Austin and Artole looked up and saw a giant, broad chested young man and slim agile woman heading their way.

"Cason, do you know something more?" Austin asked.

"No but Kierra does," Cason replied.

The twins were almost always together. They fought like wild animals when they were angry at each other, and that happened more often than not, but they still refused to be without one another. They seemed to think alike, and many times Austin found himself wondering if the two even needed to speak to communicate with each other.

"Kierra, what do you know?" Austin asked.

"Artole is correct," Keira replied as the twins joined the two men on the ground. "I snuck into the main camp last night and was able to hear several conversations. They are impressed with their ploy, making you focus our defenses in the East, but they are going to move on the Western flank within a few days, maybe sooner.

"They have fashioned weapons out of rocks, including slings, and war hammers. They intend on sending a large part of their forces to make it appear they are attacking the East, while the rest swing around and take us from the West," she explained.

"So they have stone weapons. Any word on if Queen Emma will allow us the use of our steel?" he asked them.

"Yes, the wagon with our weapons just showed up a few minutes ago," Cason replied. "I just came from there. She also sent us our armor to help."

"Excellent. I knew the Andrayan's wouldn't abandon us," Austin said with a smile. For the first time in a month, he actually felt like there was hope.

"Not only that, but she sent word to the Rangers to converge on the quarry. We should have archers to support us from the upper ring," Keira added.

"We couldn't hope for better news," Austin said. "Alright, well if they want to catch us between a rock and a hard place, what do we do to counter?"

"Well," Artole spoke up, "I've been considering that. I think we should restructure the camp."

"How so?" Austin asked.

"Move all the tents over to the Eastern flank. This will enhance the image that we are reinforcing the Eastern side of the camp," he explained. "But more importantly, it will move our medical quarters away from the western attack."

"Okay, but doesn't that seem a strange play to make; shouldn't we keep our medical barracks on the west if we expect fighting on the east?" Austin asked.

"No. Remember, these aren't men with your level of strategic training, High General," Cason replied. "To a layman, it makes more sense to keep the medics close to the fighting."

"You can't really think they'll buy that, do you?" Austin asked, bewildered.

"Not until we convince them," Keira replied with a grin. "I'll go back into their camp tonight and pass it off how you're buying the ploy to defend the East to the extent that you're moving the medics closer to see to the wounded. I'll even make it sound like you expect large numbers of casualties and that this battle is a foregone conclusion."

"Excellent!" Austin replied. "Okay, so now we have the camp moved and we have knowledge of the trap that is coming. Well, I think it's time we came up with a trap of our own.

"Artole, you and Cason get the men to start weaving grass blankets. Get as many as we can, and make them as large as we can," he commanded. "We will use those natural sink holes that dot the area as hiding spots for our men. Then as the enemy attempts to sneak up on us from the west, our troops will spring forth from the ground and attack."

"That just might work," Artole said with a smile.

"It works for us against the Northern tribes. We use it all the time up on the front lines. Let's hope our men are as blinded by battle lust to give us an edge," Austin sighed. "Speaking of an edge, has anyone heard anything from Matt lately?"

Everyone shook their heads no around him. "Yeah I didn't think so. The last message I received wasn't good. Sounds like Kiamet is starting trouble," he said softly.

"One war at a time High General," Artole said, clasping his friend on the shoulder.

"Of course. Excellent work you three. When this is over, I plan on giving you all a massive promotion!" he said with a wink, sending everyone off to begin preparations for the battle to come.

Chapter 25

In the Age of the Eland Civil War

Austin, Chloe and Al'bet walked through the massive doors, and turning, watched as they closed behind them. Then with a loud clanking noise, they heard the giant locks snap into place with a reverberation that seemed damning in its finality. But this is what they set out to accomplish and so they decided to move on.

The path before them was as dark as the deepest caves of any mountain path. Austin could hear his uncle beside him struggling and finally the darkness was cut by a flame as Al'bet lit a torch.

"There, now let's get on with it. We know what we're here for," the thick cored Dwarf said.

"I have no clue what we're doing here, uncle," Austin said with a deep sigh. "What did I get us into?" he said, sitting on a large boulder, his face in his hands.

He felt a gentle hand on his shoulder and heavy one fall on his knee. Looking up he saw Chloe smiling at him at his side, and his uncle before him.

"Son," Al'bet said gently, "sometimes life leads us down the strangest of courses. Even though it seems that our life has been a random smattering of events, it has been to some greater good, some greater cause.

“We are on this path, not only to free your father’s name from the dishonor it has suffered, but to free his people,” Al’bet explained, sitting down next to his nephew. “I sat and watched those people railroad your father, knowing his pride would lead him to that end and I did nothing. His own father did nothing. Once Ba’rel was banished, Ba’toth became a shell of a man, easily duped into choosing Ba’lain as his successor. Still to this day, I don’t know why I didn’t do anything to stop them. And when it was too late, I just walked away.

“Now we walk forward to earn the honor your father should have held within these hallowed halls of the Great Kings. So young man, we are doing this because it is right,” Al’bet explained calmly.

“Thank you uncle. God has blessed me by sending you to guide me,” Austin said with a smile. “Alright, what do we do first?”

“Well this is a path, let’s follow it,” Chloe said, glancing around her. The cavern was much smaller than the ones in Verengrath, and she was beginning to feel the walls close around her.

Taking her advice, the three began to walk away from the gates of the Dwarven kingdom into the darkness.

They attempted to see what was ahead of them, but the darkness was so complete that they could see nothing more than five feet around them, and that was all rock. Once or twice they heard the squeaking of a rodent in the darkness, but other than that, the path was devoid of life.

Onward they walked, searching for a sign of the challenges they would face, until finally they stopped, foot sore and tired from the miles they must have already travelled.

“This path seems to have no end,” Austin said, rubbing his feet as he sat on a rock beside the trail.

"Oh it has an end; you just haven't found it yet. And you won't by going that way," a voice said beside him.

Leaping to his feet and grabbing for Eksils Torden hanging at his hip he spun towards the source of the voice. Chloe and Al'bet quickly came to his side staring at the hooded figure that sat on the same rock Austin had just been resting on.

"Lower your weapons travelers," the figure said, his voice floating from within the darkness of his hood, "if I wanted to attack you, I would have had ample time to do it before now."

"Who are you?" Al'bet asked.

"I am the Pathfinder. Your guide on this quest," the figure said.

"Lower your hood so we might see you," Chloe said, trying to sense anything from the figure before them.

"That wouldn't be advisable," the Pathfinder said with a chuckle.

"Why do you say that?" Austin asked.

"To gaze upon my rotting flesh would kill you instantly," the Pathfinder replied. "You see," he said as he stood and turned towards them, "I am not alive, and haven't been for millions of years. During the age of the giants I lived, a craftsman you might call me. For I used magic to create all measure of wonders in the world. This very test is one such creation.

"I was commissioned to create the path you now stand upon as a test of a warrior's valor and worth. Unfortunately, when I completed the commission, I was cast into my own creation and I haven't been allowed to leave because I fear to face the challenges you must to complete and exit this trial," the dark creature explained.

"But others have completed the task, why haven't you attempted to do so?" Al'bet asked, uneasy at the undead being before them.

"No man has ever completed this quest. There was a time, shortly after you Dwarves took over the mountain," he said nodding towards Al'bet, "when your people would send someone through the doors and then let them back in again after they sat waiting for several days. But no Dwarf has ever come this far, and lived."

"So, you made your trials so difficult that you yourself couldn't overcome them? Can we know what we are to face in hopes of leaving this cave alive?" Chloe asked.

"As I said, I am your guide. I will lead you to your trials and help where I can. But I warn you," the creature explained darkly, "these trials are no laughing matter. I will give you information, and what you do with that information is up to you, but I will not overtly help you as your guide.

"You will face three challenges. A test of strength, wisdom and faith. For a true warrior must contain all three. But there are three of you, which of you is the warrior who faces the trial amongst you?" the creature asked.

"We take this trial together. We shall face the judgment as a whole," Chloe said with a stern force in her voice.

"Interesting," the voice said with a hiss. "Never before has the trial been taken as a group. There was always a single champion. Regardless, if you wish to face the dangers as a group, I see nothing within the guidelines of the trial that excludes that option.

"But be told true, being three will be no easier than being an individual. The challenges you face will test your steel, your endurance and most importantly, your minds. Everything you experience can and will kill you if you allow it. But you must challenge your senses, and trust within yourselves." He said ominously, "What you are about to experience will change you all."

"So be it. Let us be gone so we can face whatever comes and defeat it," Austin said, his confidence filling the air around him.

"Excellent!" the ghostly figure replied. "Then we shall go. Follow me and prepare yourselves for what comes!"

Chapter 26

In the Age of Yelantas Porthanaclies

Austin stood at the rim of the rock quarry looking down at the enemy camp below him. He still had a hard time considering his own men "the enemy" but here they were on either sides of the line he drew in the sand.

Sure it shamed him that he failed his kingdom and didn't take the city as he was commanded to. But after meeting the people of Andraya, seeing the lengths they went to limiting the bloodshed and seeing the cowardice of his own king, he had already come to terms with the folly of the entire campaign to begin with. He tilted his head northward, as if by staring in the direction of his home, he could see what was happening there.

As much as he wanted his countrymen to prevail, he knew King Williams' claims upon Eland were valid. He also knew that the men left behind to defend the kingdom could not stand against the might and whit of the full Andrayan army.

Sighing deeply, he turned his attention back to the problem before him. He didn't have the luxury of a Kings Way as was found in Czariana, nor did he have a hope that cooler heads would prevail. There was no leader in the camp before him who had the wisdom of the battlefield. All he faced now were soldiers who missed their family and friends and wanted to go home. No amount of reasoning would help him convince them to keep their word.

"What do you think High General?" Artole asked, creeping up behind him.

"That this isn't going to end well," Austin said bluntly.

"For us or them?" his second in command asked.

"Doesn't matter. Elander spilling Elander blood is never a good thing," he said with a frown.

"Well," Cason said, standing at his other shoulder, "war rarely offers the ideal. Those men had their honor to maintain. They chose their desire over their responsibilities. They chose this route, not us."

"I agree," Austin said, and turning to his two generals he smiled. The two men were so different from each other. Artole was athletically built, and preferred the use of a sword in combat. His armor was a medium scale, average for a soldier.

But Cason was a massive man. Standing over six and a half feet tall, the giant of a man wore a massive suit of armor that would crush an average man. He swung a huge, studded mace and although he carried a ton of metal into combat, he could fight for hours, without losing his stride. He simply couldn't get where he was going very fast.

Looking down at the camp below one more time before moving towards the path down to their camp, he thought of Cayson's twin sister Kierra, somewhere down amongst the enemy troops. Keira was the exact opposite of Cason. She was light and agile. She could move and swing through the enemy as if a feather on the wind. Her leather armor was designed so she had knives at her every reach, so no matter where her hands were near her body, she could grab a blade and set its edge to work.

Their parents were both high ranking members of an Assassins' Guild. When they realized that Cason was too large and muscular for the work, they focused his education on tactics and as is the case with all assassins, he was taught to use his body as a weapon, not just the tools in his hands. And thus, he was best suited for war. But Keira was exactly what was needed in an assassin, a role she fit to a tee.

“Have we rearranged the camp?” Austin asked his men.

“Yes sir,” Cason replied. “Everything is ready for the morning. We laid an amusing trap on our Western flank,” he chuckled deeply.

“Trap?” Austin asked.

“Let’s just say, their confidence will not last long when the fighting starts.” The large man chuckled deeply. “We had time to adapt your idea a bit.”

The next morning’s sun rise was warm and welcoming. Austin had been up for hours, preparing for the battle to come. Keira had returned in the night and told him that the enemy would attack at dawn.

The High General sat in a hole in the ground, surrounded by a handful of men, waiting for the signal to attack to come. He wasn’t sure what he was doing here, or why, but he knew to trust his men and if Cason said he should sit in this hole until he heard the trumpets, then he’d sit in the hole. Suddenly there was the sound of marching in the distance. Then the nervous whinny of war horses. He knew the only horses on the field of battle were with his men, so it was clear that the enemy was on the move.

He could picture the huge frame of Cason, standing with a hundred or so of his men, tapping his mace against his left hand. He was told that Artole would be in a similar hole across the battlefield, and that a large number of these holes were spread out, a trap for the over confident men from the quarry.

Suddenly the sound of marching became the rushed stomping of an army running forward. His heart began to race as he sat in the hole, waiting for the trumpet calling him and his men into battle, but none came. He sat, watching shadows race past the opening, covered with grass, twigs and leaves, oblivious to their existence. *'This is going exactly as Cason had described it!'* the High General thought in amazement. Realizing that things were finally going as planned, he calmed himself and waited, knowing his general would give the call when it was time.

But the High General didn't have to wait for long, for as soon as he calmed himself, the trumpet blared and he and his men launched out of their hiding place and began fighting with anyone within reach. It was a bit disorienting, but since his men were the only ones with armor, they quickly picked their targets and began to fight.

Soon he was able to work his way to where he saw Cason and Artole fighting side by side and the three of them began to cut down a swath of Elanders before them. But the day was a long way from over, and the odds were not in their favor.

Austin was growing concerned. His numbers had begun to dwindle and his men were tired. The day was old, and there was no clear victor on the horizon. Their weapons and armor had held the day, but they couldn't take another. They had to finish this today, or they were lost. Now he was surrounded by a small group of his men, including Artole and Cason, fighting valiantly, but he knew it wouldn't be long before they too fell. He had no clue if Keira was okay, leading the troops across the camp in the distraction zone, but he hoped she was alright.

He swung his sword again and kept another enemy at bay. He wasn't sure he had a lot more left in him and with his spirit failing, he knew his hope would soon be gone. It appeared that his short lived position as Elander High General would be filled with failure.

But just as he was considering how to save his men by sacrificing himself he heard another battle cry fill the air. The battle ceased for a moment as everyone turned to see who had the energy to shout like that. Looking out past the battlefield he could see a massive cavalry surging towards them, the Golden Lion of Andraya flying high above the newcomers. It was Brody and the Andrayans! They had returned just in the nick of time!

Spreading far across the battle field, Brody's men were driving forward in a typical wedge formation, but that's when Austin noticed that it wasn't a single wedge, it was three! The Andrayan Cavalry were driving between all the Elander forces, dividing them into smaller and easier to manage groups.

Brody drew up next to the Elander High General atop his charger and smiled. "I heard you could use some help," the master tactician shouted.

"Not really, but if you're here, stay for a spell," Austin shouted back, and as the two punched gauntleted fists together, they once again turned back to the battle front. But the surprises didn't end there. Soon Austin could hear cries of pain coming from near the back of the quarry. He had no idea what could be causing them until he looked up and saw Chloe, bow in hand flanked on either side by Andrayan archers, surrounding the upper edge of the quarry.

He later blushed but at that moment he thought that no woman had ever looked as beautiful as she did. He gazed up at her as she fired volley after volley into the men below, turning the flow of battle to their favor, one arrow at a time.

The battle carried on for the next several hours, until sunset made the battle impossible and both sides pulled back to their camps. Austin's camp was now filled with Andrayans who had shifted their focus to saving the wounded, and burying the deceased.

When Brody, Chloe and William's eldest son, Logan, entered the camp they did so to the cheers of Elander and Andrayan alike, including Austin who met them warmly at his tent.

"I can't believe you guys are here!" he said, joy filling his smile.

"We left the battle front as soon as we received word from Emma," Brody said, getting down from his mount and taking Austin's forearm in his.

"I'm sorry for the behavior of my men," Austin said. "I thought they had more honor than this."

"It's hard to press an ideal such as honor, Austin," Chloe said as she shook his hand. "Those men in the quarry are most likely very honorable, when things are good. It's a difficult principle to live by when times are less than ideal."

"That's true, and they have shown that. I'm afraid the Merc's we hired are at the center of all this," Austin said, shaking his head. "They've been eliminated, but the fire they lit didn't die with them.

"But come and join me at my fire, please!" Austin said, and leading them to his tent, he urged them to rest by the fire he had going. "Brody, Chloe and Logan, I would like to introduce you to my command team, Artole Telaries, Cason Rolwaith, and his sister Keira Rolwaith."

“Glad to meet you all,” Brody said to them with a wave as he sat on a log. “How are things looking tonight?”

“We've lost fewer men than we initially thought,” Keira said quietly. “It looked a lot worse for a while there. But thanks to the medicines and healers you brought with you, I think many will survive that we thought were lost.”

“Excellent news,” Logan said with a smile. “How much trouble do you expect tomorrow?”

“That's hard to tell,” Cason piped up with his deep voice. “Keira has been going into their camp for weeks gathering intelligence, but enough of them have seen her fight on our side that we can't send her in anymore.”

“But,” Austin said pouring a cup of coffee for the Andrayans, “I don't think it is likely. We now not only out number them, but we have archers on the quarry wall, and all of us have the benefit of armor. I'm confident this is over by sun up.”

“I hope so,” Brody said staring down at his cup. “There has been enough war between our people to last a lifetime.”

Everyone nodded quietly as each of them stared into the fire lost in their own thoughts of home.

Chapter 27

In the Age of the Eland Civil War

Almost immediately after the Pathfinder spoke, a strange light began to glow from around his body. "You may douse your torch, Master Dwarf," he explained. "I shall light the way now."

Doing as he had been instructed, Al'bet cut the end off of his torch and placed the remaining branch in his pack.

"You'll not need it so long as I'm with you, I assure you," the Pathfinder explained.

"I'd prefer to have it with me. It's sentimental," Al'bet replied gruffly.

"As you will. Well, follow me," the ghostly figure commanded as he began to lead them. "As I explained earlier you shall be tested in mind, body and spirit. But the type of test will not be obvious until the end. Remember, to never rely on your senses here, for they will betray you. Your eyes shall see what the Trial Master wishes; your ears shall hear what they will."

"If we can't trust what we see and hear, how do we hope to succeed?" Austin asked as they walked behind the hooded figure.

"I never offered you any hope, nor did I welcome you into this cave. As far as I'm concerned, you have none," the ghostly figure replied.

"That's reassuring," Austin replied sarcastically.

"Again, I offer no reassurance. I am not your friend, nor your ally. I simply lead where you must travel," the Pathfinder explained.

Sensing he had nothing more to offer, Austin, Chloe and Al'bet began to follow him silently. The light that radiated from the creature's body was enough to illuminate much of the room around them. For the first time since they started on the path, did they notice the incredible carvings on every surface they could see. Images of heroes battling mythical creatures surrounded them. The floor was as polished as that of the Great Hall of Verengrath and it reflected everything with the gentle reddish glow emanating from their guide.

"These carvings are amazing," Chloe said in awe.

"Thank you. I've had quite some time to perfect them over the centuries," the Pathfinder said, continuing to walk without turning.

"You did all of these?" Chloe asked.

"Yes," the undead creature replied.

"You come from the age of ancients you said. These are images from that time?" she continued to probe.

"Indeed they are," the Pathfinder replied.

"I've never heard of these tales. They must be lost to time," she added.

"Yes. These are the images of true heroes. Men and Beasts who roamed the lands of Arene long before your races were formed from the dirt," the Pathfinder answered her.

"Arene?" Austin asked.

"The name of the planet upon which we walk. We live on a large ball, floating in the heavens, surrounded by others. The stars in the sky are each a sun like ours, with planets just like this one. Ours has been named Arene, by the Creator," the Pathfinder explained as they walked.

"We have a lake in Andraya named Lake Arene. I often wondered at the origin of the name. You have met the Creator?" Chloe asked.

"Nothing as official as that. But my life continues on, even after my body died long ago. The force that drives it on in this form comes from the Creator. I am as much His creation as you are," came the reply.

"Pathfinder, do you have another name?" Chloe asked.

"Indeed, in another time I was Etherion," the Pathfinder replied.

"May we call you such?" Chloe asked. Austin was listening to her exchange with their guide closely. She was up to something.

"You may, but it bears no difference on your quest," he replied.

"That's fine, but if you are to be our guide, and possibly the last creature we shall come to meet, I wish to know more of you," she explained.

"Very well. I wasn't born of a mother and father as beings of this age are. Instead I was created from light and wind. I once was a Wind Walker, a race of elementals that commanded the skies.

"During the age before even the Giants, all the elementals ruled Arene, and the face of her was very different than it is now. The Creator had just fashioned the planet from his voice, and it was only just beginning to bring forth life. The green that covers so much of the world was almost non-existent. Instead, we elementals covered Arene's face and lovingly shaped her as the Creator commanded us.

"The Fire Lords flowed upon the surface, moving rock from the mountains across the planet. The Rock Titans, working side by side with the Fire Lords, shaped the ground and all upon it. They were the ones who began to tend the gardens.

"Next were the Water Sages. Brilliant minds, flowing together in the depths of the seas, guided the flow of rock and air alike. Finally were my people, the Wind Walkers. We carried word back and forth between the lands, separated by the seas. We all worked together to shape the planet in all her beauty," Etherion explained almost poetically.

"It sounds awe inspiring." Chloe said, enthralled.

"It was. It was violence and peace all as one. We never waged war with each other, but we moved mountains with our sculpting," the ghostly shape said fondly.

"But where are the Elementals now?" Al'bet asked.

"All of them are gone, except for me. All things come to an end, Master Dwarf, even I someday, when the Creator is finished with me. They were all called to the place of our final home to rest with He who created us," he said solemnly.

"That's sad," Chloe said gently.

"No, it's truly not. Your kind could never live side by side with mine in our glory. The violence of what we were capable of would have destroyed you in your frailty. No we had our time, to work at the will of the Creator, and when we had completed our piece, we moved on. Your races too shall disappear someday, lost to time, only to be found by what you leave behind.

"That in part is what this trial is about. What are you leaving behind? Your wars will fade from memory, your heroics, and your contribution to Arene. All but the important things that you yourselves must figure out before your time is up. Remember, we all have our time. Now is yours, so don't let yourselves be forgotten," Etherion explained gently.

"But you said we shall be forgotten," Austin replied.

“Oh your names, your forms, even your greatest pride shall be gone to time. You didn’t even know about Wind Walkers, and yet here I stand. But what my people left behind you can see every day. Every valley, mountain, waterfall and sea. Our hands have touched all of it, and as you sail the oceans, fight your wars, harvest your crops, you reach out and touch our hands who were there before,” the Pathfinder replied, a smile in his voice.

“You mentioned that you didn’t speak directly with the Creator,” Austin said, “yet you mentioned that He directed you. How did He do that?”

“The angels brought us His commands,” Etherion replied.

“Angels?” Chloe asked. “Like the ones in stories?”

“Well, it’s doubtful that the stories could do them justice. There were many forms of angels. Cherubs, who were small and playful. They tended to be mischievous and played little tricks on people. They were innocent, and they rarely did anything that we could see in a serious context.

“Next is the Host. This army of angels was incredible to witness. Giant, even next to a Rock Titan. They had a pair of large feathered wings, and did the most in the Creator’s name. They were the most frequent messengers who came to us.

“Finally,” the elemental said almost hushed in awe, “were the Arch Angels. Massive creatures even compared to the Host. They had six wings, and were incredibly powerful. They led the Creators army, the Host, and were His most trusted commanders.”

The three friends followed him silently, giving more attention to the reliefs etched into the walls all around them trying to comprehend the incredible creatures explained to them. All they had worked for, freeing their people, guiding them, uniting them, killing them. It meant nothing in the agelessness of what they were learning.

As they walked they began to notice a change in the hue of light coming from their guide. It was now going from red to a more gentle orange color. So too did his demeanor. Now when they spoke, he replied lightly, listening to their stories, urging them to tell him more.

"And now your people feel free?" Etherion asked Chloe.

"They are free, Etherion. No man holds their lives in the balance. They can be who they were meant to be," she explained.

"And this is freedom to you and your people?" Etherion probed.

"Yes, it is. Why, Pathfinder, what is freedom to you? Are you free?" Austin asked.

"No, I am far from free. I am a captive here, both of the prison I built, and the fear that keeps me from facing the challenges to release me from it. But, most horribly, I am also a captive of this corporeal body.

"As a Wind Walker, my body was air. I could coalesce into a man shape if I wished it, but in my original state I was a breeze. When I was thrown into this prison as its guide, I was forced into this form. And when this body began to die and fail, I was stuck, rotting within it. I am very far from being free," Etherion explained.

They all watched as his aura again began to turn a gentle red.

"I'm sorry Etherion," Chloe said, "it must have been amazing to be so free. I suppose what we consider as freedom seems so limiting to one such as you."

"Yes, but I would gladly live that life to finally see the end of this prison," he said with a deep sigh.

"Who did this to you?" Austin asked.

"An evil mountain giant. When our age was nearing its end, we began to disappear from Arene one by one. We Wind Walkers stayed the longest. Being carefree and able to float upon the wind we were happy to just exist.

"So we spent our days relaxing, using our magic to do anything that interested us. We watched countless wars, waged by the new inhabitants, the Giants.

"These creatures were like little brothers and sisters. They lived on the ground, the oceans, the gardens and everywhere that we had once worked. But they were angry with each other, and fought ceaselessly.

"It was at this time that a lord among their people, Tyris, commissioned me to create a test for his men. He said he wanted his people to prove themselves to him in heart, mind and body. So it was that I created the Path of Fire.

"I was innocent to the ways of deceit and so when I began to do as he wished, I never noticed the darkness that settled upon him. Year by year I built these tunnels in time and space, creating the jumbled maze we walk through today," he explained.

"Etherion," Al'bet interrupted.

"Yes," their guide replied.

"I haven't seen a maze. It's only been a straight line," Al'bet replied.

The body of the Pathfinder gently shook with laughter within the folds of his robes. He must have been truly amused by the question because his aura shifted briefly to a tint of pink. "That's because I am leading you. With me, this maze is a direct course. Without me, it is a myriad of twists and turns. As I said, it doesn't simply exist on Arene's surface. It passes through time itself. Look behind you." He said.

They all turned and saw the gates they had entered hours before a mere hundred steps behind them.

"But how?" Austin asked incredulously. They then watched in amazement as the ground began to stretch before them, pulling the door, two hundred steps, three hundred, five and on and on until they could no longer see it at all.

"I am in complete control of this place, General," Etherion explained.

"That's incredible," Al'bet said, truly amazed at the craftsmanship.

"Thank you Master Dwarf. As I was explaining though, when I was finished my work, Tyris sent his son into the trial. He was certain that his own flesh would be true to him. But I hadn't designed the trial to be a measure of their devotion to him. I created it to test their complete strength of mind, body and spirit. So it was that the young giant failed, and was the first to perish in these dark tunnels.

"Tyris went berserk and much to my dismay, he flung me into the labyrinth while I was in a more corporeal form. But no matter how hard I tried, I couldn't leave. You see, the magic is as such that if you go in too deeply, you instantly get locked inside. So great was Tyris' rage, and so full was my confusion that I was flung past the point of no return. Worse yet, because as an air elemental I could not be trapped, the labyrinth did something I never expected. It stole my powers from me, and formed this body around me. It trapped me, within my own creation," he said, his pain thick in his words. Chloe watched as his aura changed to a shade of purple, as blue seemed to set into the shades of red normally around their guide.

"I am truly sorry to hear this tale, Etherion," she said, and suddenly she grabbed him and drew him to her. Holding him close she simply hugged the ancient creature, who led them to their trials.

Etherion didn't know what to take the sudden sign of compassion, and wanted to lash out, yet something stayed his hand. A gentle word in the back of his mind calmed him in his madness, and he accepted the gift openly.

Chapter 28

In the Age of the Eland Civil War

The two stood holding one another for a moment more before the Pathfinder pulled away.

"It has been a long time since I felt the embrace of one who cared, Princess Chloe. You have my thanks. But we have to move on," Etherion explained, sadness still in his aura.

"Etherion, since you are in control of this place, could you not just bring us to our trial?" Al'bet asked.

"Eager to begin, are you Master Dwarf?" their guide chuckled.

"No, but my feet can't take much more of this," Al'bet explained with a grumble.

The ancient Pathfinder chuckled again, and nodded. "Yes I can do that for you. All whom you will face are prepared to kill you, and in fact, after so long without prey are eager for it I'm sure."

The others nodded silently and waited for what was to come. Suddenly, without warning a door began to open in the wall next to them. The corridor was bathed with bright white light, which intensified as the door swung open. Soon they found themselves standing at the entrance way of a room filled with candles.

Etherion motioned them forward and the three companions walked into the lit room, cautiously. They didn't notice, but their guide followed them in and the door closed behind them.

There, sitting upon a shimmering mountain of gold, sat a massive silver dragon. Her scales shone in the candle light, flickering around them.

"Good day, Etherion," the incredible creature spoke. "It's been a long time since you graced my presence."

"Indeed Zenatha. It has been long since anyone wished to face your trial," the hooded figure replied.

"And who comes before me, to challenge this trial?" she asked.

"We come to you, great Dragon," Austin replied. "I am Austin Ironfist, with my friend Chloe Duthain and my Uncle Al'bet Ironfist."

"And Etherion, the Pathfinder!" Chloe suddenly shouted. Her companions looked at her, and the Pathfinder rushed to her side.

"What are you doing?" he asked, rage and panic in his voice and his aura.

"You wish to be free," she explained suddenly, "free from this prison, but you have always been afraid. You no longer have to be afraid. You have friends with you. We will not fail, so you will not fail. Do you accept my offer?"

He paused, his aura red with anger, while bolts of yellow went streaking through it. But as he looked to Austin and Al'bet, who nodded their agreement, the aura shifted from bright red to pink, down to yellow and then began to glow a faint blue.

"I stand with my friends as well, Zenatha," he replied loudly, fear edging his voice.

"Well, that's unexpected. Who will be the pathfinder when you've either escaped or been destroyed?" she asked.

"That is for time to tell, and is no longer a worry of mine, silver one," he replied.

"Indeed it is. I almost feel a draw to join you all in your quest to be free from this place," she said but then she sighed, "but alas, the world outside isn't what it used to be. The age of dragons has passed and this horde is all I need now," she said, taking up mountainous handfuls of gold and letting them fall between her giant, clawed talons.

"Great dragon," Austin said loudly, "what is it you would have us do?"

"High above my head hangs a pendant," she replied. Each member of the group looked up and saw it, hanging from a hook in the middle room, suspended high above her. "That pendant is called the Qua'drac. It has been placed in my care by Forthozan, the Fallen. Retrieve it, and you can go on," she replied calmly.

"Who is Forthozan?" Chloe asked.

"Forthozan is a fallen angel," Zenatha replied. "During the age of the Voice, the great Creator did not only give us the Elementals to shape our world, but He also created the angels.

"During this time, it was the angels' duty to paint the sky with the planets high above our own. Several of the angels grew prideful of their creations, and demanded that they be allowed to govern those planets," she explained, "but the Creator, in His infinite wisdom, told them that the cosmos was a playground, but only for a short while. That all things are happening based on a master plan that He alone understands.

"Some of the angels rejected this answer, and turned from the Creator, the fools that they are. For truly, how could one who was created expect to rival the power of their creator? And so it was that those who rebelled were forced to take on other roles in creation.

"Garatories, his youngest brother, was forced to become the Keeper of Time. Unisorin, the middle of the three, waits until the end of time as the Keeper of Energy. Then finally, Forthozan the eldest, was made to become the Keeper of Knowledge. Each of these angelic brothers waits, fulfilling their duties until the end of time, energy, and knowledge, at which point they shall come together before the Creator who will judge them, and end all of this," the dragon explained, raising her talon, indicating everything around her.

"Each of the fallen has expended a great deal of energy to fulfill their tasks. Because the Creator only punishes us as a lesson, He gave each brother a powerful tool to assist them in their task, by giving them the ability to harness their trials into physical forms.

"Garatories, as the Keeper of Time, created the Harkin, a long golden staff which acts as a celestial hour glass. It allows him to monitor time as it flows. Unisorin created the Mace of Esrit, which hangs at his side and controls the flow of energy to all things.

"Neither Garatories nor Unisorin have ever come to me, but Forthozan came looking for a safe place to store his Qua'drac, the pendant above us. He had held it in his presence since his punishment began, but he nearly lost it once by a star far from Arene, and nearly damned himself for all eternity. You see the Qua'drac is a receptacle that slowly fills with all the knowledge of the Universe. Of the three relics it is the most powerful. For you see, as the other two diminish with time, the Qua'drac becomes stronger. So once he heard that this labyrinth had been created, he decided that this would be the best place to store it.

"Thus it has come to me to protect. I neither care for this bauble, nor the power within. And I have no love for Forthozan either. Therefore should this jeweled relic leave my presence, I would not be disappointed," the shining creature before them explained.

"Is there a time limit?" Al'bet asked.

"None. Do what you wish, try what you will, and take what time you see fit," Zenatha explained lazily.

The four challengers searched high and low for access to the chain upon which the pendant hung. None of them could find any way to reach it. It was much too high stand upon each other's shoulders to reach. There were no ladders, and although there were some treasure chests, there weren't enough to build up that high to grab it. Even when Austin attempted to knock it down with Eksils Torden he failed.

They all sat staring at it as hours passed, none of them able to come up with anything fruitful. They lay down upon the ground and slept, thinking that a nights rest would help clear their heads and help them come to a solution in the morning. That is, everyone but Etherion, who said he never slept. Instead he sat, watching them sleep on the ground before him.

"These mortals are strange, aren't they Pathfinder?" Zenatha asked.

"Yes. The female is most interesting," he agreed.

"She's bonded to you it seems?" the dragon replied softly.

"Yes, as a friend. It's been a long time since I've felt someone want to be my friend. They've always been afraid of me," he said quietly.

"We've been friends for a long time," Zenatha replied.

"Yes, we certainly have. If it wasn't for you coming to me wanting to hide your horde, I never would have allowed you into this life, you know," he said sadly.

"I know, Etherion," she replied gently. "Do you think they can succeed?" she asked.

"I don't know. They are different than the others," Etherion answered his friend.

"Perhaps it is time for the Labyrinth to come to an end," she said with a gentle huff.

"But your horde would be at risk," he said, stepping next to her and stroking her eye ridge. She shivered with joy at the sensation.

"True, but I think it might be time that the Creator would welcome me home," she said.

"It's been so long since we've been near Him," Etherion said mournfully. "I'd like to feel His presence again."

"As would I," she said with a huff.

"Well then, I think it's time, don't you?" he said, turning to face her.

"Yes, I believe it is," she replied, and reaching out her talon she allowed him to stand on it, and lifting him to the ceiling, he unhooked the pendant and held it as she lowered him to the ground. "Good luck, Etherion," she said. "I hope to see you in paradise."

"And I you, Zenatha," he replied, his aura glowing a contented gentle blue. And suddenly the candles, the gold and the silver dragon disappeared. "And I you, old friend."

Chapter 29

In the Age of the Eland Civil War

"Wha...where'd she go?" Austin said, waking and seeing the darkness around them, as Chloe and Al'bet began to stir and take in their surroundings.

"She's moved on," Etherion replied.

"But why? Did we fail the trial? She said there was no time limit," Al'bet asked.

"She's gone because we succeeded, haven't we Etherion?" Chloe asked.

The figures aura shifted to a bright shade of yellow as he proudly held the amulet out before him.

"Yes," he replied, "we did."

"But how?" Austin asked.

"It doesn't matter how he accomplished it," Chloe replied with a gentle smile. "What matters is that he did it, and we are one step closer to clearing your father's name."

Although she was looking at Austin, her attention focused on the elemental at her side. She could see the shades of red nearly completely gone now, where before they seemed to be a constant part of their guide's emotional state just the day before. She turned to hide a smile, knowing a little love and friendship may have saved their new friend from another prison. Not one of his design, nor one of dead flesh, but one of his emotions. If she could free him from a single prison that was the one she was most concerned about for the ancient creature at her side.

"Chloe's right," Austin said with a smile, patting the hooded figure on the shoulder. "It doesn't matter how you did it my friend, but the fact that you did. Thank you for joining us in this quest."

"I'm strangely glad for the opportunity," Etherion replied. "I've been too afraid to do it myself, but with colleagues it seems possible."

"So we have two more trials to face. What trial was the one we just experienced?" Al'bet asked.

"I can't answer that," their guide replied, "because we won't know until the end. What appears to be a challenge of one sort could easily be that of another."

"Well do we eat, or should we move on to the next challenge?" Austin asked.

"I suggest you eat if you've brought provisions with you," Etherion replied. "I don't require food to sustain myself. But the upcoming trials will be more difficult than the last one, I assure you."

"You designed this maze," Al'bet said as they ate, "what can you tell us of what comes next?"

"Nothing, unfortunately," Etherion replied.

"How can you know nothing of what lies ahead?" Austin asked.

"Because that is the nature of the challenges," the Pathfinder explained. "I knew Zenatha was within these halls, since I allowed her to enter. But I didn't know we would be brought to her. The other trials will be performed by magic and I will have no control over where they come from, and by whom."

"You mean you didn't design the trials?" Chloe asked.

"No," came the reply. "I simply provided the environment for them to take shape.

"I have led many such as you through this trial, and I've seen many of them make different levels of progress. There was one young Elf who I was sure would succeed. But his weaknesses were amongst those of the spirit, and although he was intelligent and strong, his will was weak and he failed at the last moment of the final trial. I watched as a giant Basilisk devoured him whole.

"Several encountered Zenatha herself," Etherion explained. "She always has something interesting to confuse those who come to her. As a Silver Dragon, she has the power to fool your mind's eye into seeing what she wants you to see. So some of her trials have been quite entertaining.

"Then there were some she simply devoured because she didn't like their tone of voice," he said with a shrug. "Dragons are like that, you never know how their moods shall present themselves."

"Well it's a good thing we caught her in a good one then," Al'bet said with a chuckle.

"Yes, but something else is strange about your experience with her," Etherion said, confusion in his voice.

"What do you mean?" Austin asked.

"She's never been this easy to overcome," the elemental replied. "She's tricky, but this time she seemed to have lost the heart to try."

"Maybe her time in the labyrinth has taken its toll?" Chloe suggested.

"Perhaps. It has been such a very long time that we've been here," he replied softly.

"Well lad," Al'bet said turning to his nephew sensing the conversation needed a change, "have you given any thought of what you would ask from the kings when we're successful?"

"Some. You?" Austin asked.

"Certainly. I'll ask that your father's honor be returned, and that all the transgressions against him be erased," Al'bet said, chewing some jerky.

"How about you Ms. Chloe," Etherion asked, "have you given thought to what you would ask?"

"You know of the promise made to those who complete the Path of Fire?" she asked.

"Yes. It is a tradition handed down from the very first Lord of the labyrinth," their guide explained. "All those who came after were lulled into a sense of security offering it with impunity, since they knew no one ever overcame the trials."

"But the Dwarves who are said to have successfully completed the trial?" Al'bet asked.

"They turned out to be great leaders among your people, didn't they?" Etherion asked.

"Yes, they are some of the greatest names in our history," Al'bet said, disappointment in his voice.

"Politicians use such events to overcome strife at home. Po'than Greatstone was the first of your people to do so, if I recall correctly," Etherion replied.

"That's right," Al'bet said with a smile. "He was my ancestor."

"I can see the resemblance," Etherion said kindly.

"You knew him?" Austin asked.

"No, but I watch all who enter the gates, waiting for them to step past the gateway into the labyrinth itself," the elemental replied.

"It is said that during his reign, our people faced a war with the Drugar," Al'bet explained. "Drugar are dark Dwarves. Their skin has turned grey after so many generations without stepping into the light. They dwell deep within the rock, and although they entered the mountain with our people, they delved too deeply and found some form of religion there. A strange and dark power.

"This power has, for the most part, always kept them close to its source. But one of their leaders whipped them into a frenzy and they attacked Verengrath. All Dwarves use magic, but by and large we only use it to imbue strength or beauty to our creations. There is no real use in using magic to attack a Dwarf, our hides are too thick and it has no lasting effect on us. But a blade made strong by a spell can pierce us and kill us like any other.

"Unfortunately the Drugar found a way to twist magic, and worse yet, how to attack us with it. So when they attacked, although our weapons were superior to theirs, their magic was catastrophic. It killed hundreds of our people and would have wiped us out if not for Po'than Greatstone.

"It is said," Al'bet continued, "that Po'than took the Path of Fire to find strength to overcome the Drugar. So it was that after a week within the great doors, he returned and turned the tide of battle against our dark enemies."

"That's true but he didn't receive any magic or special strength here," Etherion replied. "Instead he camped right by the doors for the week, and hammered on them when he was ready to return. But he told everyone that he had a great power and gave your people what they really needed, master Dwarf."

"What was that?" Al'bet asked, his disappointment back in his voice.

"Faith. They believed they had a great leader and these beliefs led them to victory, closing the Drugar deep within the mountain after their victory," the Pathfinder explained. "There is nothing to be ashamed of Al'bet," he added, "Po'than used the prestige of the Path of Fire to stir the hearts of your people. I'm proud that my creation could do that for you in your time of need."

Chapter 30

In the Age of the Eland Civil War

They were preparing to move on when suddenly the cavern began to shake around them. They reached for one another, to steady themselves as rocks fell around them and the floor cracked open exposing bright red and yellow veins of molten rock swirling below them.

"Steady yourselves!" Etherion shouted. "The Labyrinth has detected our success in the first challenge and is reacting!"

Horrified, they watched as the smooth stones under their feet began to separate and the heat began to rise up to them. But to their relief the gaps in the stones weren't very wide and the swirling, liquid rock never rose towards the surface.

Then when the shaking around them finished they looked around, amazed at how the floor had changed. Instead of a solid surface, it was now as if a cobblestone path was before them, illuminated by the glowing below.

"It's done," their guide explained calmly.

"What's done?" Al'bet asked, his chest heaving as he attempted to calm himself.

"Did you never wonder why this was called the Path of Fire, Master Dwarf?" Etherion asked.

"Never gave it much thought," Al'bet admitted. "I was so focused on the trials; I never gave it any attention."

"Well, this isn't just about three trials," the elemental explained. "This entire construct is a test. From the confusion of the labyrinth, to the very ground you walk on, this structure is aware of you and all that you do."

"How can a structure be aware?" Austin asked, gently feeling the ground with his foot.

"Remember when I said I was the last elemental left? Well that isn't entirely true," Etherion said, with what sounded like shame in his voice.

"One of the weaknesses of my people," he explained, "was our arrogance. We looked at everyone as below us because, well, they were. Not in the sense of importance, but we were the only flyers, and as such we always flew high above everyone else.

"It was thanks to this arrogance that when I stumbled upon Graltor, a Fire Lord, I never gave him a lot of credit for his intelligence. But I realized that I needed someone like him to best control my labyrinth. So it was that I fooled him into joining the labyrinth, and it is he who controls the very nature of these tunnels."

"You fooled him, and forced him into an eternity of being captured here?" Chloe asked, sadness in her voice.

"Worse than that, young half Elf," Etherion replied, his voice full of remorse, "I did it while I thought I would be free from this place. I chained him here, in ignorance." Suddenly the bright red aura returned to his presence, signaling that the madness had returned again. "I would accept it if you wished to sever our friendship," he said dryly with a tone of anger.

"We all make mistakes in our youth," Al'bet replied. "Your sacrifice to this test over the years appears to have humbled you."

"I agree," Austin said, nodding gently. "Would you enslave him again, if you were to redo it all?"

"No," Etherion whispered, hanging his head in his shame. "No, I could never build this, if I knew then what I know now. What pain this place has caused. My only legacy is torment and loss; I have nothing of valor to speak of, for my existence."

"Well then, is there any way to free him?" Chloe asked.

"Not unless we destroy the Labyrinth," their guide replied.

"How do we do that?" She asked.

"I would have to get out of the maze. The exit rests on the top of a mountain, far away from Verengrath, deep within the continent. There, I could begin the chain reaction that would destroy the entire path," he replied.

"Well then, it sounds like we have more than the four of us to save now," Chloe said with a gentle smile. "We'll work together to make right this wrong, Etherion. Let's focus on getting free of this, so we can set everything straight again."

Their guide nodded slightly, as the red faded and was once again replaced with a purple hued blue instead.

"Well then, we better move on," Austin said. "Are we ready to face the second trial?"

"Yes, let's move forward so we can get this over with," Al'bet replied. "How long do you think we've been gone from Verengrath?"

"Time hasn't passed outside since you entered," Etherion said.

"It hasn't?" Al'bet questioned in awe.

"Well not really. As far as the world outside is concerned, you've just entered the hall for mere moments. By the time you leave, it may have only been an hour by their time," the elemental explained.

"Alright, then that gives us time to get home once we're done," Austin said with a smile, and grabbing Eksils Torden he bowed, ushering the Pathfinder forward. "If you will, Etherion, take us to our next trial."

At that, Etherion stepped forward and taking two steps began to lead them on. "We will have to walk a bit for the next one. Now that Graltor has opened the floor, I have to be careful how fast I shift the maze. That molten rock below our feet can, and will splash, and it will burn the flesh from your bones if it hits you," he explained.

So they walked a while, following their guide, trying to prepare for their next challenge.

They had walked for nearly an hour when they finally came to a dead end. "This isn't right," Etherion said, confusion in his voice. "There are no dead ends to me."

"Then perhaps we are where we were meant to be," Austin said. Walking forward, he reached out and touched the wall. But instead of hitting solid rock, his hand pushed through causing the wall to shimmer like a pond that had been disturbed. He quickly drew it back with a yelp and moving all his fingers made sure everything still worked as they should.

"A portal!" Etherion said in wonder. "I've never seen a portal in this cavern."

"So this is new?" Al'bet asked, testing the open void with his hand.

"Yes. It means we will be taken from within the Path of Fire to another place all together," he said excitedly.

"Well then, we should go," Austin said, but as he was about to walk through, Chloe grabbed his hand.

"Let's go through together, alright?" she said with a small smile. Austin, thinking she was simply afraid, smiled and nodded, and while holding her hand he took a step into the wall.

Chloe rushed close behind to follow him in. Once they had disappeared, Al'bet took a deep breath, then as if he was about to jump into a cold river, hopped towards the wall with his eyes closed. His large Dwarven nose squished against solid rock, as the wall, now solid once again, bounced him onto his backside. "What the heck!" he shouted, and quickly got to his feet, his face turning a bright crimson.

Etherion moved forward and reached out to touch the wall. It was for the first time that Al'bet saw any part of their guide. The hand was shriveled, almost leather like, and tightly wrapping the bones in his hand.

"It's solid. Apparently, it was meant for only them to go through," the air elemental replied.

"Or only for him," Al'bet replied, dusting off his behind.

"What do you mean Master Dwarf?" Etherion asked.

"That girl has never once led me to believe she was afraid. Even in this labyrinth, where she is obviously terrified of the enclosed space, she follows without a sign of fear.

"Yet the way she grabbed his hand, I thought I saw a sign of terror in her eyes for a moment. I think there's more to that Elf than meets the eye," Al'bet explained.

"A truer statement could never be made, Master Dwarf," the Pathfinder replied.

"Do you know something I don't?" Al'bet asked.

"A great deal more, I should think. But on this, it is an instinct. It was almost as if she knew he alone would be allowed through," the elemental replied.

Chapter 31

In the Age of the Eland Civil War

Chloe and Austin held their breath as they were swept through a tunnel made of light. All around them, colors flashed and streaks of colored light flew past them. Still holding each other's hands they were whisked away until finally, when the colors and lights faded away, they found themselves floating in nothingness.

"Where are we?" Austin asked.

"I don't know," Chloe replied, looking around.

Austin joined her as they searched all around for anything in the darkness that surrounded them.

"This is strange," Chloe said gently.

"I'll say. It's like we're floating in a river," Austin replied.

"Not that, but I can see you clearly," she said to him.

"Why is that strange?" Austin asked.

"Because you would think, that like in a dark cave, we shouldn't see each other at all," she replied.

"You're right," he said, realizing he saw her as clearly as on a sunny summer's afternoon.

"It's almost as if the light is coming from within us," she added.

But he didn't have time to answer, as suddenly they felt a rushing of wings and three creatures flew by them drawn to a single point of light that hadn't been there before.

Carefully, Austin and Chloe moved towards them to listen to what they were saying.

"Greetings Brothers," one of the three said.

"And to you, Brother. It has been a long time," another spoke.

"Indeed, far too long Garatories," replied the first.

"So Time, Energy and Knowledge are all that is left," the third said.

"Yes," replied the first. "All that was is undone. Our Father should be here soon to finish where He started."

"How do you think He will receive us, Forthozan?" the third asked.

"We have spent our existence doing as He commanded. He shall be pleased, Unisorin," the first, who was apparently Forthozan, replied.

"They are the fallen!" Chloe whispered to Austin.

The Half Dwarf could only nod as he watched them. Something didn't feel right. Where was Arene? Where were the stars? Why were they floating in nothingness?

"Do you feel any weaker brothers?" Forthozan asked the other two.

"I feel…diminished," Unisorin replied. His two feathered wings shone brightly in the darkness. His bare chest was only covered by a long yellow sash, hanging from his right shoulder, down to his left hip. Hanging from a belt tying a loin cloth around his waist, the golden mace Esrit pulsated gently at his side. His only clothes besides the sash was a white cloth covering around his waist and a pair of sandals upon his feet. He was handsome, Chloe thought to herself, and his long blond hair shimmered as if made of light.

To his side, stood the red headed Garatories. As his brother, his hair sparkled as if made of strands of light and he too had a sash but it was tied around his waist as a belt. He wore a white tunic that extended to cover him until it reached his thighs. Instead of sandals he was barefoot, and instead of a golden mace at his hip, he had the staff he named Harkin in his hand. The staff appeared to be made of a rich, dark wood, and upon the top sat an hourglass. Austin looked closer at the hourglass and realized that the bottom bulb was nearly full of a bright golden sand. And although the top bulb appeared to be empty, a steady stream appeared from nowhere, to fall into the lower chamber.

Finally, the most glorious of all three, stood Forthozan. Instead of two wings like his brothers, he had four, and each time they moved they made a gentle fanning noise. He was covered in armor, golden and silver upon white bands of metal and it shone brightly upon him. His long black hair would have been lost in the nothingness, if not for the characteristic shining as if it were made of a dark shimmering light.

Chloe once again listened closely to what they were saying. "Diminished?" Garatories asked. "Yes, that makes sense. There is little energy left in creation, isn't there?"

"Very true. All that is left is here in this small area," Unisorin replied. "And you brother, how do you feel?"

"Weak," Garatories replied. "Time is nearly up." He turned to their brother, silently listening to them speak. "How about you Forthozan? How do you feel?"

"Complete and powerful," he replied, his confidence flowing from him as he spoke. It was then that Chloe noticed the Qua'drac hanging from his neck. She quickly looked over at Austin, and saw that it was still tied to his belt.

'How is that possible?' she asked herself, but she was quickly cut off.

"How is it that we diminish the closer we get to the end, and yet you flourish?" Garatories asked, frustration clear in his voice.

"Because, as time and energy draw to an end, I hold all of the knowledge of the ages. It is within me, and to know all has taken me to the pinnacle of power!" Forthozan shouted into the darkness.

"What do you intend, brother?" Unisorin asked cautiously.

"I shall face Father, and I shall destroy Him!" he said, laughing as if madness had descended upon him.

"You can't brother!" Garatories whispered, quickly looking around to see if they had been overheard. "Forthozan, please. Come to your senses!"

The second angel couldn't move fast enough to dodge his brother's hand as Forthozan back handed him across the face. "Silence, brother!" he replied angrily, the words dripping with disdain. "I know now that our Father's only power is what I am in command of. Knowledge. Knowledge of all time, since the beginning of time. I am his equal. No, I am his superior!"

The other two seemed to grow weaker as the moments passed, and Chloe was sure this was because as the keepers of time and energy, as those forces passed from existence, so too did they.

"Now watch, as I face our *Father* and recreate all things as I wish them to be!" And they watched as he pulled the Qua'drac from his chest and began to hum into it.

Austin and Chloe watched as it began to vibrate at first, as if reacting to the resonance of his voice. Then as it began to vibrate harder, a light began to shine from the dark jewel in its heart.

"Austin we have to do something," Chloe said turning to him. But Austin wasn't listening. He was enthralled by what he was seeing.

"Austin," she said a little louder, but still he was mesmerized by the light.

"Austin!" she shouted, finally getting his attention. But it also caught the attention of the three angels beyond them causing them to take notice of their presence.

"You!" Forthozan shouted, and extending his arm towards them caused their bodies to be drawn forward.

"What do you mean, you?" Austin asked. Angry at being pulled like a puppet on strings.

"You don't remember me?" Forthozan asked, rage seething through him.

"We've never seen you before," Chloe gasped. Austin didn't know what was happening but she was acting like she was being suffocated. He watched as she struggled to breathe.

"What are you doing to her?" Austin shouted, trying unsuccessfully to rush to her side.

"I am crushing the life out of her. I am bringing her miserable existence to an end!" the angel before them shouted.

"Leave her be!" Austin yelled, trying desperately to stop their steady movement towards the power crazed being before them.

"I will crush her first, so you can feel the pain of her loss. A pain akin to the crushing pain you caused me for all those centuries!" Forthozan laughed.

"Pain? What pain?" Austin asked, desperately trying to turn their tormenters attention to him and away from Chloe. "We've never met you before!" he said again.

"You have! And you have caused me to suffer greatly. But this time I assure you, I won't allow you to use the Qua'drac! It caused a pain that I still carry to this very day!" the massive creature replied. Austin hadn't realized how huge the three of the creatures were until now. From a distance they looked to be the size of regular men, just with wings. But as he and Chloe were drawn nearer, he found that they were giants, over ten times their size and he was powerless to stop the crazed creature.

"I will not let you harm her!" Austin shouted. "I don't know who you are, and I have no desire to, but I will destroy you if you do not free her!"

"Destroy me?" Forthozan laughed. "A mere gnat could harm you as you could harm me. No, puny mortal, prepare yourself for the end, for it has finally come!"

Austin tried to think of something, but he couldn't reach the giant angel, and even if he could, he could never inflict damage on one so huge. He looked to the other two for help, but they were cowering behind their brother, terrified of the insanity that filled him. In an act of desperation, he reached down, and grabbing Eksils Torden, he lifted it and began swinging it faster and faster by the leather strap at the end.

"What's this? A hammer? You think to destroy me with a simple hammer?" the angel shouted, laughing again. Austin wasn't sure what to do, but a sudden thought came to him. Faster and faster he swung Eksils Torden and then in an act of pure desperation, he released the strap, letting it fly towards his foe.

Straight and true, Eksils Torden flew towards Forthozan, causing the giant angel to laugh at its approach. But the laughter caught in his throat when he saw the hammer, spinning end over end through space, heading not for him, but for the amulet he had let drop to his chest. Desperately he tried to stop it, but he missed the spinning weapon as a moment later it crashed into the gem in the center of the Qua'drac.

A loud cracking sound shattered the stillness around them, as bright white lines moved along its face, opening into thick beams of light.

Forthozan screamed in pain as the cracks opened wider and suddenly the Qua'drac exploded in a blinding light. Instantly after the explosion dissipated, Forthozan's armor fell from him and evaporated into the nothingness.

The crazed angel reached out to crush Austin with his bare hands, but he was stopped by an invisible barrier that formed around the two half humans. The giant angel, now thrashing wildly trying to reach Austin and Chloe, slammed as hard as he could against the barrier screaming in rage. Then suddenly a warm light began to envelope them all. Austin felt an overwhelming feeling of peace come over him as he watched the light grow brighter and brighter. The Half Dwarf General turned his attention to Forthozan and his fallen brothers, trying to understand what was happening. He quickly realized that the three angels were familiar with this new force that had joined them. He watched as all three bowed their heads low, looking to the center of the light as it continued to grow all around them.

"Garatories and Unisorin," a deep and calm voice spoke from the light, "you've done well my sons. Time to go home, you've redeemed yourselves."

Both angels bowed low, and whispering thanks to the speaker, they walked slowly into the light, glancing sideways at their brother who was now on his knees shaking in terror.

"Forthozan, I had such hopes that you would be able to handle the responsibility I set before you in being the Keeper of Knowledge. But as I warned those before you, and your leader who is now being cast into a fiery pit for a time, so few can handle the knowledge that you possessed. For knowledge is power, and you contained so much power. But, even with all that knowledge at your disposal, you still hadn't learned that my power isn't encompassed in a single strength. Mine came before you, and shall remain after all has gone away.

"Now go, join your brothers. Because although my wrath is intense beyond all others, my compassion is greater still. You failed, as I knew you would, but in this failure, you will have learned a great deal. Now go, and we shall see to correcting the damage done within you," the voice in the light said.

Austin watched as fear was replaced by remorse on Forthozan's face, and tears began to roll down his giant cheeks. "Father, I am unworthy of your love."

"My love is mine to give my child. Now go home," the voice said. It was then that Austin realized he was in the presence of the Creator. He instantly clasped his hands together and bowed his head before the presence before him.

"Young Austin Ironfist," the voice called to him.

"You know me?" Austin asked, an incredible joy filling his chest.

"Child, I knew you before you were you," The voice replied with the sound of gentle laughter.

"What will you do to me, to us?" he asked, as Chloe was brought into his arms.

"I am sending you to where you came from. You aren't of this time, and as such, don't belong here at the end," the Creator replied.

"What of Chloe, can she be saved?" Austin asked.

"She is fine, child. Forthozan was using his knowledge of her greatest fear, that of enclosed spaces, to cause her to lose consciousness. When she awakes, she will be shaken, but unharmed. Now go, you have friends who fear for you," the Creator replied, and it was then that Austin realized that Al'bet and Etherion were not with them.

The young Half Dwarf nodded in reverence, and soon felt the driving force of movement as the lights and colors returned, and he and Chloe were flung back through the tunnel from which they came.

Chapter 32

In the Age of the Eland Civil War

Austin emerged from the wall, carrying Chloe in his arms. She had yet to awake from the fright she experienced and laid limply against his chest. As soon as he stepped out, Al'bet and Etherion rushed to him to see if they were alright and what had happened.

"We came face to face with the three fallen angels," Austin replied. "I'm not sure, but I think we were at the end of time," he said quietly. The other two just stared at him in amazement.

"You seem, different, General," Etherion said softly.

"I feel different," Austin replied

"You met Him, didn't you?" Etherion added.

"Yeah, yeah I think I did," Austin replied.

"Who? Who'd you meet?" Al'bet asked, concern etched on his face. Austin just gently laid Chloe down on the floor and walked away silently, by himself. "Who'd he meet, Etherion? Who hurt my boy?"

"No one hurt him, I assure you Master Dwarf, but I expect that he came away a changed man," the Pathfinder explained.

"Who changed him?" Al'bet asked, growing frustrated.

"The Creator," Etherion replied bluntly, turning his hooded head in the direction of the fuming Dwarf.

"The… what?" Al'bet asked incredulously.

"That's right Master Dwarf, the one and only Creator. I expect it will be a long time before he'll be able to answer questions about what he's experienced. No one enters the Creator's presence and comes away unchanged," the elemental replied softly, as if remembering his own past. Al'bet noticed that the aura around the creature's body went from deep blue to an almost white hue.

They all sat quietly while Chloe slept. No one knew how long she would remain unconscious, and Austin seemed to have all the fight drained from him for now. Al'bet knew better than to push him, so they made camp for the night by the now sealed portal. Austin hardly moved from where he sat, hardly ate and refused to speak in more than one or two word sentences to any form of conversation. The elemental was right, the Half Dwarf had been changed.

Austin sat with Chloe's head in his lap, as he gently stroked her hair. He had never given faith a whole lot of thought, and he didn't know what it meant for his life now that he came face to face with his Creator. But he knew something had to change.

He awoke suddenly, as the cavern began violently shaking around them. Looking down he saw that Chloe was still unconscious, so he quickly snatched her up and looked around for Al'bet and Etherion.

"What's going on Etherion?" he yelled, his years of combat training causing his body to jump into action.

"It's Graltor! He's angry!" Etherion replied.

"About what?" Al'bet asked.

"I don't know yet," Etherion replied. "I'm trying to reach him with my mind, but he's incensed. Quick, flatten yourselves against the walls!" he shouted.

Instantly doing as they were told, Al'bet and Austin pressed themselves hard against the walls as debris fell around them, and then to their horror the stones in the floor began to shrink even more, creating large gaps between them. They could no longer simply step from stone to stone, now it would require more of a hop.

"Can you communicate with Graltor?" Austin shouted over the noise.

"Barely. He's raging. Something about a higher being entering the labyrinth!" Etherion replied with a shout.

"A higher being?" Austin quickly became afraid for all of them.

"No, not Him, but a creature of immense power all the same!" Etherion shouted, sensing Austin's fear.

"How do you know?" Austin asked.

"Because Graltor would welcome the Creator. This is a being that the Fire Lord despises," the elemental replied. "This isn't stopping. Come, follow me. And be careful!"

Quickly Etherion began hopping from one small stone island to the next, moving down the hall as rocks showered down around them, crumbling on the labyrinth floor. They knew he wouldn't be able to move them automatically to where they were going, since the lava within the wide open gaps would surely splash and burn them all, so they followed where he led instead.

The air elemental would stop every few minutes, concentrate and then would bound in a new direction, as if being guided to the cause of the Fire Lords distress. On they jumped, until finally they came to a large black door.

"The cause of the problem is beyond this door!" Etherion replied with a shout as more rocks fell around them and the ground continued to shake violently.

"So, let's go in there and find out what's wrong!" Al'bet replied.

"It isn't that simple." Etherion shouted.

"Why?" Austin asked, still carrying Chloe in his arms.

"That's the door to the final trial!" Etherion replied.

Al'bet and Austin looked at the door, and then one another, the same thought crossing their minds. Were they ready to enter? Suddenly a huge chunk of the ceiling crashed behind them shattering the floor, giving them no way back.

"I guess Graltor isn't giving us any options!" Austin yelled, staring into the swirling yellow and red sea below them. Reaching forward he grabbed the handle and pushing hard on the door he forced his way into the room.

Once they entered all the violence they experienced in the outer chamber stopped, as everything came to a rest. Etherion and Al'bet quickly followed Austin and stopped just inside the door. They all froze where they stood, as they stared at the creature before them. Etherion had heard the description of the being before, but Al'bet had no clue who they were in the presence of. The only one, who knew for sure, was Austin.

"Forthozan!" he said through gritted teeth.

"It is. But who are you little mortal?" the angel asked. In their last meeting, he was a giant. Here, he was still clad in armor, had four massive wings and stood in all his splendor, but he was only around 10 feet tall. Austin had seen larger frost giants in the north. It appeared the angels could control their size at will.

"You don't remember me?" Austin asked incredulously.

"I don't concern myself with mortals. I honestly cannot tell any of you apart," the angel replied smugly.

“You should remember me,” Austin said, his anger rising to a boil. But he calmed quickly as Etherion stepped in front of him.

“Of course he doesn’t remember you, he hasn’t met you,” he said and then turning towards the young Half Dwarf spoke softly, “yet.”

Suddenly Austin understood. When he first met Forthozan, the angel spoke as if they had met before. Austin didn’t remember then because he hadn’t met the angel at that time. Now their roles were reversed and it was the angel who didn’t know him.

“What is it you’ve come for, Forthozan?” Etherion asked.

“I’ve come for my pendant. Word reached me that Zenatha lost it in some paltry game. So I came to retrieve it and find a more suitable keeper,” the angel replied.

“Zenatha didn’t tell you who had it?” Etherion asked probing deeper.

“No. But I never gave her much time. It is far too important to leave to the wrong hands. It is a major component to accomplish my goals. So when she wouldn’t tell me, I killed her,” he said, speaking as if he had stepped on a bug.

Etherion went silent. Austin and Al’bet took a step back as his aura went from the baby blue it had been previously, back to livid red, now with bolts of lightning arcing from it. It hadn’t taken them long to realize that the aura showed the elemental’s state of mind, and how thanks to their patience and friendship they seemed to have expelled most of the demons within their guide. But now, stripped of his dearest friend, the silver dragon, he appeared on the cusp of insanity.

Reacting quickly, Austin handed Chloe to his uncle and stepped before Etherion looking into the blackness of his hood. “She is with Him now, Etherion. Calm yourself. We need to overcome this together. And know this, if I understand anything that happened in the second trial, we can inflict a major hurt on this devil to defeat him!"

Hearing the reference to the Creator, the elemental worked to regain his composure. Taking deep breaths to steady himself, he calmly turned his attention back to the arch angel.

"Well then," the Pathfinder spoke with a great deal of determination in his voice, "what if I told you the Qua'drac wasn't available to you?"

"Not available to me?" the fallen angel laughed. "Honestly? Do you realize whom you are in the presence of?"

"I do. I am with Forthozan the Fallen. The eldest of the brothers who turned their backs on their place of honor, serving He who created all things! Forthozan the Fallen, who has been condemned to spend his eternity collecting all the knowledge through time. But most importantly, you are Forthozan the Fallen, the demon who murdered my dearest friend!" the elemental said, nearly choking on the last word.

"Yes, all of those," the angel replied with an angry hiss. "But I am also Forthozan, the Arch Angel! The Creator may have forced me into this task for my disobedience, but he did not take away my rank! Have care what you say to me, little creature!"

Etherion would have launched at the angel in his rage, but Austin calmly laid a hand on his friends shoulder, and pulled him behind him.

"I'm sorry, Forthozan," Austin said calmly, "the Qua'drac is required by us for the time being. We won't be able to give it to you now."

"You have it?" the angel said, rage filling his voice. "You played these silly games with me, wasting my time, and you had it all along.

Give it to me now, worm, or I shall take it and destroy you and your companions with little more than a thought!"

"I think not, Forthozan," Austin replied. The Half Dwarf General quickly grabbed the amulet that hung at his side and lifting it before him, he held it high so everyone could see it. "What do you expect to do now, little creature?" Forthozan asked with a sneer.

"Something you taught me!" Austin replied and holding the amulet at arm's length directly in front of his mouth, he began to hum. Louder and louder he hummed hoping he didn't have to be an Angel to make the magic work. But to his relief he didn't, because soon the amulet began to shimmer and pulse with light in his hands. This didn't faze the Angel at all as he stood his ground and smirked at the show he was watching. The air crackled with energy as the amulet shook violently in Austin's hands, yet he hung on as hard as he could, getting louder and louder. Yet the more he hummed, the more he worried nothing would happen. This looked like what Forthozan had tried to do, but Austin hadn't seen what it took to release the energy buildup since Chloe interrupted the arch angel before it could happen.

Still he carried on, filling his lungs and humming over and over again, until his fingers burned as if on fire. His fear rose as it appeared that the Angel had grown tired of watching this spectacle and began to move towards him, with his hand stretched out to take the amulet away. Not knowing what to do, Austin suddenly let out a loud shout, and still nothing happened.

Finally in an act of desperation he yelled, "Forthozan!" and a bolt of energy exploded from the amulet. It smashed into the chest of the angel, violently throwing him back against the wall. Falling to the ground, Forthozan looked up as Austin changed the direction of the amulet's energy down towards him, carving a deep groove in the rocky wall. The Angel screamed in pain as it hit him where he lay on the ground, as Austin turned all of his anger and rage towards the being flailing on the floor. He wanted nothing more than to kill this creature, who in his arrogance would turn away from the amazing power of the Creator he himself had only briefly come to know. Who would try to kill Chloe, by using her terror against her. Who killed the Silver Dragon, Zenatha, without care. Who would kill them all as if they meant nothing.

But then the words he heard during his time with the Creator broke into his mind, '*Because as my wrath is intense beyond all other, my compassion is greater still.*'

Coming back to his senses, he turned the beam away from the angel, blasting a huge hole in the wall, causing the room to fill with dust and debris. The beam from the Qua'drac sputtered and died, causing the amulet once again to become just another pretty bauble.

As the dust settled, Austin stared in disbelief at the hole he just blew in the wall. For the first time in days, he saw the sun just above the mountain tops. The room they stood in was at the very pinnacle of the mountain, and he was looking out at the world from the mountains peak. Austin strode across the room and helped Etherion and Al'bet to their feet, and picking up Chloe, he led them to the hole in the wall. As they passed the wounded and bleeding Angel, Austin stopped them. Then, throwing the amulet down beside Forthozan, he shook his head in disappointment at the creature and walked out of the Path of Fire, victorious.

Chapter 33

In the Age of the Eland Civil War

With Chloe still held closely against his chest, Austin walked out of the mountain followed by Al'bet and almost hesitantly by Etherion. Each of them drew a deep breath and a sigh of relief as they stood upon a rocky shelf looking out at a huge mountain range before them. It was done, they were free of the Path of Fire. Suddenly, a glimmer at his side caught Austin's attention. The Eland High General turned and let out a gasp at what he saw.

There at his side stood a stranger, wearing Etherion's robes. The elemental had lowered his cowl and stood with his head back taking a deep breath of the chill mountain air.

"Etherion?" Austin said quietly, almost hushed.

The elemental smiled and nodded. Instead of the visage of death that they were warned about, the Air Elemental looked like young man, in his twenties. His hair was short, unkempt and shone like silver in the light of the setting sun. It reminded him of the angels he saw during the second trial, as it seemed to shine from within. His eyes were a bright, vibrant blue, but had a deep wisdom within them.

"Is it really you, lad?" Al'bet asked with a tone of near reverence.

"Yes, master Dwarf, it is I," Etherion replied, and lifting his hands he floated inches from the ground. "You all freed me, and now that I am out of the Labyrinth I have been freed from both of my prisons!"

"Is this your natural form?" Austin asked grinning.

"No," replied the elemental, "but I'm having trouble reverting completely. It doesn't matter though. I feel so incredibly free!"

He shouted as he spun quickly around, and then turning towards his friends he flashed a mischievous grin at them and shot off like a bolt into the sky with a shout of delight. Austin and Al'bet watched in wonder as the elemental rose so high that he burst through the clouds above them, creating a hole with the up currents that followed him.

"Warms the heart, doesn't it?" Al'bet asked.

"Yup," Austin replied.

"Sunset's the prettiest thing I've seen in a lifetime too," the Dwarf added as they watched the orange-tinted sun dipping behind the mountains.

"Yup," Austin replied again.

"Could make a Dwarf cry," Al'bet said.

"It could," Austin agreed. Then looking down at his uncle, the two exchanged bright smiles as the Dwarf punched him in the side and laughed a deep belly laugh. He then turned and walked away, grumbling about dust in his eyes.

Austin then felt movement in his arms, and looking down he saw Chloe as she awoke. She smiled at him, and reached up to wipe the dust from his hair. "Anything happen while I was asleep?" she asked with a chuckle.

"You could say that," Austin laughed back at her, and putting her down, he held her against him as they watched the last rays of sun fall below the horizon.

Being overjoyed at being free, they wandered the mountain peak by the light of the full moon. Soon, Chloe stumbled upon the remains of an old eagle's nest, which they used to fuel a small fire. They decided they would sleep outside, rather than going back into the chamber. They claimed it was because they were glad to be free, but in truth they were afraid the Labyrinth's magic would ensnare them again.

When they fell asleep they slept as soundly as babes and only woke when their empty stomachs forced them to the next day. Taking out the last of their provisions they made a simple breakfast of dried meats and some fruit brought to them by Etherion, who had returned sometime in the night.

They sat around discussing the events they faced in the labyrinth and how to get down from the mountain when Etherion spoke up. "My friends," he said meekly, "I have to ask you for help, yet again."

"Anything Etherion," Austin replied. "What do you need?"

"I need to destroy the Path of Fire," he said gently.

"Destroy it?" Al'bet said amazed. "You can do that?"

"Yes," the elemental replied. "I built into the mountain a mechanism that would allow me to destroy it, should I ever see a need. But it could only be triggered from out here, and since I was stuck, there was no way to do so.

"But now that I'm free, I must destroy what I created. I know now that it is only a thing of darkness, evil and pain. I couldn't live with myself if anyone else had to face its madness," he continued, then hanging his head he added, "And I must free Graltor.

"I have been in contact with him telepathically, and he yearns to be free as I. He must never be left to suffer alone," he said with desperation in his voice.

"Show us what you need done," Austin said resolutely.

"I knew you would help," Etherion said with a smile. "Come with me master Ironfist. You and Eksils Torden are all I need!" Then floating into the air, the elemental lifted Austin on an air current and gently lifted them both up to another landing around fifty feet above the exit they had created.

The air elemental lowered Austin to the ground and then floated over to a large pile of rocks. Swinging his hands above his head, he caused the pile to float into the air, rock by rock and moved it over the back edge of the platform, clearing everything but a single narrow pillar sticking out of the ground.

"This pin," he explained, "holds a very complicated mechanism in place. By driving it into the ground, we will release that mechanism which will collapse the entire labyrinth structure."

"What about Graltor?" Austin asked.

"He'll be fine," Etherion replied. "Once the pin has been dropped, I will signal him to prepare to leave and once his chamber is released from the magic he will swim out. He knows the magma flows through the planet very well. Once he is free, he will swim clear of the mountain, deep into the heart of our world. He is very excited, as it is there that his people used to dwell."

"Okay then, let's do it!" Austin replied with a smile, and taking his hammer from his hip he walked over and prepared himself for the first strike. "Just drive this post into the ground?"

"That's right. Straight down," his former guide confirmed. Austin nodded, and swinging his hammer as hard as he could, he drove the post down over a foot. He hit it again and again, driving it down into the mountain. He pounded it down until it was only inches left above ground when it stopped dropping.

Austin struck it again with no luck. Frowning he tried again, but again, the pin didn't move.

"It's stuck!" Austin said with frustration.

"It can't be," Etherion said in near panic.

"Easy Etherion," Austin said gently. "Maybe Uncle Al'bet has some ideas. He's worked with stone his whole life. Can you bring him to me, please?"

The elemental eagerly nodded and jumping off the edge of the shelf he flew down to where Chloe and Al'bet waited for their return. Austin waited until he saw his uncle, tumbling end over end as he was lifted on air currents up to where the general stood. The Half Dwarf almost burst out laughing as he listened to his uncle cursing and shouting that this wasn't any way for a dignified Dwarf to travel!

Austin continued to watch as Etherion then floated Chloe up, who giggled with joy and spinning around gracefully pretended she was a jewelry box ballerina. Once Al'bet got up and dusted himself off, all the while grumbling to himself about wishing he had his ax, Austin brought him to the pin and explained what they needed.

Al'bet gently tugged at his beard and considered what he was being told. "So you made this pin absolutely straight?" Al'bet asked.

"Yes, most definitely straight," the elemental explained.

"Well, mountains shift with time, and that must be what happened here. The rocks in the mountain have moved just far enough that they are putting tremendous pressure on the pin. There isn't a force in the world that could move it if that is the case," the Dwarf explained seriously.

"That's it then," Etherion said, defeated. "Well if Graltor cannot be free, then neither can I."

"I didn't say there was nothing to be done," replied the Dwarf. "We simply cannot drop the pin by hammering it straight down. Son, hand me your hammer," he said, turning to Austin.

Austin handed his uncle his hammer who then grabbed a small stone, and using the hammer to give it an edge created a small chisel. "This won't work as well as metal, but it'll help."

The Dwarven smith then knelt down next to the pin and began to chisel the rock around it, trying to widen the hole. He worked for hours, crumbling stone chisel after stone chisel, and digging deep into the mountain. He stopped and leaned against the peak to rest after working tirelessly to release the pin.

"That is a deep hole." He panted as he rested. "This is going to take me a while," he explained.

"If only we had some metal tools for you to work with," Austin said from his seat next to his uncle.

"Etherion," Chloe said. "How much control do you have over the air currents?" she asked.

"A lot of control. I have the ability to manipulate the air in all sorts of manner," he replied.

"Have any of you seen what a river's current can do to rock over time?" she asked.

"Sure, it can carve deeply into it. But that takes time, and a lot of water," Al'bet replied.

"That's true, but what if Etherion took a pile of sand and grit, and spun it around that pin like a drill? If he could spin it fast enough, with enough downward force he might be able to cut into the rock faster than we can without steel," she explained.

"You know what, the girl's got a point," Al'bet replied, then added, "besides the ones on her ears, that is," with a wink.

Chloe laughed and turned to Etherion. "Do you think you can do that, Etherion?"

"If Master Al'bet can try for as long as he has, I can certainly try now," he replied, and spinning his hands around his head he began to use the air to sweep the mountain shelf clean of all debris, swirling it into a large ball floating before him. He then moved the ball of air and grit towards the pin, and spinning his finger around before him, caused the grit to form into a spinning funnel. Once it was moving fast enough, he shifted his hands, causing the funnel to slip over the pin down to the ground, and began to use the grit to eat away at the rock.

Nothing happened at first, then adding extra currents to support the funnel, he strengthened it further and began to press down even harder. Soon the sound of a drill press on rock began to fill the waning hours of the day as inch by inch the elemental drove his air drill into the ground. Chloe, Austin and Al'bet walked to his side and as the four of them looked down, they watched as Etherion drove his drill deep below the surface of the mountain shelf.

The elemental had to lift the spinning rock and air up out of the hole several times, dragging debris with it, which he added to his drill, lowering it again and again into the mountain.

Suddenly, without notice, the pin dropped down the hole, disappearing in to the darkness below. Etherion stopped his spinning hands and the all four of them looked down in to the empty hole, waiting for a sign.

A moment passed and then the sign came. At first it was just a vibration. Then it was a shimmer, followed by a shake until suddenly the whole mountain began to violently ripple below their feet.

"All of you, jump off the mountain!" Etherion shouted and without thinking Al'bet, Chloe and Austin all leapt off the edge of the shelf falling off the edge of the mountain. But before they could fall, Etherion caught them up on a gentle air current and floated them all high above the mountain.

"What's happening?" Chloe shouted.

"It's a massive earthquake!" Al'bet replied. "I think you did it Etherion."

"Quick Etherion," Austin called out, "warn Graltor!"

The Elemental nodded and closing his eyes he reached out to the Fire Elemental deep inside the mountain.

"He's free!" Etherion shouted. "He's swimming out of the labyrinth. The rock is falling all around him. He's having to swim deeper than he expected to escape the collapse around him. Oh no!" he exclaimed.

"What?" Austin shouted.

"He's trapped. The collapse has blocked his path," Etherion yelled in reply. "No wait! My word I had no clue he was so powerful! He just blasted the collapsed wall aside as if it was nothing!" he explained as he kept his eyes shut tight. "He's now so confident he's not even swimming below the rock. Tons of it are falling about him but he's letting it bounce off of him as if pebbles. He's laughing!" Etherion nearly screamed with joy as he began laughing himself. He suddenly stopped and went silent.

Austin, Chloe and Al'bet all waited impatiently to be told more when the earth stopped shaking and the noise stopped.

"The earthquake, is it over?" Austin asked.

"It might heave a bit yet," Al'bet explained, "but I would guess that the worst of it is over. Any word from Graltor?"

Etherion remained quiet, his eyes closed tight as he reached out to the Fire Elemental down below them. Then he opened them and smiled, “He’s free, and floating in the rivers towards his old home!”

All four of them shouted with joy in celebration. They had done it. The Path of Fire was no more!

Chapter 34

In the Age of the Eland Civil War

The day had been lost trying to destroy the Labyrinth, so they once again made camp on the mountain top. Etherion flew off and collected wood to allow them to once again have a fire to warm themselves in the cold mountain air. "Well, what do we do next?" Austin asked the others as they sat around the fire.

"What do you mean?" Al'bet asked. "We go back to Verengrath and restore your father's honor."

"But how will they know we succeeded?" Austin asked.

"You will tell them the truth," Etherion replied. "I will come with you and explain who I am. Together we will tell the Kings our story and we shall show them that the cavern beyond the doors to the Path of Fire has collapsed."

"But isn't there normally a sign that you succeeded?" Austin asked.

"Certainly, you return alive," Etherion replied.

"In all previous 'attempts' made by the Dwarves, they returned the same way they left. They also did it after a week or so, you said," Chloe reminded them. "We will neither be able to return by the same way we entered, and if time has stood still, we will only have been away for a couple of days."

"That's true. But it will still take us a few days to get back there," the air elemental replied. "I will fly you home, of that you shall have no fear. But even at that, we are many miles east of where you started. In fact, we aren't even in Eland anymore. We are well past the Ten Kingdoms."

"Okay, but we are still going to enter by the main gates of Verengrath," Austin replied.

"Of that there is no alternative," Etherion shrugged.

"Let's cross these bridges when we get there," Al'bet replied with a yawn. "I, for one, need some sleep. I'll see you all in the morning." And with that he slipped into his bed roll and promptly began snoring.

"I think I'll fly around a bit. It's been so long since I've been free, I'd like a bit of time in the air," Etherion said with a smile, as he slowly floated up and then flew away.

This left Austin and Chloe alone. "Are you alright now, Chloe?" Austin asked.

"I'm fine. The nightmares didn't return last night, so I'm hoping I'm through with it," she said with a shrug.

"If you were so terrified of the caves, why'd you come? You could have waited in Nord Byen. I would have found you there," he questioned.

"Like I told you before, where you go, I go," she said, looking at him straight in the eye.

"I was terrified that I lost you," Austin said.

"I'm difficult to lose," she replied with a grin. "How was it? Being in the Creator's presence?"

"Incredible. I was terrified and calm at the same time. My emotions knew no bounds, but I felt welcome, as if I was standing at my parents' front door. It was a kind of love and peace I never experienced before," he said, trying his best to put it all into words.

"But you never felt threatened?" she asked.

"No, never. I did feel like there was an expectation placed on me. I've heard others say that He loves us unconditionally. But there are conditions, we must all be aware of that," Austin replied, playing with the fire.

"Will you be alright?" she asked.

"Yes, I'm fine. But I see things so very, very differently now," Austin replied.

"Still want to be King?" she asked with a smile.

"I'm not sure where I shall sit. But I know one thing. No matter where my feet take me, I know my place is with you." He looked up and saw her smile a little smile at him that melted his heart. He then watched as she went to her bed roll and lay down. The Half Dwarf General then watched her back for a while, still playing with the fire and he smiled. It felt good to say what had been in his heart for so long.

The morning broke clear and bright, and once again the friends shared fruit they had never tasted before. Etherion was quickly trying to relearn where everything was, since many of his visual markers on the ground had long ago disappeared. But still, he had dreamed of flying again for so long, that even without visual markers, he knew where he was just by feeling things out around him.

But it was time to go, and so they packed up their things and prepared to leave the mountain for a final time. "Now, just sit, with your leg's crossed," Etherion explained. "I'll take care of the rest." And following his instructions, the three friends sat and waited until they felt fingers of air rushing all around them, gently lifting them and then in an instant they began to fly through the air.

They had never experienced anything like it before. Everything looked as if they studied a huge map below them. The trees were nothing more than green bumps; animals bound across the plains, oblivious to the travelers flying above. Rivers twisted and turned and all the while, they watched. But Etherion's powers were still weak and after only six hours of travel they had to stop so he could rest.

"We'll camp here tonight then," Chloe said as she helped him to a cushion of grass so he could rest. "We don't have to rush back."

"No, we will take our time. But I am concerned about how the war effort goes back home," Austin said.

"Your commanders will prepare the troops they can. Trust me Austin, you won't fight alone," Chloe said with a smile.

"I should have taken your brother up on his offer," the High General said with a sigh.

"Like I said, you won't fight alone, Austin. Have faith," Chloe said softly.

"Aye lad. If I were a King, I'd call the troops of Verengrath to stand at your side," Al'bet said with a smile. "To see Dwarves on the battlefield again after so long would be glorious."

Austin listened to his uncle sing Dwarven battle songs, their music filling him with pride in his people. '*No,*' he thought to himself, '*I won't let my people down.*'

And so it was that they travelled across the great distance between the Labyrinth exit and the Ten Kingdoms. When they finally began to recognize the land to be that of Eland, they knew it wouldn't be long before they reached the massive doors of Verengrath. Sure enough, after travelling for a few more hours they soon began to descend outside of Nord Byen.

"We must be cautious," Al'bet replied. "Ba'lain won't be expecting us to ever return, but his spies will inform him the moment they see us. Let's go to the Wounded Hand and see if Le'stal and Kierra are there."

So it was, under the cover of darkness, the four companions carefully worked their way through the village to the Wounded Hand. As before, the pub was full of people, all laughing and enjoying themselves. They peeked through the windows to see if they could see either of their friends but when neither appeared, they crept to the back door of the living space behind the pub and gently knocked upon it.

Taking to the shadows once again, hoping someone would answer, they waited. Soon, the door opened a crack and they heard a very timid voice call out to into the night. "Hello?" the voice said. "Is anyone there?" it asked a bit louder.

Etherion stepped into the light coming from the doorway. "Hello, I'm looking for Le'stal Strongarm. Might you know him?"

"I might, what is your business with him?" the voice in the door asked.

"I have news of his friends," Etherion replied calmly.

"You do!" the door flung open as Le'stal stepped out into the night. "What do you know of my friends?"

"That they are waiting for you to open the dog gone door!" Al'bet said, stomping over to the young Dwarf and giving him a friendly hug.

"Al'bet, you're here!" Le'stal said in excitement. "How about the others?" he asked.

"We're here too, my friend," Austin said stepping forward, with Chloe at his side, smiling at the Dwarf.

"Oh you can't believe how happy I am to see you all," Le'stal said, reaching out for all of them. "And who's your companion?" he asked, taking Etherion in before him.

"Do you want us to tell you the story out here or should we go inside where no one can see us?" Al'bet asked, kicking Le'stal in his good shin.

"Of course, come in! Kierra will be excited to see you all." Le'stal said, ushering them in to the kitchen of the back room. "Kierra and a few others who might be of interest to you," he added.

"Others?" Austin asked cautiously.

"Yes, five others showed up yesterday asking for you and Miss Chloe," the blonde Dwarf replied. "I was afraid you had died in the cave in and told them I didn't know what had happened to you. They stayed the night last night and decided to wait a few days, just in case you returned."

"Cave in? What cave in?" Al'bet asked.

"Around a day and a half after you entered the Path of Fire, there was an incredible earthquake. It was more violent than any we had ever experienced before," Le'stal explained. "Our engineers said that it originated from beyond the Path of Fire's great doors. So Emperor Di'an had them opened to see what had happened and when we did we saw that the entire cavern had caved in on itself. There was no way to clear out the path, and we didn't know how far you had travelled so a rescue effort was quickly disregarded at Ba'lain's urging."

"Of course that motherless Drugar would suggest we be left for dead," Al'bet replied with a grumble. "Well he has a surprise coming for him!" he laughed.

"What surprise?" Le'stal asked.

"We'll tell you all about it later, but first," Austin replied, "who are these people looking for us?"

"They are in the pub," Le'stal said. "They have taken to sitting at the big table by the door. Sneak a look through the kitchen, and you'll find them sitting there."

So Austin and Chloe carefully snuck through the kitchen towards the energetic sounds of the common room. Coming to the door leading to the tavern, they opened it a crack and peered inside. Scanning the room they saw their old friends, Nardok and his crew, and a few others they had no knowledge of. They spotted some Dwarves keeping to themselves, who seemed awfully out of place, but it wasn't until they saw the table by the door that they got excited. For it was there, sitting as a small group, that Austin's Commanders were waiting, enjoying the music being sung by a young lady. Lyra and Artole sat cuddling one another; Matt sat with his eyes on the Dwarves that Austin had also noticed, while Keira and Cason argued with each other over some unknown topic.

Austin and Chloe pulled back from the door and creeping back into the Inn's living quarters, he smiled at her. "You saw the same faces I did?"

"Yes, it's a good sign," she said, returning the smile.

"Who was it?" Al'bet asked.

"Friends. Le'stal, could you get them back in here?" Austin asked.

"I can try. Should I get Kierra?" He asked.

"Yes, I want to see all of them. But be careful. There is a table of Dwarves out there that don't appear to belong here," Austin warned. Nodding, the blonde Dwarf rushed out of the smaller, living space kitchen and into the open tavern. He returned a few minutes later with Artole at his heels.

"What is this news of our friends that you said you ha…," he said, but then seeing Austin and Chloe he quickly rushed over, followed by the others as they all warmly welcomed them.

"What happened to you all?" Kierra, Austin's aunt asked.

"It's a long story," Austin replied.

"Then we best make ourselves comfortable so you can start, shouldn't we?" Lyra replied.

"Yes, we best," Austin said with a chuckle.

So it was that Kierra went out and informed everyone she was shutting down early tonight and ushered everyone out. Then barring the doors and windows, she came back and had everyone join her in the Tavern where there was more room.

Everyone took a seat as Austin, Chloe, Al'bet and Etherion told their story. The group was silent, amazed at the story as it unfolded. Then when Austin came to the part about meeting the Creator, they were spellbound. It was more than any of them could have imagined.

"But once we were free," Etherion said, drawing the story to a close, "I had to keep my promise to Graltor, to free him as well. So thanks to Austin, Chloe and Al'bet, we worked together to destroy the Path of Fire completely. That's why there was a cave in."

"But, as I said, it only happened a day or so after you left." Le'stal replied.

"Time flows differently in the Labyrinth," Austin said shrugging.

“That’s incredible,” Keira, Austin’s commander replied.

“Yes, it was quite incredible. But we have successfully completed the trial, and now, we have to go to Verengrath to finish this,” Austin replied.

“Be careful in the Under Kingdom,” Le’stal warned.

“What’s happened?” Al’bet asked.

“Ba’lain has been on a tangent since you left,” the young Dwarf replied. “He tried to get them to seal the doors, but they said that was against the law of the trials. He then tried to get me arrested on trumped up charges. When that didn’t work he had me thrown out, saying I could no longer return. He knows there is trouble brewing, his witch of a mother has warned him as much. But there is something else. I overheard him speaking to her one day, and it appears Ba’rel was right, someone was in league with a dark Elf. And from what I gathered, it sounds like it really was Ba’lain the whole time.”

“That makes perfect sense. He is probably trying to ascend to the Jeweled Throne without the rite of victory,” Al’bet replied, rubbing his chin.

“Well, we have a nasty surprise to give him, don’t we?” Etherion said with a smile.

“That we do. The laws of the land say that we have the right to ask for anything we wish. Nothing is too great to ask for, and all Dwarves must humble themselves at the request,” Al’bet explained. “It is the right of completing the trial.”

“Do you know what you’re going to ask for?” Cason asked.

“Yes. It’s what we set out to do. We are going to restore my father’s honor,” Austin said. “But what are you doing here?” he asked. “What required you to find me?”

"Duke Wesset has been forced to withdraw his bid for the throne," Matt explained. "His official position is because he couldn't get enough troops together to make a real attempt, which is partially true," the spy replied.

"I thought he and the other Aristocracy were hiring an army of mercs? They should have had more than enough money to do that," Austin said incredulously.

"No, that was just the excuse to throw fancy parties. They tried, but you know how those blowhards are, all talk no action," Matt explained. "But that isn't the real reason they stopped. The real reason was Kiamet turned them. I don't know what he did, but their will to fight him simply vanished."

"I know what happened." Chloe said softly.

"What?" Matt asked, ever interested in finding the answers to life's little riddles.

"Neamith the Dark is a dark Elf who is in league with Kiamet. I would say he put a spell on them, as he did to Austin and to the Kings of Verengrath," she explained. "He will have bent their minds to his bidding, and caused them to turn from their desired goals."

Chapter 35

In the Age of the Eland Civil War

"Well, that being said," Austin pushed on. Seeing how uncomfortable Chloe was becoming with the current topic, he decided to change the direction of the conversation, "It doesn't explain why you are all here."

"Well we hadn't quite got to that part yet," Lyra replied.

"Kiamet has made his move. He is marching towards the capitol region and expects to face us there," Matt explained.

The news hit Austin like a boulder. "Already?" he said with an incredulous whisper.

"Yes. He has amassed his army, but they aren't all Elanders," Cason replied. "They're largely Northern Tribesmen."

"What?!" Austin nearly shouted.

"It appears," Matt injected, "that when you sent him back to the Northern Front, he used the opportunity to ally himself with them."

"When did this come to your attention?" Austin asked his most trusted spy.

"Only recently. When you sent me to the front, I was only there a short while before the Andrayan war broke out and I rushed back to help you," he replied. "He must have done it after I left and kept silent since then. I never should have left my post. You never needed me in Andraya."

"You have always done right by me, Matt. I simply never thought his ego would cause him to turn his back on his people," Austin said.

"He's wanted nothing but power since he joined the military," Artole replied. "Having no heir to the throne simply allowed him to set his sights higher."

"Well, where do we stand with our own troops then?" Austin asked.

"We have around a half of the numbers he has," Commander Keira replied.

"The other Elanders are watching to see who wins," her brother Cason replied.

"Yes, that's to be expected. And the Elander troops, whom do they support?" Austin asked.

"We have most of them," Lyra said looking at a scroll she pulled from her bag, "but the rest all went back to their homes to defend their villages. Everyone is scared, Austin."

"Yeah, well so am I," he said, rubbing his face with both of his hands. "Alright. Tomorrow we go to Verengrath to finish what we started. As soon as it's done we will head south to muster our troops."

Everyone nodded in agreement and, heading to their rooms, retired for the evening.

"Austin," Etherion said gently, "I won't get involved in a war."

"Huh, oh. My friend, I never expected you to," Austin replied. "I'll be honest, your magic would go far in helping me, but I would never ask you to involve yourself in a battle that isn't yours."

"I've done so much wrong for so long with my dreaded creation," the elemental said, "I just can't bring myself to compound it."

"My friendship has never been contingent on you doing anything other than being yourself, Etherion," Austin said, putting his hand on the Wind Walker's shoulder. "I am simply honored to have walked on this quest with you."

He smiled when Etherion looked up at him.

"Your meeting with the Creator did change you, didn't it?" he asked.

"More than you know," he said with a wink, and turning, he went to his room to sleep.

It was mid-morning when they marched to the giant doors of Verengrath. Al'bet walked up to them and hammered on them to open. The smaller man door opened, and out walked Ro'tan Sureswing.

"Who requests entr…" he said gruffly, then seeing who stood before him, he stopped and his jaw dropped in a look of shock. "Al'bet? You've returned?"

"Aye, you great boulder dome," Al'bet laughed. "And we successfully completed the Path of Fire."

"You what?!" Ro'tan shouted.

"We completed the quest, old friend," Al'bet said with a grin.

"But you didn't return by the Path's door," Ro'tan replied.

"That way's been blocked," Etherion replied, moving forward. He sensed that Al'bet was going to expose the history of their kings as frauds and stopped him. Al'bet looked up at him, but Etherion never moved his gaze from the Commander of the Guard at the gate.

"Yes, I know. But who are you and the rest of these people?" Ro'tan asked still in shock.

"Ro'tan," Chloe said gently, "we don't have a lot of time to discuss this now. We've received word from our friends here that the

High General's enemies are on the move. We must finish what we started so we can meet them on the battle field."

"Um, yes. Certainly. Come with me. I'll vouch for you all!" Ro'tan said and leading them forward they rushed deep into the mountain kingdom.

When they arrived at the great chamber Ro'tan ushered them in and told them to have a seat in the front row. He then rushed over to another room and suddenly a deep, loud trumpet sounded, echoing all around them.

"He's calling an emergency meeting. Stay close. This room's going to get REALLY full this time," Al'bet explained.

Full was an understatement if Austin had ever heard one. When they first stood in this room full of Dwarves, it was standing room only. Now, every bench was doubled up, the back row was filled, and every stair was blocked. It appeared that every Dwarf in the kingdom had come to see why the emergency call was used.

Ro'tan had moved back into the smaller meeting chamber the kings had used earlier, to inform them as to why he called everyone to the chamber was Austin's guess. Al'bet chuckled thinking how Ba'lain would nearly wet himself at the news.

Finally when everyone who could fit had entered, and those who couldn't, huddled around the doors to see what they could of the proceedings, the trumpeters came forward and announced the arrival of the Kings. The rulers of Verengrath entered the chamber with as much dignity as they could, yet you could see their eagerness to confirm the news from Ro'tan. As each one climbed to their thrones and sat, they stared, unsure if their eyes deceived them or not. When they had all taken their seats, Emperor Di'an stood and addressed them. “Al’bet, High General Austin, and Princess Chloe of Andraya, please step forward.”

Doing as they were told, the three got up from their seats and walked down to stand directly before the thrones.

“We are glad to see you safely returned from your quest. But to cut to the chase, how are you here?” he asked.

“We completed the Path of Fire, milord, and have returned.” Al’bet spoke loudly so everyone could hear him.

“But the door to the Path of Fire is blocked,” Di’an replied.

“True, but that isn’t the way we exited.” Glancing over his shoulder he saw Etherion who sat motionless, allowing him to decide which direction to take the discussion. “Because of the cave in, we were forced to find another way out of the labyrinth.”

“Labyrinth?” King Shar’tal, ruler of the Ruby throne questioned.

“Yes, my king,” Al’bet answered. “The Path of Fire is a massive labyrinth. It is literally an incredible maze where all who enter will surely be lost.”

“Then how,” Ba’lain nearly shouted, “did you find your way?”

“That would be thanks to me,” Etherion said, and floating on an air current, rose from where he stood and landed gently beside the others.

“Who are you?” Emperor Di’an asked in amazement.

“My story is too long to tell here, but needless to say I am the architect and guide within the Path of Fire,” the elemental explained.

“The architect?” Ba’lain said with a laugh. “That would make you…”

“Many thousands of years old, yes highness,” Etherion replied.

“Impossible!” Ba’lain charged.

"Only to a closed mind," Etherion replied seriously.

"How dare you!" Ba'lain shouted, jumping to his feet.

"Enough Ba'lain," Di'an called, trying to keep things under control. "The fact remains, that they are here when we expected them to be dead within the cavern."

"You believe them?" Ba'lain shouted.

"We saw them enter the gateway to the Path. We felt the tremors. We saw the cave in, and now we see them here. Not only that," Di'an said as if schooling a child, "they return with a being that can float as if on air. I think the more incredible question here is you DON'T believe them?"

"No, I don't. As far as I know it was all an elaborate scheme. They may have snuck out of the doors when no one was looking and been in hiding this whole time. And this person, could just be a sorcerer!" Ba'lain argued.

"A Half Elf, a Half Dwarf and one of our most esteemed citizens, snuck out of a guarded door, unseen, and hid for a week?" King Mar'kal, king of the emerald throne questioned. "I think you insult an awful lot of people with that line of thought."

"Indeed," King La'met, ruler of the diamond throne added, "These three are heroes to our people! We should receive them as such." To which many in the chamber cheered, drawing a thunderous applause from everyone else in the room.

Motioning for silence, Emperor Di'an quieted the chamber. "For the sake of governance, let us vote as a people. Tell us your story," he said, speaking now to the four standing before him, "and we," he continued motioning to the room at large, "shall vote."

And so the long and detailed story of what happened, what they saw, what they experienced and most importantly, who they faced began. Each member of the group spoke in turn, adding their point of view, enhancing the overall story.

The massive chamber sat quietly as they were told of Zenatha the silver dragon, of Fire Lords, Wind Walkers, Water Sages and Rock Titans. They told of the Qua'drac, and the fallen three, Forthozan, Garatories, and Unisorin. During the telling of his meeting with the Creator, Austin spoke with such conviction that none seemed to even breathe.

Then, when they told of their efforts to free Graltor from his chamber, deep within the center of the labyrinth a massive cheer erupted from all those assembled as they described the pin falling. Finally when the commotion ended, and they told of their voyage home, flying upon invisible air currents the four story tellers stood silent.

A hush fell over the massive chamber. The emotion of it all filled the room as Dwarf after Dwarf attempted to assimilate what they had heard. Dwarves are known to be isolationists. They don't mingle with other races often, and when they do it is rarely beyond their own front door. To hear of the wonder that the people before them experienced was an incredible amount to grasp for them all.

"I have a question." Emperor Di'an spoke when it was all done and he had thought for a while.

"Yes, majesty," Chloe replied.

"Your tale is very different than the Dwarves that came before you," he said, "Why is that?"

"I can answer that for you, milord," Etherion said stepping forward.

"Please," the Emperor replied.

"The Path of Fire does not contain a single trial that is repeated each time you go through it," he explained. "With the addition of the Qua'drac to its walls, the magic that works within it changed the trial for the four of us. I have walked with others through their trials and witnessed many different experiences. Once I watched a giant face a tribe of Ogres, another faced a burning village in need of his help, and still another faced a dark representation of himself. The trials we faced were selected by the magic within the labyrinth itself, because it suited our own weaknesses."

"Convenient," Ba'lain grumbled from his Sapphire throne.

"But consistent," Di'an replied with a frown. "My questions are answered. Are there any others?"

"Yes," Ba'lain replied, "I don't believe a word of it. What single bit of evidence do you have that any of it was true?"

Etherion chuckled. "Are you sure you want the answer to that majesty?"

"I most certainly do!" Ba'lain replied with a smirk.

"Okay, but remember, you asked for it." And gently swinging his arms around he caused a sudden surge of air to form around him and then moving it forward he caught the King of the Sapphire throne up in it and floated him above the dais where all the kings sat.

Higher and higher he floated shouting and screaming until he was high enough to be seen by everyone in the chamber. It was then that Etherion began flying the panicking Dwarf around the room in wider and wider circles. The crowd stared in awe as Ba'lain flew through the air, his black beard pressed against his chest, and his face pulled back by the wind. Everyone assembled was lost in amusement until a squawking noise came from behind the kings.

Everyone's attention turned to Ba'lain's mother holding her chest in panic.

"That will do Mr. Etherion," Emperor Di'an said softly. The Wind Elemental nodded his understanding and as gently as a mother caring for her child, he lowered Ba'lain back, onto his throne.

"Ba'lain," King Shar'tal, sitting at his side said quietly. "did you wet yourself?"

The comment was instantly caught by everyone in the chamber, thanks to the caverns design, causing them all to break out in laughter.

"I assume," shouted Emperor Di'an over the noise catching everyone's attention, "that your question is answered?"

Ba'lain couldn't find his voice but nodded quickly.

"Good. Then it is time to vote," Di'an said with a smile. "To my people, I put this vote. Do you agree that these three have successfully completed the Trial of Fire? All who agree, please rise, those to disagree remain seated."

Austin watched as no one moved. The lack of votes concerned him. Did they tell too extraordinary of a story for these people? Was the fantasy of their reality that unimaginable? He turned watching everyone, to see if anyone at least agreed with them. Then, as he turned, he saw Le'stal rise from his seat. He was followed by Mar'di, Li'sa, and soon, row upon row, seat after seat, each Dwarf rose. Like a bearded wave, each Dwarf in the room stood. Following their lead, as a sign of support, so too did Matt, Cason, Kierra, Artole and Lyra.

Finally he turned and watched as four of the five kings rose from their jeweled thrones, as they too cast their votes. Everyone in the room stood silently, except for two, Ba'lain and his mother. All eyes turned to the Sapphire throne, condemning the blue king for his abstinence.

"It is decided," Di'an said smiling at his people surrounding him. "We the people, of the Dwarven Kingdom of Verengrath, accept your testimony and we recognize you for your successful completion of the Trial of Fire. You honor us with your presence," he finished, and bowing low, signaled all his people to do the same. As he rose clapping began all around them and soon the room thundered with applause.

After what seemed an eternity, the clapping slowly died away and everyone took their seats.

"As Dwarven law commands," Di'an announced, "You have earned the right to ask of anything of our people. What is it you wish to ask of us?"

Al'bet walked forward confidently, "We wish to return the honor to my nephew, Ba'rel Ironfist's name. To have it returned to the books of our people, and to have him recognized as a fallen amongst us."

"So it shall be done," Di'an pronounced to everyone in the room, to which all assembled nodded with approval.

"I humbly submit, milord," Al'bet added, "that if we restore his honor, we too should take his charges of sabotage seriously as well. I believe a formal inquiry should be called for, if you see fit."

"Since Ba'rel was exiled because of his dedication to this belief, then I agree. I shall call for an official inquiry into the cave in of the old tunnels," Di'an pronounced.

"Thank you my king," Al'bet said and bowed low.

"And you three, what would you have of us?" King Mar'kal asked.

"What do you mean majesty?" Austin asked.

“All of you completed the trial,” Emperor Di’an replied. “All of you have earned anything you wish from us. Princess Chloe?”

“I went on this trial only to support my friend, the High General,” Chloe explained. “But as an official representative of Andraya, I request that a formal trade agreement, one of skilled labor and goods, be drafted between our people. To be ratified by my brother, King William Duthain of Andraya and you, your Majesty, Emperor Di’an.”

Again everyone in the room seemed to be pleased with the request.

The emperor nodded sagely and replied, “This is a welcome request. I believe our people shall benefit from this agreement.”

Then he turned to Etherion. “My lord,” the elemental replied, “swimming in the veins of molten rock below this mountain is a gentle giant named Graltor. I wish that if any Dwarf of this kingdom meets him, they will show him the respect one of his kind deserves. He is my friend, and I wish no harm to come to him. If he should need your help, I ask that the people Verengrath do what they can to aid him.”

Once again the people of Verengrath seemed to like the request and once again the Emperor found it simple to grant. “Let it be known,” he declared, “that the elemental, Graltor, is a friend to the Dwarves of Verengrath. He shall be treated with respect and we shall help him, should he call upon us.” He then turned his attention to Austin who stood there, silently. “High General Austin, what would you have of us?”

Chapter 36

In the Age of the Eland Civil War

Austin stood silent for a moment. He had never thought of doing anything but returning the honor of his father, which had already been accomplished thanks to his great uncle. He looked up at the sea of Dwarves before him shifting his gaze from face to face, when he saw an old Dwarf amongst them. His beard was very gray and he carried a heavy oaken staff in his hand that he obviously used as a cane. The Half Dwarf General had never seen this Dwarf before, but he recognized his eyes immediately, almost as if they were his own. They were his father's eyes, and he knew the Dwarf to be his grandfather. It was then that the request sprung to his mind.

"Emperor Di'an," Austin said loudly, "my uncle has told me that my father would have been the chosen champion of the Bronze Clan if he had been here to take part."

"Yes, it was well known to all of the clans that he was the clear choice," Di'an replied, avoiding looking at the current representative of the Bronze Clan. "In fact, I looked forward to facing him. When he was exiled, I was disappointed in not being able to battle against him."

"My father was a powerful Dwarf, Emperor. I believe he would have held your seat should he have been allowed to compete," Austin said with a grin.

Many of the Dwarves in the stands chuckled, since many agreed with the young Half Dwarf's belief. "That is very possible. He was an incredible Dwarf," Di'an said cocking an eyebrow.

"Since the Bronze clan wasn't prepared for his absence, I believe they chose hastily in their replacement champion," Austin said loudly.

"Now wait a moment!" shouted Ba'lain.

"Be silent, Ba'lain!" came a voice from behind the royal dais. Everyone turned their attention to the speaker, who was none other than the Dwarf Austin saw in the crowd, his grandfather, Ba'toth. "He's correct, on both points!" he added, slowly working his way down to where his grandson stood. "I never would have chosen you if I wasn't lost in my grief over Ba'rel's exile," he continued, until he hobbled in front of Austin.

"I am High General Austin Ironfist," Austin said bowing his head in respect to his grandfather, "son of Ba'rel Ironfist, grandson of Ba'toth Ironfist. A son of Verengrath."

"Yes my boy, you are," his grandfather said with a grin and a wink. "Now finish what you were saying son," he said as he turned to face the kings, moving to his grandson's side.

"I request that with my father's honor returned to him, that we honor his memory as a powerful Dwarf, and that of his clan that he was to lead," Austin said loudly. "I would not presume to remove you from your high seat, Emperor, but my request is that my uncle Ba'lain Ironfist be removed from the royal council, and that my other uncle, Al'bet Ironfist be given the seat my grandfather held during his time, that of the Emerald throne." He finished to a shocked exclamation from the Dwarves assembled. He turned briefly to look at Al'bet at his side. The Dwarf never moved, never flinched a muscle. He stood as if he were a statue, frozen in time. Austin had no clue what his uncle was thinking.

"This is a major request you ask of us, but our law requires that we follow it. Might I ask if we could get acceptance from the rulers you would be affecting?" Di'an asked, concern etched on his face.

"I agree," Austin said, afraid his request would be thrown back at him.

"What would this shift entail?" King Mar'Kal, the current holder of the Emerald throne asked.

"I suggest the simplest would be to shift everyone to the next seat," Di'an replied.

Mar'Kal thought a moment, his shimmering green robes adorned with gold embroidery, shifting as he considered what was being asked of him. "I am not ashamed to say that your father," Mar'Kal pronounced, "was my better in combat. I would have fallen to him on the field. I accept."

"I too, agree, your father was without equal," King La'met added. "It gladdens my heart to honor Ba'rel in this way."

"As do I," King Shar'tal agreed. "Ba'rel was my friend, but I believe your choice of a representative to replace him will do our people great honor."

"Well then, we only have one other to ask," Emperor Di'an replied. "Al'bet, do you accept this request made by your nephew?"

Al'bet was silent, and still hadn't moved since Austin made his wishes known. He stood, staring in the distance.

"Al'bet?" Di'an urged.

Still the Dwarf never moved.

"Al'bet, do you have an answer?" Di'an asked growing frustrated with the delay.

Again Al'bet never moved a muscle. In all his years he had never been put on the spot like this. It was well known that the former Dwarven General was far from humble. He rarely hid his opinions and was never afraid to speak his mind. But now, with this honor laid at his feet he couldn't get his body to respond.

Suddenly Ba'toth lifted his cane and slammed it into his little brother's foot, snapping him out of his trance. "Answer, you darned fool, before I take your place," Ba'toth admonished.

"I accept!" Al'bet yelped, trying not to grab his foot in pain. A massive cheer erupted from everyone in the room at his answer. But a loud shout echoed from the Sapphire throne.

"Silence. Silence all of you fools! I do not accept!" Ba'lain nearly screamed. He was visibly shaking and his face was red with rage. "I have earned my place, and I shall keep it!"

"Ba'lain of the Bronze clan," Emperor Di'an called out, to try to get the situation under control, "As a citizen of Verengrath we respect your opinion, but as you are no longer one of the Ruling Council, your vote only counts when a general vote has been called."

"I am not a simple citizen!" Ba'lain shouted.

"But you're wrong," Di'an replied, remaining calm and even a touch smug. "Each of the council accepted being shifted to their new title, and with the acceptance of your uncle Al'bet to the Emerald throne, you were essentially removed from the council. You are no longer a ruler of Verengrath."

"You fool!" Ba'lain shouted. He then jumped onto the long arching desk that ran before all the kings and grabbing a knife from his robes grabbed the Emperor and held the blade up under his throat. "I shall be Emperor. None of you insignificant roaches understand my greatness. I shall lead our people, and we shall rule with an iron fist!

No more shall we trade with outsiders. No, we will build a horde that the dragons of old would envy! I shall become the greatest ruler of all time.

"None of you believed my brother when he accused me of sabotaging the tunnels, but it was true! I hired the dark Elf to cut the support cords. His hatred of us is incredible! We hold something he longs for, deep within our vaults! With his help, I shall ensure that our people fall into place."

"Ba'lain," the Emperor calmly spoke, "by your own admission you have confessed to crimes against this kingdom, your family and your people. I hereby grant you one chance, and only one chance. If you walk away now, I shall allow you to leave in exile, as your deception caused your brother to do. But I warn you, if you do not accept it now, by releasing me and leaving this kingdom, I will sentence you to death."

Everyone stood at their seats, silently watching the drama on the dais unfold. They waited anxiously for his answer.

"Emperor Di'an," Ba'lain began, "I decline!" he shouted as he quickly slashed the blade across the rulers throat. He smiled as he threw the Emperors limp body down on the desk before him. But as soon as the body fell, a loud thud echoed in the large assembly hall. Everyone turned in shock to see Le'stal, standing with his arm stretched before him, and his knife in Ba'lain's chest.

The crazed Dwarf grabbed at the hilt, but it was too late. He gave a gasp as he dropped to his knees, and fell over dead on his side.

The surrounding Knights rushed to Di'an; to see if anything could be done to save him. But when the Dwarven Emperor stood, shakily at first a cheer went up from everyone assembled, including the humans watching in the front row.

The cheering went on and on and finally when it calmed, Shar'tal turned his friend by the shoulders to face him and shouted, "But how?"

"I don't know," the bewildered Emperor replied.

"Well, I might be able to answer that," Etherion replied with a coy smile.

"Please do, Master Elemental," Di'an requested.

"When he raised the knife to your throat, I wrapped the blade in a cocoon of air. It was as if he attempted to slice your throat with the sheath still on," he laughed, and once again a cheer exploded from all the Dwarves assembled.

It was late in the night and the celebrations had just gotten started. The Bronze clan seemed to ignite with pride in their new king, who was settling into his role as a Verengrath ruler quickly.

"What can I say," Al'bet said to Le'stal who sat with him in his royal mansion. "It suits me," he laughed.

"It doesn't matter what title they give you," Le'stal replied, "you're still a know it all, you know that, right?"

"Would you have it any other way?" Al'bet asked.

"Not on your life, my king," Le'stal laughed loudly.

Suddenly a beautiful Dwarf walked into the room with a robe in her hand. "It's time for your bath, my liege," she said with a smile.

"Why thank you Au'drey," he said with a grin, and looking at Le'stal he said, "Well a Dwarf's got to bathe." And jumping from his seat he chased her out of the room as she rushed ahead of him giggling.

Chloe just laughed quietly to herself as she watched them go. She turned her attention back across the room to where Austin sat with his grandfather. The two of them spoke quietly by a massive fireplace, the red and yellows of the flames casting their long shadows across the floor.

"They're still talking?" a voice asked from behind her.

Matt drifted out of the shadows and leaned on a pillar beside her, as he too watched them.

"For the last four hours, at least," she replied.

"They have a lot to catch up on it seems," the spy said, nonchalantly pulling a long stem pipe from his belt. He then pulled out a leather pouch of tobacco, filled the pipe and began to gently smoke as he returned his attention to Austin and his Grandfather across the room.

"You're loyal to him, aren't you?" Chloe asked, her concern deep in her voice.

"It's hard to trust a spy, isn't it?" he asked. She shrugged her agreement. "Yes, I am loyal to him. He not only spared my life years ago, but something about him makes me want to follow him. He's a great man, with incredible potential."

"He is at that," she replied.

"Can I ask you a question?" he said.

"You just did," she replied with a chuckle.

"Another then," he said with a smile.

"Sure," she said.

"What's your interest in him?" he asked.

Getting to her feet, she began to walk away. But before she left the room she smiled and looking over her shoulder she replied,

"Something about him makes me want to follow him." Then turning her back to the thief once again, she left to retire for the night.

"I've heard that he has that effect on people," Matt replied, and pushing off the pillar, he melted into the shadows to watch Austin and Ba'toth long into the night, until they finally fell asleep where they sat. The only sign of his presence was the smoke wafting from the shadows.

Chapter 37

In the Age of the Eland Civil War

The celebrations marking the return of the Champions of Fire began bright and early the next morning. The festivities were planned to go the rest of the week, but Austin and his commanders knew they had to leave almost immediately.

"I'm sorry uncle," Austin spoke to Al'bet, "But with Kiamet on the move, we can't stay to celebrate with you."

"What are you going to do, son?" Al'bet asked his nephew as he and Ba'toth walked them to the great doors of Verengrath.

"I don't know, but my people deserve to be free, and I intend to make it happen," Austin replied, his face filled with concern.

"Well whatever happens, just know you have a family who cares for you," his grandfather said. "No matter what happens out there, you will always have a place here," he explained.

"You have my thanks, grandfather," Austin said with a smile. "But I don't believe I will be returning from this fight if we fail. Kiamet's pride has been deeply wounded by our histories together; he will see me die on the ground at his feet if he has any say."

"Then you shall have to see to it that he doesn't have his way," Ba'toth replied calmly. "I just found out that I had a grandson around two weeks ago, I think I'd like a bit more time with him."

Austin's smile faded a bit as he nodded his head. He too wished to have more time with his new found family.

"Any words of advice?" Chloe asked as she followed behind them, giving them this time together.

"Sure, aim for the ankles. Gets you big folk every time," Al'bet chuckled. This caused Ba'toth to join in laughing as well, followed by Austin and the rest of his command team. "Son, Eksils Torden will guide your hand. It does have magic, but as you yourself have seen, it is powerful all on its own. It is made of the stars, so let it shine brightly when things look their darkest.

"And young lady," he said turning to Chloe, "watch his back. He tends to forget he has a behind that needs minding."

"I'll be there, you can be sure," Chloe said, smiling at the new king.

"I have no doubt you will, lass," Al'bet said with a wink. Then as they rounded the corner they stood before the massive golden doors of the Dwarven Kingdom.

"You've met the Creator, son," Ba'toth said to Austin. "You know He exists; call to him for help. Perhaps He'll favor you in this."

"It can't hurt to ask," Austin said, a look of hope crossing his face.

"And no matter what you do, never give up!" Al'bet replied. "No matter how dark it appears, help will always find you."

They stood on the outskirts of Nord Byen, strapping everything onto their mounts. They had said their goodbyes to Al'bet and Ba'toth at the Verengrath gates, and now prepared to head south.

"How long do you think it'll take?" Chloe asked.

"At least a week," Artole replied.

"Yeah, and with the pack horses, maybe longer," Kierra added.

"Well then," Austin said, mounting his charger, "we had better get started."

"Um, if I may," Etherion said softly from above them. "The horses won't allow me to float you there, as I did before," he said, "but perhaps I can help you a bit. Mount up all of you and break into a hard gallop. Try to keep pace with one another," he warned, "you're a large group, I won't be able to do this if you spread out too far."

Everyone mounted and getting a nod from the elemental, they urged their horses forward, gradually getting to a gallop they could all maintain together. Etherion flew behind them, rising and falling on the currents, and when he saw that they had found their stride he gently sent a current under the horse's hooves, raising them a couple of inches above the ground. Then propelling them with a breeze he sped them up, causing them to nearly double their speed. Austin looked over his shoulder and smiled at their new friend and nodded his thanks. The former Pathfinder just nodded back and concentrated on keeping them all moving ahead at a uniform rate.

It was late on the third night of their travels as they lay on their bellies, scanning the open plains below. In front of them lay the city of Lytton, and surrounding it were thousands of campfires, illuminating the tents surrounding them.

"Are they Kiamet's?" Lyra asked.

"I don't know," Austin replied. "I don't see any emblems."

"Well then, we better find out," Matt said, sliding back down the hill out of the sight of any who may be keeping a look out.

"I agree," Kierra replied.

"Okay," Austin said, catching their meaning, "you two infiltrate their ranks. Try to find their command tents and bring back any information you can about who they are. Meet us back here in the morning."

Both of his best spies nodded, and sneaking into the forest to descend from different directions, they moved off to find out what they could.

"Alright, that leaves us," Austin said to Cason, Lyra, Artole, Chloe and Etherion. "I suggest we make camp. No fire tonight. We don't know if they are with us or against, so let's not give away our positions. We will take shifts keeping watch. And be prepared for trouble, we don't know what's going on."

Everyone nodded and set out to prepare to sit tight until their informants could return. Austin was walking towards his horse when Etherion stepped up to him.

"Austin, do you have a moment?" he asked.

"Certainly my friend. How are you feeling? You must be exhausted from the long journey. We never would have made it like this without you," Austin replied, clasping him on the shoulder.

"I am fine, I'll need rest shortly, but for now I'm okay. General, I wanted to say I appreciate you and the others helping to free me from the Labyrinth," he said softly, hanging his head. "To float amongst the breeze again is invigorating."

"No Etherion," Austin said gently, "it is we who have been blessed to know you. You have been our guide inside and out of the Trial. It is thanks to you that we are free as well."

"That is kind of you to say. It warms to me to have found friends such as you. Which is why this pains me even more," he said, taking a deep sigh. "General... Austin, I have to leave soon."

Austin stood quietly for a moment looking at the torment crossing the elemental's face. He could see the being before him was in conflict within himself.

"For millennia," Etherion continued, "my creation trapped and murdered so many beings. Trolls, Ogres, Giants, even my friend the Silver Dragon Zenatha, all died because of me. I can't take another life," he explained.

Austin thought a moment, and then, smiling at his friend he spoke gently to him, "Etherion, I never expected you to fight this fight, as I already explained to you," Austin said. "I wish to free my people, that's my fight. Each of these people who follow me, they took this on themselves because they each want to be free. We all believe in this cause, and we will gladly die for it.

"But the last thing I want is for others to suffer because of this," he continued. "My father always told me to fight for what I believed in. It was thanks to my parents suffering that I was able to live the life I did, and come to this position in my journey. But it isn't a position that I would ever force on anyone. No my friend, stay until you feel you must go. Even watch from the breeze if you wish, but don't feel any guilt for not taking part. You've done my friends and I a great kindness in getting us here as quickly as you have. Not only quickly, but silently, giving us this opportunity to find out if we face friend or foe out there. You are my friend, and I am simply glad to have met you. That is all I want from you, I assure you," he said with a smile.

The elemental lifted his head, and returned the smile and nodded his thanks. He then floated gently off the ground, and crossing his legs underneath him, floated before Austin, a look of contentment on his face. "Thank you, Austin. I feel at peace now, thanks to your kindness. I will go and rest, but I will return before you find battle," he said, and floating away he left Austin alone.

Austin returned to the others and helped them set camp. Then taking to his bedroll, he went to sleep, allowing Cason to take the first watch.

Morning broke brightly, as everyone awoke under Austin's watchful eye. He was given the final watch, to allow him to rest to prepare for the coming day. He helped the others break camp, and then sat to eat as they waited.

A couple of hours passed uneventfully, when his ears picked up a gentle rustle of leaves. He sat waiting, his body loose, preparing to fight if he had to. He glanced around at the others, and he knew they too had heard it and were ready.

Suddenly Keira and Matt quietly moved in amongst them, much to their relief and joy. The two exhausted spies moved to where they all sat and, taking a seat themselves, began to give them the information they had collected.

"They're mostly ours," Keira said, taking a sip of ale from her brother's mug.

"Mostly?" Austin asked.

"Yeah, mostly," Matt added. "They don't realize it, but they've been infiltrated. Keira and I recognized some of Kiamet's people mixed in with them."

"Probably spies," Artole replied.

"That's our guess," Keira said.

"Okay, so how do we deal with the spies?" Chloe asked.

"We don't," Austin replied. "We don't know how many there are, and we don't know how much they've already reported. No we will go down to the camp, find the leaders and we shall prepare for battle."

"What if they're saboteurs?" Lyra asked.

"They are. They are also likely back stabbers and cut throats," Matt said. Everyone turned to him with curious looks. "What? It comes with the position," he shrugged.

"He's likely right. We can't leave them to attack during battle. Instead, we will continue as if nothing is out of line. Once we can be sure of who doesn't belong here, I'll have Matt and Keira eliminate them quietly," Austin explained. Everyone agreed that this made the most sense and packing their things they moved down into the valley to join their troops.

Everyone in the camp was excited to see their command team with them, and instantly spirits rose among those who had seen them. Austin was sure that within a half hour the entire army would know they had returned. He scanned the faces as they walked through the lines of tents and was concerned. Old men and women nearly equaled the able bodied men amongst their numbers. He was going to lead many of these people to their deaths, it suddenly occurred to him.

This troubling thought ate at his mind as he worked his way to the command tents, nearest the city walls. When they all entered the secured perimeter they were surprised to see knights surrounding a tent with the royal emblem on its side.

Austin instructed the others to wait as he walked to the royal tent, unsure of what he would find. As soon as the knights recognized him, they saluted and stood at attention. Then the captain of the king's guard, who stood closest to the tent flap, entered the tent and quickly exited, walking to the confused general.

“High General Austin,” the captain of the guard Todd Asiries said, coming to him with a salute, “his majesty, King Yelantas Porthanaclies, would like to see you in his quarters.”

Austin quickly nodded and following the Captain entered the king’s tent. There, sitting on a wooden throne sat his ruler. Austin quickly fell to his knee and bowing his head honored his king.

“High General, I am glad you finally found time to see me,” Yelantas said, annoyance in his voice.

“I apologize my king,” Austin replied, “I was away until this morning.”

“Yes, that is what I was told by *your,*” he said the word with emphasis, “people.”

“They are still your people, milord. They simply follow me in my bid for filling your role when you are called from this plane,” he said humbly.

“You still know your place, don’t you young man?” the king replied, softer this time.

“Milord, my place has always been at your service. But with the loss of your heir and your failing health, I felt I must secure the people’s future,” Austin said.

“So why don’t you simply marry my daughter and take the throne by ascension?” Yelantas asked.

“That is because I do not love Princes Jasmine,” Austin replied simply.

“Royal marriage is rarely about love,” the king replied.

“True, but I am not a royal my king. My heart is held by another, and I’ll not give my hand to anyone else,” he said matter of factly.

“And if I commanded you to?” the king asked.

"It would be the first time I would ever have had to disobey you, milord," Austin said, looking his ruler in the eyes.

"I thought so. Do you remember when I chose you to be High General?" King Porthanaclies asked.

"Yes sire. Like it was yesterday," Austin replied.

"I had been paying attention to you and Kiamet for some time, based upon the recommendation of Lethus. He had been watching you two for a lot longer than that," Yelantas explained. "When the two of you walked into the royal court, I could see such a difference in you both.

"Kiamet always felt he belonged there. He was a soldier to better position himself politically, not to defend our people. But you, you were there because you wanted to better our people. At the time I never thought anything of it, and to be honest the only reason I chose you over him was because he got too mouthy," the king said with a shrug. "But after the war with the Andrayan's and seeing their young king in action, I realized I was wrong. I had chosen the better man completely by accident.

"Young man, should you be victorious in this coming battle, I will step down as king. All I ask is that my daughter and I live out our lives somewhere comfortably. Then you may rule this kingdom as you see fit." His statement startled Austin. Was he actually getting his king's blessing?

"Milord, I never intended to ascend your throne until after..." he paused, struggling to find the words.

"After I was dead? Yes, you would have that intention, wouldn't you? As I said, I chose the correct man for High General, without a doubt," the king replied with a nod. "None the less, that is my position. Do you accept to allow Jasmine and I to retire in comfort?" he asked.

This turn was more than he had expected, but he was trained to quickly assess all the angles and quickly made up his mind. "Yes my king," Austin replied, "I agree."

"Excellent. The throne is a heavy burden. I grow weary of it in my age," Yelantas replied. "Captain, you shall witness this." He said turning to the Captain of his guard who nodded his agreement. Then taking a quill and a piece of parchment, he wrote out the terms of their agreement and signing his name made it a royal decree. He then passed it to Austin to read, and once he was able to assimilate all that was happening, he took the quill and signed his name as well.

"It is done then," King Yelantas said, laying the scroll out to allow the ink to dry. "You will be responsible for keeping this safe. Trust me; the aristocracy in this Kingdom will require it. With this and my word, they will have no choice but to accept their places."

"Thank you my king," Austin said, bowing low once again.

"Young man," Yelantas replied, "lead our people well. Better than I. That is all I can ask of you." And with that he nodded his dismissal allowing Austin to leave his presence.

Chapter 38

In the Age of the Eland Civil War

Austin slowly exited the tent, shocked, surprised and relieved by what his king had said. He never expected to get the king's blessing to essentially overthrow him, but there it was, in his grasp none the less. He walked slowly to where his friends stood, waiting for him to return to them.

"Well?" Matt asked, concerned by the confused look on Austin's face.

"What?" Austin said, starting to come to his senses.

"What did the King want? Keira asked

"Oh, he wanted me to marry his daughter," Austin said, still kind of dazed.

"And what," Chloe asked, her arms crossed across her chest, "did you tell him?"

Austin, hearing the tone of her voice replied calmly, "I said yes."

Everyone stared at him in stark disbelief. Chloe looked like she was about to pass out.

"Oh come on," Austin said with a laugh. "Of course I didn't." A loud rush of air escaped from everyone around him. "I told him that wasn't the path for me."

"You're darn right that isn't your path," Chloe said, punching him in the jaw, dropping him to his behind as she stomped away.

Everyone cringed, as Austin sat there, flat on his back trying to understand what had just happened. Seeing Matt stretching his hand out to him, he grabbed it and allowed the former thief to help him to his feet.

"That wasn't what I had expected," Austin said, feeling his jaw.

"It's better than you deserved," Lyra said, rushing after Chloe.

"I'd have stuck a knife in your guts," Keira said, following after them.

"What?" Austin said looking at the men who remained behind.

"Oh, you'll figure it out soon enough," Artole replied with a chuckle.

"Alright," Matt said seriously, "now what did he want?"

"He wanted me to marry his daughter, that wasn't a lie. And yes I did decline. But instead he gave me this," he said, handing them the declaration. "Do any of you know where Etherion is?" he asked.

"Yes," Artole replied, "he's sitting at our camp. He wants to limit his interaction with everyone."

"Alright, let's get out there right away then," Austin said, and rushing through the crowd, he hurried to where they had left their things the night before.

There, just as Artole had said, sat the air elemental staring into space.

He rose as they approached, genuinely happy they had returned. "General," Etherion said with a smile.

"Pathfinder, my friend. I have something important I need you to do," Austin said, returning the smile. "I know you are torn about your role in this coming battle. You don't want to hurt any others, yet your loyalty compels you to do something. Well I have something very important for you to do for me.

“This document is my royal ascent decree, given to me by King Porthanaclies. When we are victorious at the end of the coming battle,” he explained, “it will prove to the current aristocracy that I am the true king of Eland.

“Take it my friend. Take it and keep it safe from harm or theft,” he said, handing it over to Etherion. “When we set forth to battle, please fly away, and remain away. Return at the end of the day, every day, until you are sure we are victorious, and then I request that you return it to me. Can you help me in this way?”

“I would be honored, General,” the air elemental smiled. “I appreciate your sensitivities to my position.”

“You never should have allowed yourself to feel that way, Etherion,” Austin said gently. “I am your friend, no matter how this turns out.” Turning, he said gently, “Now I have to prepare to move our people out. I don’t know how we can face Kiamet with only a handful of men.”

“You have more than that,” Lyra said, walking up behind the group of men, followed by Chloe and Keira. “You have all of those people down there.”

“I can’t go to war with women and the elderly,” Austin replied.

“Why not?” Chloe asked, her brow furrowed.

“They’re not soldiers. A battlefield isn’t the place for women and the aged,” Austin said incredulously.

“Each of those people,” Keira said, adding her voice to the others, “is willing to die for our vision of freedom. They have heard what life is like in Andraya, and they want that vision for themselves and their families. This isn’t about land or a title, Austin. This is our freedom.”

"And don't forget," Chloe said seriously, "a woman dropped you on your behind."

"Oh, I assure you," Austin replied, "I won't forget that too soon. But how do I live with their deaths on my hands?"

"The same way you would if they were men," Artole said, coming to his side. "They are Elanders, and they will make us proud on the field."

"That they will," Matt added with a nod.

Cason grunted his agreement, his arms crossed across his massive chest. Austin looked at each of them, taking in their body language and nodded his agreement. "It's agreed then. We have our army."

"Now how do we arm them?" Artole asked.

"The city armory has what we need. I will request to see the king and see what I can do about getting some of those weapons made available to us," Austin replied.

The day finished with weapons being handed out to any able bodied member in the camp. During this time Austin and his friends moved their things to join the rest of their people, as they planned their next move.

Austin couldn't help but feel a sense of pride in his fellow countrymen. They had come together to be free, and being with them once again made him smile.

As the small group sat around discussing their plans for moving out, a guard entered the tent that had been set aside as the war room. "High General," the guard said, "there is a man and a woman out there who demand to see you."

"I see no harm in seeing them. Send them in," Austin replied.

The guard bowed and exited the tent, leaving everyone to wait for the new arrivals. Austin was shocked to see the most unlikely pair enter his tent. For there stood his adopted grandparents, Lonny and Mary Ann!

He rushed to them and, embracing them, he was overwhelmed with joy.

"What are you doing here?" he asked.

"We've come to fight at your side," Mary Ann replied.

"Wha...but why?" Austin said in shock.

"Because you are our family, Austin," Lonny replied. "We would never let you face this alone."

Austin was deeply touched, and after the warnings he received from his friends that afternoon, he didn't argue. Instead, he ushered them to the table, where he held out his seat to Mary Ann, and Artole gave his over to Lonny.

"As much as I am glad to have a few more sets of able hands," Austin said, "I'd prefer it if you could lead my engineering core. I have no lead smith yet, and I could use some armor and arrows for the battle to come."

"I can do that," Lonny replied without hesitation.

"And Mary Ann, I could use someone to help with the wounded. Forgive me if it seems I am keeping you from battle," he said sheepishly, "because, although a part of me wants to, I know it wouldn't be right to do that to you. No, I truly need skilled people to lead my support ranks, and I couldn't find a better couple to rely upon."

Both of his elderly friends beamed with pride.

"We'd be honored to help you in any way we can," Mary Ann said.

"Well," Lyra said getting back to the information on the table before them, "it still looks like we're outnumbered. How do we face an army of superior numbers, such as theirs?" she asked.

"We don't face them head on," Matt said looking at a map on the table. "We have to attack from the trees, and retreat, picking off as many of their people as we can."

"Yes, that is the logical course of action. But unfortunately, it won't work," Austin said with a sigh.

"Why not?" Keira asked.

"Because Kiamet will be expecting it," Artole replied for Austin.

"He knows warfare; no matter how much I despise him, he is a brilliant battlefield commander," Austin added with a nod. "Our best course is to do the exact opposite, and face him as equals."

"But we aren't equals," Matt replied.

"True, but I guarantee, if we try guerilla tactics, it will turn out worse for us than facing him on the field," Austin replied.

"Then we face him, and beat him regardless of his superior numbers," Chloe said with a shrug.

They all agreed with her. It was clear to everyone in the room, this was an all or nothing gambit, and it was one where the stakes were incredibly high.

Chapter 39

In the Age of the Eland Civil War

Austin's army had moved well away from the Capitol city of Lytton to protect it from the coming battle. Instead they chose the Plains of Tumare in the North Western area of the kingdom nearly two days from the capitol city. It was here that Austin's scouts felt Kiamet would surely come through.

They had waited for their enemies to arrive for a week, preparing weapons and people for the coming conflict. While they waited Austin walked amongst the tents, trying to give a reassuring presence to his people.

"High General!" a voice called out from behind him. Austin stopped and turned to face Matt as he rushed forward. "Can I have a word with you?" he asked.

"Certainly. What is happening with our unwelcome guests?" he asked.

"That's what I've come to you about," the thief turned spy replied. "Several of them have gone missing."

"So they've left to deliver our whereabouts to Kiamet? Good, it'll make it harder for him to miss us," Austin replied, still walking and smiling at everyone he met.

"That's what I was thinking too. But sir, I had another thought," Matt said with a grin.

"I know that smile Matt, and it rarely bodes well for someone," Austin said with a chuckle.

"Well let's hope this time it doesn't bode well for Kiamet," his friend laughed in reply. "We know they inhabit locations around the northern camp. Let's plant a rumor that we will be attacking from the forest, guerilla style, and maybe we can divide Kiamet's troops."

Austin nodded in agreement. "I like that. Considering we only have one option really open to us, and that's a head on rush, giving him the wrong idea would help," he replied. "And knowing Kiamet as I do, he'll think this is just like me, being predictable, and it'll be easier for him to buy. Alright, you and Keira do just that. But make it quick. All the reports we've received say he's only a couple of days away," the High General warned.

"Aye sir, consider it done," Matt said, but continued walking at his friend's side.

"Is there anything else?" Austin asked.

"How are things with Chloe?" Matt blurted, unsure how to address the delicate topic.

Austin sighed deeply and shook his head, "You have no tact, whatsoever do you?"

"Well, what can I say; tact is usually a long way to a subject. I just prefer to get the heart of things as quickly as possible," his hooded friend replied.

"Well, it isn't great. She has hardly talked to me since the other day. I guess I screwed up," Austin replied, rubbing his temple.

"Most likely," Matt said with a shrug. "We always screw up at some point, General. Women are difficult to understand."

"Yeah, but I didn't mean to hurt her when I said it. I was caught between being in a daze and joy at the news from the King that it just burst from my mouth," Austin replied, furrowing his brow. "She's taken it kind of personally though."

"She's put an awful lot on the line for us, you know?" Matt replied.

"Why, what do you mean?" Austin said stopping dead in his tracks and turning towards his friend.

"From what I've been able to learn, King William of Andraya wasn't pleased with her leaving to come here without support of some kind," Matt answered. "He believes in you, from all I can tell, but she is his sister, and he wasn't impressed with the idea that her life be placed in danger like this. He would have gladly sent his entire Andrayan army to stand at your side, rather than his beloved sister. But she demanded that he let her go, and he did, grudgingly. She knows if anything happens to her, he will be devastated."

"Yeah, I figured as much. She's independent, but she's still his only sibling. So what do you think I should do?" Austin asked.

"I have no clue. That's why I tend to avoid long term relationships. They get complicated," Matt replied.

"That and the women tend to throw you out the same window you snuck in through after a couple of visits," Austin laughed.

"That too," Matt said with a frown, causing Austin to laugh even harder.

"Well, I'll deal with it in due time. But right now, I have to worry about what is coming," Austin said, growing serious again. "Go and put your plan into action. Keep the real plan limited to the command team and let's try to get these people through this mess as quickly and safely as possible."

"Yes sir," Matt said, and turning he instantly disappeared into the maze of tents around them.

Austin sat upon his charger staring at the incredible site in the valley below him. There Kiamet's army had setup camp, and it seemed to stretch for miles. It was true; he had allied himself with the Northern Tribesmen, just to claim the throne. He had no clue what his former colleague had offered them in exchange, but he feared the worst.

Just how many troops were down there, though, was unknown to the young Half Dwarf. None of his spies could enter the camp. Somehow every time they attempted to infiltrate the border, guards would instantly detect them and chase his people away. Proving just as frustrating was trying to surveil the camp from a distance. Each morning, a fog would settle above them, hiding their details from anyone who tried to get any information from their movements. Kiamet's camp was an enigma, and that lack of information could be costly.

Austin turned his steed and rode back to his own camp, just a half hour ride away. When he arrived he was met by a very excited Artole searching for him.

"General Austin. You must come quickly!" his most trusted commander urged.

"What's going on?" Austin asked.

"It would be better if you saw for yourself," he replied, and handing his horse's reins over to an attending soldier, Austin ran after the man. They rushed by the curious faces of those around them, but they never stopped until they reached Austin's command tent.

Before they entered, Artole checked to make sure no one was looking and then ushered the High General into the tent, quickly drawing the flap closed behind them. Austin had no clue what he was about to face inside, but what he saw nearly caused him to fall on his face.

"Well, now. Did ya miss me?" came the cheerful call from his uncle, sitting at the table with the other command team members.

"Uncle, Al'bet?" Austin said in shock.

The hiss from around the room sounded like a snake den as everyone hushed him.

"We took great strides to hide him," Lyra said. "Don't muck it up by being a big mouth now."

"Sorry," Austin replied in hushed tones, "but I never expected you, Uncle. What are you doing here?" he asked.

"I'm not alone. I couldn't convince the council to move the entire Dwarven army to support you, but as leader of the Bronze Clan, I was able to mobilize our people," the King of the Emerald throne replied.

"How… how many?" Austin asked, his shock hitting him even harder.

"Twenty thousand battle hardened warriors," Al'bet said with a grin.

"But why?" Austin asked praying he wasn't dreaming.

"Because son, you're one of us," his uncle said, growing serious. "And if there's one thing a Dwarf would never do, it's leave their kin to die alone."

"I don't know what to say," Austin replied.

"There's nothing to say," Chloe said. "It's what family does for one another."

Austin nodded his understanding and smiled at his uncle. "I'm glad to have you here, Uncle," he said, genuinely happy.

"And I come with more than just that," Al'bet said with yet another grin.

"Oh, and what's that?" Austin asked.

"Tactics. I've seen my share of battles too, lad," his uncle replied, and pointing at an open seat at the table, he turned his attention to the map in front of them.

Austin sat inside the Parlay tent waiting for Kiamet to arrive. It wasn't as formal as the old laws decreed, but it would have to do. At his shoulder stood Artole, waiting in his capacity as Austin's second.

They didn't have to wait long though, as the flap to the tent quickly opened and in walked a messenger.

"What is the meaning of this, soldier?" Austin asked.

"I'm sorry High General, but Lord Kiamet couldn't make it," the man replied.

"High General? Lord Kiamet?" Austin asked, arching his eyebrow in amusement.

"Yes, General," the soldier replied straight faced, "it is a title befitting a king."

"Alright, so what does your General have to say for himself?" Austin replied goading the messenger.

"*Lord* Kiamet," the messenger said stressing the title, "commands your unconditional surrender."

"This sounds like the last time I was in one of these tents," Austin said with a sigh. He was really beginning to wonder if these pre battle parlays were worth the effort.

"Commander?" Austin said looking at Artole. The silent man simply shook his head no.

"Soldier, you can tell your General that we decline. We go to war tomorrow morning," he said calmly.

The messenger simply nodded, and clicking his heels together reeled around and strode out of the tent.

"Well now, that wasn't so hard was it?" Artole chided.

"Kiamet certainly knows how to do things efficiently, doesn't he?" Austin chuckled.

"Well, let's see if we can efficiently separate his head from his royal shoulders," Artole replied, shaking his head. "I never did like that guy."

"Who, Kiamet?" Austin asked.

"No, the messenger. You didn't recognize him?" Artole asked.

"Not that I recall. Who was he?" Austin asked in return.

"Maddox Youngen. He was a captain of the Eastern defenses," Artole replied.

"A captain, demoted to messenger? He must have done something to upset Kiamet," Austin chucked.

"Doubt it. That boot licker probably volunteered," he said with a frown. "*Lord*," Artole chided and spit on the ground. "What an idiot."

Chapter 40

In the Age of the Eland Civil War

The morning was cold, and a fog had settled upon the green grass of the open plain. There, in the middle of the field upon which he was to face his enemy, Austin stood with his uncle and Chloe at his side. Behind them stood around a hundred men, all armed and ready for battle.

They stood silently as they waited for Kiamet and his troops to appear. Soon the distinct sound of marching feet echoed in the grey, and they knew that their enemy approached. As they stood waiting, Austin took a deep cleansing breath to release his mounting tension.

Without looking Al'bet spoke gently. "That's it lad, let it out. We'll need our wits to win the day."

"You think we can win this one, Uncle?" Austin asked, staring straight ahead.

"If there's one thing we Dwarves know, it's how to win an in hill battle," Al'bet said gruffly.

"Don't you mean *up*hill battle?" Austin asked.

"Son," Al'bet replied, "when you live in a mountain it doesn't matter if you go up or down, you're always stuck between a rock and a hard place."

Austin chuckled softly but held his position. He was genuinely glad that his uncle was there with him. He glanced briefly out of the corner of his eye at Chloe standing at his left hand side, wondering what she was thinking. She hadn't been very open with him since he made his wise crack about marrying the Princess. He tried to explain he was only kidding, but she seemed to have taken it to heart.

He turned his attention before him again and watched as dark shapes began to form far across the plain. He continued to watch, until he noticed a small group heading towards them.

"Easy now son," Al'bet said cautiously, "this is where you prove your metal."

Austin had been in many battles before, but simply hearing his uncle's calm voice at his side made him feel even more confident. Slowly the shapes that moved toward them began to take on a more distinct form, and soon Kiamet rode forward with Captain Youngen at his side.

"Are you kidding me?" Kiamet laughed seeing the three of them standing alone. "No generals, and what, a handful of troops? Did they all abandon you last night?"

"The people who support me are our countrymen, Kiamet," Austin replied. "They are farmers and merchants. They aren't warriors. I sent them all home."

"Yes, my spies told me you had done that," his adversary said from his mount. "Are you a fool?"

"I'm wiser than you think Kiamet. I simply didn't feel they had to be standing here with me to defeat you," Austin replied.

"You will find," Kiamet sneered, "that it will take a lot more than a handful of men, a Dwarf and a woman at your side and a bunch of rebels to the crown, hiding in the woods to defeat me."

"Then I suggest we start, or do you simply surrender. Either way, it isn't going to end well for you, I assure you," Austin again replied, his voice stern in the chill morning air.

Kiamet spit on the ground before him and turning his mount quickly rode back to his troops to begin giving orders.

"Well played," Al'bet said with a grin.

"He's got a huge ego," Austin replied, "I simply made it the first casualty, hoping his anger would help him make mistakes."

Al'bet just chuckled and continued to stand still, watching. The morning fog had already begun to burn away with the rising sun, making Kiamet's army a lot clearer. Austin was surprised at how few Elanders were with him. After the battle in Andraya, he was sure more would have sided with his former classmate. But it appeared that the majority of Kiamet's troops were men from the Northern Tribes.

You could clearly see their white polar hide adorned bodies. Many had trophy teeth, skulls from small lizards and even a few jaw bones of massive sharks from the Artillian Sea wrapped around their necks. Most of them had fur lined helms with horns on either side. A few of them had a single horn in the middle of their foreheads, as if they were charging beasts in man form. They were not warriors to be trifled with, as his years of experience could attest, but Austin knew that their greatest weakness was their inability to take orders.

Northern Tribesmen were large proud men. As a sign of status, many of them had large braided beards, setting them apart from their fellow tribesman. Austin counted at least fifteen chieftains amongst the throng before him. Their beards were not only braided, but decorated with thick, colored beads. He wasn't sure if his troops could handle their berserker style of fighting, but it was too late to call it off now.

Suddenly the massive army began to race down the hill towards Austin and his small group of soldiers. It appeared that Kiamet had no intention of going easy on Austin, just because he had such a small force. This was exactly what he had hoped, and taking yet another deep breath watched as the surge of warriors rushed towards them.

'Hold,' Austin said to himself, steeling for the right moment to make his move. 'A bit more,' he said again, waiting as the enemy continued to rush forward, weapons high above their heads. "Stand firm!" he said out loud, watching the ground as the first of his enemies passed the imaginary line that marked where they would meet their surprise. "NOW!" he shouted and suddenly the hundred or so men behind him lifted great horns into the air and blew hard on them all at the same time.

The noise echoing from the horns filled the clearing with an almost physical force. So much so that it caused nearly the entire advancing army to slow a step, causing chaos to erupt amongst the ranks, as men bounced off one another. Almost immediately, Austin's troops launched into attack. Using the same strategy they used in the Andrayan quarry, the Half Dwarf General's troops sprang from hidden pits all around the enemy troops, surging onto the battlefield.

Suddenly, instead of bearing down on a nearly nonexistent defensive force, Kiamet's men were surrounded by shouting and charging warriors, both human and Dwarf alike. Austin looked close and saw his commanders leading people from all points around their enemy, slashing and killing anyone who came close enough to their weapons.

Kiamet was set on his heels momentarily, but soon his battle hardened sense took over and he began to shout orders. Now his commanders began to take control of their regiments trying to slow the momentum gained by Austin's surprise attack.

"See," Al'bet said, "tactics."

Austin nodded and rushing forward he charged ahead giving the silent order to his hundred men to follow him into battle.

The battle raged for hours as Elander fought Northerner. The sun rose high above them, marking nearly midday as they fought. Austin had left his sword at his back for the entire battle and instead relied heavily upon Eksils Torden, launching any who stood before him back into a crumbled heap. With each swing, he defeated any man that approached him. Occasionally he would hear a whistle by his ear and would see men fall deeper in the horde before him, assuming that Chloe's bow was singing at her fingertips.

He kept swinging, slashing enemies with the pick ax half of his weapon and smashing bones with the hammer head. Al'bet was right, this was an incredible weapon, and although he could feel the weight in his hands, he could hardly feel its effects on his muscles.

All around him was chaos. Screams echoed everywhere, the clamor of metal on metal as men fought filled the morning air, and still he fought on. Finally picking the best moment he could, he began to pull back, signaling for Chloe and Al'bet to do the same.

As they stepped out of the massive battle comprised of three armies he quickly assessed what was going on. His people were handling the enemy troops well, but he knew they couldn't last forever. The sheer numbers of Kiamet's army was simply overwhelming.

He turned to his signal bearer and commanded him to call his commanders to him. Then falling back he, Chloe and Al'bet waited near the forests edge for them to join him.

Soon all of them, Lyra, Artole, Cason, Keira, and Matt rushed to his side. They took another look at the battle below to ensure it could carry on without them for a short while, and then they entered the forest.

"What are you all seeing?" Austin asked not wasting time.

"We're doing alright," Lyra replied, "but our people are going to grow tired quickly."

"I agree," Keira said. "We're already seeing injuries caused by fatigue."

"The good news is the Berserkers aren't making any more of a difference than the regular soldiers," Matt said with a shrug. "They're just not full of battle lust today."

"I've noticed that, too," Austin agreed. "Their hearts aren't in this."

"Maybe they don't like following an outsider like Kiamet?" Chloe said.

"Possible, even likely," Austin agreed. "But it's also possible he has disrespected them. Well whatever it is, let's keep using it. Do we need to shift tactics then?" he asked.

"We don't have any other troops other than hand to hand," Cason replied, his huge chest still heaving as he tried to catch his breath. His heavy armor made him almost unstoppable in combat but it took a heavy toll on his endurance as the day went along.

"That's true. We don't have archers or anyone else to help," Artole added. "We have no choice but to carry on as we have."

"Well then, let's get out there and help. This battle isn't going to be won without us!" Austin ordered and turning he began to walk back towards the plains outside the forest tree line.

But as they walked back towards battle, still catching their breath they suddenly heard a shout from behind them.

“General!” a voice called out as a scout rushed from deep in the forest towards him.

Chapter 41

In the Age of the Eland Civil War

"General!" the scout shouted again.

"Yes soldier, come here," Austin ushered.

The young man rushed up to them. His red uniform was stained with sweat. This solider had been running quite a ways. "General we're in trouble," the scout said, panic etched on his face.

"You're just catching on now?" Matt asked sarcastically.

"No Commander, we're in REAL trouble!" the scout panted.

Suddenly, as if to emphasize the point everyone at the top of the hill felt the ground vibrate below their feet. "What was that?" Cason asked, scanning the forest around them.

A booming roar echoed through the sounds of battle behind them. "Oh no," Keira said, suddenly terrified.

"What?" Chloe asked, concerned by the looks all around her.

"Not that kind of trouble," Cason said, staring at his sister.

"Yes Commander, that kind of trouble," the scout replied staring at the forest as it shivered with each heavy thud.

"What?" Chloe asked again, this time a little louder and with more urgency as her panic began to rise.

No one answered as they all waited, staring into the depths of the forest before them. The ground shook harder and harder as something large moved towards them, roaring as it approached.

"I think," Chloe said pulling her hood over her head and reaching for an arrow, "I'd rather not know."

"Matthew!" Austin shouted.

"Yes General?" the scarred ranger replied.

"It's time," Austin said turning to the man at his side.

"It is; isn't it?" Matt replied, a self-assured smirk on his face.

"It's time? Time for what?" Chloe asked, watching the two men before her.

"You don't think I keep him around for his good looks, do you?" Austin said with a grin, and turning towards his friend he watched as the spy began to move forward.

"Well," the former thief injected, "that too, I'm sure."

Then pulling his rapier from its sheath he kissed it, twisting it so the steel of the blade caught a glimmer of sun. "Well Bernadette," he said to the blade as the steal glistening in the sunlight, "time to dance my love," and turning, he immediately began rushing towards the noise.

Chloe watched as huge trees rocked violently back and forth, as whatever it was coming towards them got closer and closer. Then, just as Matt reached the edge of the small clearing they were in, a massive creature burst out of the bushes. Chloe couldn't believe her eyes, for there, bearing down upon them was a huge mountain troll!

No one moved, except for the former thief turned spy and ranger, who never slowed down, even as the massive beast emerged, roaring from the tree line. Instead he jumped and landing on the giant trolls arm he ran up it, straight for the beast's bulbous bald head. The Princess of Andraya was spellbound as she watched the man, only a fifth of the beast's size run up its body as if sprinting up a hill. She had never seen a mountain troll before. The mountains behind her village of Czariana, the capital of Andraya, were tame. They had large cats and mountain goats, even rampaging boars and feral pigs, but nothing as incredible as the beast that had her mesmerized.

She stared at the huge creature, which only stopped for a moment to find his prey. The only clothes it wore was a furry loin cloth, covering its grey, thick hide. It also wore boots of a similar creature, tied with a crisscross of leather banding.

Matt continued to run up its arm, ducking and sliding on his knees for a moment as the beast attempted to swat him off with its free hand. Quickly bouncing to his feet he ran the last few steps towards the creatures head and slammed his weapon into its left eye!

The Troll let out an incredible roar of pain as Matt withdrew his rapier. The spy then did a flip in the air, leaping over the creatures head and away from its wildly flailing arms. Again, everyone stood spellbound as he landed on the ground behind the beast and quickly spinning with a back hand slash, rotating on his heel, he cut the tendons in the massive beast's right ankle making it fall to the ground like a mighty timber being felled. Not losing momentum, Matt jumped back onto the giant troll, ran along its back and quickly stabbed his blade into the base of its skull.

The creature let out a loud hiss as all of the air in its lungs escaped for the last time.

"Show off," Cason said as he grinned at his friend, still standing on the trolls broad back.

Firmly planting his foot on the creature's skull, Matt posed for a moment, a satisfied grin on his face. "It wasn't that bad," he said, gently panting.

"Um sir," the scout said. "That isn't what I mea..." but he was cut off as everyone realized that the shaking ground hadn't stopped with the death of this troll. Suddenly the forest exploded as twenty more of the massive creatures barreled towards them.

Matt's eye's opened wide in surprise as he turned, and ripped his sword out of the dead creature below him. Everyone could barely hear him say "Oh shoot!" as he began to run as fast as he could away from the charging creatures. Almost as if seeing him run past them was the signal to go, everyone turned and began to run behind him as fast as they could trying to elude the rampaging beasts.

"What do we do now?" Chloe asked as they ran for their lives.

"I don't know. I didn't realize that Kiamet had sold his soul to the Demon himself!" Austin shouted as they ran, darting through the trees. They ran as fast as they could, knowing that the battling armies were just outside the edge of the forest on the plains beyond.

They broke through the edge of the forest and rushed head long into the raging battle of the three armies, who still hadn't realized what was charging towards them. The beasts broke from the forest and killing anyone around them, friend or foe alike they charged after Austin's command team.

Chloe could hear the foot falls of the giants behind her as they ran, all the while getting closer with each long stride. Struggling to think of a plan she realized that they couldn’t handle these creatures with the troops that they had. Instead a single idea sprung into her mind.

The young half Elf suddenly stopped, and dropped to the ground, crossing her legs as she fell. Then linking her hands together she began to sing. The melody was low at first, slowly picking up timbre, but still remaining very deep and slow. Hearing her sing, Austin stopped and turned to see what she was doing, and soon the other commanders with him stopped and did the same. They watched as she sat in the grass, her eyes closed and her head bowed as she sang her gentle melody.

Unfazed by the music, the family of trolls all began to rush towards her, an easy target for their battle lust. As they surged towards her, the closest amongst them, a huge male grinned in anticipation of the kill.

Matthew began to move towards her to kill as many of the beasts as he could before he and his comrades fell before them, but Austin stopped him. Silently he nodded in Chloe's direction as she continued to sing. Her tones rose and fell, as if she was weaving a tapestry made of music. The raging beasts rushed towards her, but this didn't slow the young half Elf a beat. She continued to sing, her voice growing stronger and stronger until the first of the creatures, almost upon her, swung his huge wooden club, intending to launch her into the sky and to her death.

Just as the club swung towards her head though, all time seemed to slow as Austin and his friends watched in horror. The Half Dwarf General began to swing Eksils Torden, preparing to launch it at the beast in a last ditch effort to save her. But suddenly an arrow appeared to form out of nowhere, right between the beasts eyes driving it backward a step! Then the first arrow was joined by thirty more as arrow after arrow landed in its massive body, making it look like a huge porcupine. The sudden flurry of arrows caused the beast to continue to reel backwards as it slipped and fell onto its back, dead.

The air darkened as volley after volley of arrows arched through the sky landing beyond the young Princess and striking into the charging throng of Trolls behind her. Everyone on the battle field turned and looked in shock as they all realized that a fourth army had joined the fray.

Austin raised his hand to shade his eyes from a bright glowing sphere, pulsating behind the new forces, and felt his heart nearly explode in joy! For there, surrounded by a massive army of archers, sat three men on horses that he never expected to see again. His blood pounded to see King William, his massive long bow before him, its line still quivering from the release of the arrow that had struck the beast first. The half Elf king's eye still trained on the troll, dead on the ground, that a moment before was about to kill his only sister. Flanking him on either side were his most trusted advisors. To his right sat General Declan, commander of the Andrayan troops, with his sword still pointing forward as he signaled the launch of his archer's arrows. To his left sat Brody, Prime Minister of Andraya and the engineering genius of the kingdom, drawing his twin swords from his back.

"General!" William shouted.

"Yes sire," General Declan said with a nod. "FORWARD!" he shouted as everyone on the hilltop let out a massive scream and row upon row of Andrayan troops rushed across the open plain to join Austin's failing armies.

Chapter 42

In the Age of the Eland Civil War

The horses whinnied and screamed in anticipation, as Andrayan metal met Elanders' blades for a second time in less than a handful of years. Austin's shock was broken when he saw his friend, and the king of Andraya leap from his mount and, swinging his blade, began to chop down Kiamet's men. The Half Dwarf rushed to meet the half Elf king, as they both swung their weapons into any who would stand before them. They fought towards each other, carving a line through soldiers all around them until they met. The two men briefly smiled at one another as they turned, back to back, and began to circle and fight the horde bearing down upon them.

Again and again, their hammer and sword met the enemy as they fought on, as Austin found his second wind with the addition of the Andrayan forces. Both men fought valiantly, but the number of soldiers focusing on them was incredible. Austin wasn't sure why the sudden shift in attention until they saw Kiamet across the field directing the attack towards them.

Seeing that he had the upper hand Kiament moved forward and signaled his troops to withdraw, giving the general and King William a moment to breath.

"So," he laughed as the fight raged on behind the ring of men circling the two leaders, "you have found another fool to follow you."

He leapt off his horse and walked to the edge of the circle, protected by his men.

"I assure you," William said with a smile as he panted, "I am no fool. I am simply a person who knows the value of freedom. I am amongst those who convinced my friend, General Austin, to believe in himself. I urged him to become a flame of freedom for your people. It is a flame that will only get hotter, and brighter, no matter what you wish of it."

"And what of your own flame, now that it shall be extinguished?" Kiamet laughed.

"Not today it won't!" a loud shout yelled directly behind him. Turning to find the speaker, Kiamet fell on his back when a gauntleted hand struck him across the face as Declan strode across the clearing to stand next to his king.

"I agree!" another voice said several feet away, as two men screamed in agony, twin swords sticking from their chests. The dead men fell to the ground, as Brody pulled his weapons free. Then, resting them on his shoulders he walked to join the others.

"Aye, my nephew will not fall to the likes of you, dark one," Al'bet said, chopping the legs out from under another of Kiamet's men, taking his place beside Austin.

"Fools!" Kiamet screamed. "I have already won! So you took down my trolls. Do you honestly believe that is all I have at my beck and call?" he sneered.

"I have been pulling your strings for months, Austin," the general chided. "It was I who commanded that you be hunted and tormented by magic. It was I, who all along, knew when this fight would come to a head."

"Well," Austin said with a smile, "thanks to my friends, I overcame your dark magic, and thanks to your torment, I found my family and they are here fighting at my side today," he said as he patted his uncle on the shoulder. "It looks like for all your planning, fate still flows in my direction."

"Really?" Kiamet screamed in rage, his loathing clear upon his face. "Then how do you think fate will deal with this! Neamith, come to me!" he shouted.

Suddenly all the light on the field began to dim as a black mass swirled before the enraged general. The darkness then began to coalesce into a mist, then into thick clouds, and finally formed into a man in long black robes.

"I am here, my liege," Neamith hissed. None of the men in the center of the circle had seen a dark Elf before. His robes were as dark as the night, trimmed with a deep, dark purple and were covered with gold runes of protection. The skin on his hands and face were a deep, dark purple, but it was his eyes that startled them the most. Instead of the rich, vibrant blue of most of his race, his were a bright yellow, and the whites were jet black.

"Send these fools to the pits of hell!" Kiamet commanded, his rage twisting his reddened face.

"Indeed," the dark Elf smiled, "it would be my pleasure." Then weaving his hands before him, he began to conjure a spell to release at the group surrounded by Kiamet's men.

But just as he was about to release whatever magic it was that he was drawing to him, a group of birds appeared from between his hands and flew away taking the spell with them.

"What madness is this?" Neamith demanded.

"Not madness, Neamith," a gentle voice said, breaking into the group, still oblivious to the battle raging around them. Everyone turned to see Chloe striding into the circle, a strange glowing aura around her. "Me."

"You!" Neamith shouted. "I should have known your work. You've been the one freeing people from my spells, haven't you Day Wraith?"

"Yes, Dark Elf, it has been me all along. You have done yourself a great disservice choosing the side you have," Chloe said, stepping before her friends standing side by side.

"Then I shall finish you now as I should have all those years ago in Parinth!" he sneered.

"That won't be as easy as you think, Neamith," she said softly, her confidence filling her words as they floated among those who could hear them. "I see that you're falling from the light and the way is complete then," she said sadly. "Your eyes have turned to black."

"That's right, I am more powerful than you can ever imagine. I have completely severed myself from the light," he said with pride. "The sun fails you, Day Wraith. The night comes, and so too does my strength," Neamith laughed.

"Really?" Chloe smiled, as if she were speaking to an errant child. "Would you like to test that assumption?"

Without saying another word Neamith's hand shot out from his cloak as a ball of fire rocketed towards her. Chloe took two steps towards the flaming sphere, and swinging her hands around it, gained control over it, allowing it to float above her hand. She then flicked her wrist, throwing the ball high in the sky causing it to burn itself out.

Rage filled the dark Elf's eyes as he began an onslaught of magical attacks, all aimed at the young princess. Chloe simply danced into them, redirecting them, changing them and even sending them back at her attacker. Still the two fought with Neamith on the attack and Chloe on the defense. Each attack missed its mark as the two dueled with one another, dancing, weaving and chanting.

Then as if losing all patience Neamith stopped moving and instead he started to chant. His voice began growing stronger as the setting sun fell below the edge of the horizon when his strength began to grow to its pinnacle. Listening to the words, Chloe stopped, the smile wiped from her face. "Neamith, this is madness!" she shouted.

"Not so confident now, are you Day Wraith?" he laughed, again focusing his attention and energy on the spell forming before him.

"I can't let you do this to them, Neamith," she said quietly, and rushing forward she began to mix her hands within his.

"What are you doing?" he shouted in panic.

"All I can do to stop this foolishness," she said through gritted teeth, as if what she was doing was causing her pain.

"Chloe!" Austin shouted.

"No!" she yelled back. "Stay where you are!" And again, focusing on the weaving movements of the dark Elf before her she continued countering his every move, a spell within a spell. Neamith finally understood what it was that she was doing and panic flashed across his face.

"Stop, you'll kill us both!" he shouted.

"So be it," she said gently, continuing to work, the strain upon her face growing with each passing moment.

Neamith began to scream as the pain began to build beyond his tolerance, but his hands were already committed and the spell dragged him on. Darkness swirled around them, as lightening began to flash, arcing into their bodies.

"I can't allow this," Austin said, panic in his voice.

"Then don't," William said gently, and reaching up he placed his hand on Austin's shoulder. "Being a leader isn't about dying for your people Austin. It's knowing how to live for them. I give you my blessing, brother."

Clasping William by the opposite shoulder Austin turned and rushed towards the two elves as the elements ripped around them. The Half Dwarf General fought his way forward as he was hit by rocks, was bounced off invisible air currents, soaked by torrential rains and burned by lightning. On he pushed, driven forward by determination and his love for the woman in the middle of the turmoil.

Finally reaching the center of the storm he saw the two magicians as they continued to weave, the spell growing ever stronger from their combined magics. A large black disc hovered above their heads, swirling quickly, as lightning flashed from its edges. Austin could see the pain etched deep on Chloe's face as she countered with everything she had.

Stepping forward, Austin grabbed her by the shoulders and pulling her back against his chest he whispered, "I am here for you my love. I will always be here for you." And as if driven by a mysterious force he began to sing. He rarely ever sang before, but for some reason it felt right at this moment to sing this particular song. It was a song his father sung while forging steel in the smithy. Images of his parents suddenly filled his mind as he sang, his deep voice filling the raging battle of the elements around them. He saw his mother and father smiling at him. He saw Lonny and Mary Ann, his grandparents. He saw his best friends Matt, Lyra, Artole, Cason and Keira. He saw his Uncle Al'bet and his Dwarven Grandfather Ba'toth. As if no matter where they were, on this side of the veil of death or the other, they stopped to lend him their support and he sang.

He sang so loud he thought his chest would burst, his throat give way, his mind explode, but still he sung. And no matter what hit them, he sang on, through the violence of the rocks smashing into his back, the pain of the wind, rain and lightning, he sang.

He focused on his father, the origin of his strength, and his mother, the beacon of his moral compass. He saw the Human and Dwarf he missed so much, and saw pride in their eyes.

'You've made me proud son. Take her home now. We'll handle the rest,' his father said, speaking directly to him. It was then that Austin realized he wasn't seeing images of his parents, but they were both there with him, watching him, protecting him. He now realized that he was straddling between the world of the living and the dead, as Neamith's spell ripped open the veil that separated the two. Pulling Chloe to his chest even harder he began to step back, even as her hands continued to weave. Dragging her with all his might, fighting the hands of Death longing to keep her as he pulled.

He heard a scream bellow forth from Neamith's mouth, but he never lost his focus and continued to drag Chloe backwards with him. Back they moved through the sphere of elements that had surrounded the two. He desperately sheltered Chloe from the onslaught that smashed into him even harder than before, angered by his theft from their master, Death.

Finally as the raging winds around him began to subside he pulled Chloe free and the two of them fell to the ground. Chloe was already unconscious and he remained awake only long enough to watch the entire raging sphere collapsed in upon itself, taking the dark Elf with it. Then as if completely spent, he drifted into darkness.

Chapter 43

In the Age of the Eland Civil War

Austin woke as a pain shot through his chest. He opened his eyes wide at the sensation, and found that he was still lying on the ground being protected by his Uncle, William, Declan and Brody. He dared not move for fear his chest would explode again with pain.

"This isn't your fight!" he heard Kiamet scream. "He has fallen, and the day is mine!"

"You didn't declare a one on one challenge," he heard William say calmly. "You made this a war, and a war doesn't need its leader to continue on."

Austin paid close attention to the sounds all around him. By the sounds of the battle, he wasn't unconscious for long. In fact he wasn't sure if anything had changed since he fell. All he knew was that devil, Neamith, had been destroyed. The Half Dwarf General looked to the spot where the dark Elf had been moments before, and saw that he was truly gone. All that remained was a large circle of scorched earth.

"Fine, I shall finish you first, and then I will kill him," Kiamet shouted.

"You're welcome to try," Declan said, his tone mocking, "but I doubt you'll get too far."

“What makes you so sure of that?” Kiamet laughed, rage edging his voice.

“That,” Declan calmly replied. Austin struggled to see what was going on, but couldn’t from where he lay. What he could hear though was that the sounds of battle had all but ceased.

“What are you buffoons doing?” Kiamet shouted, as he turned around to see the field of battle. “The war isn’t over, keep fighting.”

“Buffoons?” a deep gruff voice reached Austin’s ears. He shifted his head to see what he could, and saw a Northern Tribe Chieftain enter the circle, followed by a group of his men, all glaring at Kiamet. “Did you just call me and my men, buffoons, little man?” the chief asked.

“Yes, you fool. Who told you or your men to stop fighting?” Kiamet shouted, enraged.

“We’re not sure why we’re even here right now,” the chief replied. “Or what we’re even doing fighting a war for a southerner such as you.”

“You are the victims,” the sound of Chloe’s voice was like music to Austin’s ears as he lay on the ground trying to control his breathing, “of magic, great warrior,” she said.

“Magic? What magic, half Elf?” the chief replied gruffly.

“His name was Neamith, a dark Elf,” she explained. Her voice sounded exhausted. Austin wanted to get up, but his body wouldn’t let him. He hurt all over.

“And he had us fighting for this coward? Where is this, dark Elf?” the chief bellowed.

“He’s dead, being tortured in the underworld. He attempted to open the curtain between our world and the next and I assure you, the keeper of the damned will not appreciate it at all. We all would have died if it wasn't for that man," she said, pointing to Austin, lying on the ground.

"I," Austin panted in pain, "did nothing but save the woman that I love."

Chloe rushed to him as quick as her weary body could take her. She was quickly surrounded by the others as they all stood watch over his bruised body. The half Elf princess knelt at his side, and gently lifted his hand to her face.

"You're hurt, my love," she said quietly. "The rocks must have beaten you mercilessly."

"I'm fine," Austin replied, trying to sound strong. "My back and my chest hurt though. And I'm finding it hard to breath."

"He most likely has broken ribs," Brody said, kneeling beside them. "We need to get him to a flat surface if we're going to help him."

"You're saying this man freed my people and saved us from death?" the chieftain said loudly above them.

"Yes. If he hadn't had the strength to pull me from the spell's grip, I would have lost control and this entire world would have been swallowed," Chloe said.

"Get five of our people," the chieftain commanded one of his men. "We'll carry him to where she tells us to."

The man nodded and rushed away shouting for his people to come to him. Soon, six large, hairy men were carrying Austin, holding him up with their arms straight under his back, trying to keep him from shifting.

Chloe refused to be carried, but did accept a ride on her brother's war horse, as they made their way back to Austin's camp. Al'bet never left his nephew's side as they slowly made their way. Finally they entered the camp, where Mary Ann and Lonny waited for them. Rushing to him, Austin's adopted grandparents quickly went before them all to prepare a table to lay him on.

While all of this happened, Artole took control of Austin's troops to bring a hasty end to the battle and the war. With the desertion of the Northern Tribesmen, Kiamet's men had nothing left. In fact, when Austin was carried away, Chief Yorgund, Chief of the Polar Clan, had Kiamet taken into custody.

Without troops, or a field commander, things quickly fell apart for Kiamet's men and they were forced to surrender. Now under the watchful eye of the Dwarves, Artole began finalizing things on Austin's behalf.

"We need to send word to the Aristocracy to let them know that the war is over and a new king has arisen," he said to Lyra, Cason, Keira and Matt. "We need to try to find Etherion and get that decree from King Porthanaclies. It is our only proof that the king has validated General Austin's ascension during his lifetime if the king tries to change his mind."

"He'll be here," Keira replied. "He was set to come to our camp each night to see what progress we made and to deliver the decree when the time was right."

"Excellent," Artole replied. "Matt, I need you to ride to Lytton and inform the king. We have to make it official. When can you leave?"

"I can leave immediately if I'm not required here," Matt replied with a nod.

"Good. Leave in the morning. With Austin being hurt, this isn't going to happen quickly anyway," Artole replied.

"What if he doesn't make it?" Cason asked, a worried frown on his face.

"That isn't going to be the case, so we don't need to wonder," Artole replied gruffly.

"How do you know?" Keira asked, her brother's fears clearly mirrored on her face.

"Did you see what Chloe did to that sorcerer out there?" he asked.

The others nodded that they had. None of them were ashamed to admit that they took vantages where they could keep an eye on their General during the entire event.

"Then you all know her power. She won't let him die," Lyra replied softly.

"It's about time those two figured it out, isn't it my love?" Artole asked her with a smile.

"We all need a push every now and again to find the answer." She turned to look at him, and gently laying her hand on his cheek she smiled up at him.

Then turning their attention back to the others, Artole continued. "Cason and Keira, make sure we have proper relief for the Dwarven troops to watch the enemy. Now that this is over, we are going to have to find a way to deal with them."

"What options do we have?" Matt asked. "We can't kill them all. Well, I doubt Austin would accept that anyway."

"No they aren't to be hurt. Send word that General Austin wants their wounded tended to, and that they are to be fed and allowed to rest," Artole commanded. "Let the healing begin now."

"Did the General give those commands?" Matt asked.

"He would if he was here, and you all know it," Artole replied. Everyone nodded their agreement and soon they all parted to do as they were told.

"Perhaps Eland can find peace after all this time," Lyra said to Artole when they were alone.

"Let's hope we can," Artole replied. "Our Kingdom can't take much more of this. And frankly, neither can I."

Back in Austin's tent everyone was working as diligently as they could to tend to his wounds. His back, arms, and legs were almost black from the bruises he received. The hair on his head was singed and matted from the lighting that struck close to his body while he fought the elements. It looked almost hopeless to everyone but Chloe.

"He's not doing well, Chloe," Al'bet said gently to her as she sat in a chair to catch her breath.

"He'll survive," she said with finality.

"Young lady, you have to prepare yourself in case he doesn't," Lonny said standing next to her.

"Listen," she nearly shouted, "this is hard enough without having to hear you naysayers make it worse. I want everyone out of this tent, now!" she commanded.

No one moved. They just stood watching her, as she held her face in her hands. She looked up briefly and seeing no one had listened she jumped from her chair and yelled, "NOW!" No one in the room disobeyed her this time, but instead hurried out of the tent as they were told.

Everyone, that is, but William.

"You too, Will," she said angrily.

"You might be able to cow them," her brother said, nodding towards the tent opening, "but I'm a different creature all together."

"This isn't a joke, Will," she said softly. "I don't think I can save him," she said, as the tears began to stream down her face.

"Of course you can," William replied, gently lifting her chin so she could look into his eyes. "Chloe, you have allowed a darkness into you. It's time to expel it from your mind, and be free from its grasp."

"I'm glad you're here big brother," she said smiling through her tears. "I don't think I could do this without you."

"Well then, let's get to work," he said, pulling off his coat and rolling up the sleeves of his shirt. "What do you need of me?" he asked.

"Your spirit," she said. "His body isn't broken too badly, but he's so weak that he can't fight to hold on. Between the transport spell I cast to hurry you to us, and fighting Neamith's Death Spell, I'm too spent to give him mine."

"What do I do?" he said, calm and serious. He knew that his sister needed him to be in control at the moment and so, doing as he always did, he acted.

"Sit in the chair. You will be very weak once this is done. So much so, you might sleep for a day or more. But you're strong big brother; you'll be fine," she assured him.

"With my life in your hands," he said with a smile, "it was never a question."

He quickly grabbed a chair and moving it next to Chloe, he sat down preparing himself. The Andrayan princess touched his chest, above his heart and that of Austin's and began to chant quietly. What she was attempting was very dangerous and in her weakened state she knew she could make a mistake costing both of the men she loved their lives. But she focused with all her might and acting as a vassal, she gently funneled Williams' life force from him into Austin, giving him the strength to fight on.

Will felt his head begin to tingle, and soon his eyes grew heavy, as if he was so tired he couldn't keep them open. But fighting the urge to sleep, he focused on Chloe, giving her all of his attention in case she needed him.

After several minutes, Chloe began to stop singing and falling back in her chair she let her hands fall to her lap, limply.

"It's done," she said with a croaking voice. "How are you big brother?"

"I'm fine," he replied, nearly sliding out of the chair with fatigue. "But I am so exhausted I don't know if I can get up."

"Then don't," Chloe said. "Just sit and regain your strength." She then smiled at him.

"What?" he asked weakly, returning the smile.

"Thank you, William," she said quietly.

"Anything for you little sister," he replied, and closing his eyes he fell asleep.

Chapter 44

In the Age of King Austin Ironfist the First

When Austin finally awoke it was dark out. Taking a moment, he realized that he was laying on a table in his tent, but when he tried to move, he found that he was bound to it. The Half Dwarf nearly panicked, until he noticed that William and Chloe sat at his side, both sleeping in chairs.

The tent was lit by lamps all around the room, and when he looked out the door he saw two knights. One bore the armor of an Andrayan Royal Guard, while the other wore the armor of an Eland Grand Knight. Realizing that William and Chloe wouldn't be captured, and still had one of William's personal guards at the door, he relaxed and lay still on the table.

He tried to make sense of everything that had happened over the last several months. He had declared war on behalf of his people, against a man he hated all through their childhood. He found his family in Nord Byen and in Verengrath. He fought an angel and won, twice. He stood in the presence of the Almighty Creator. He freed two elementals from a magic labyrinth and fought the war that started it all.

But none of it was as important as realizing that he had fallen in love with the half Elf at his side. He desperately wanted to go to her, but still, his bonds wouldn't allow him to move.

He must have made a noise, trying to get free because when he looked up, he noticed Chloe stirring. Soon her eyes opened, and when she saw him looking at her, she smiled at him, weakly, but lovingly.

She then got to her feet, and coming to his side, she gently stroked his hair. "You gave us quite a scare," she said with a smile.

"It must have been a heck of a problem, considering I'm tied down," he said grinning at her.

"Your ribs are badly broken," she explained. "This is to keep you from moving around."

"How long do I have to be like this?" he asked.

"A couple of days at least," she replied, still stroking his hair.

"Isn't that just wonderful," he said, gently shaking his head.

"It could be worse," she said with a grin.

"Oh, how?" he asked with a frown.

"You could be up and about, slicing open your innards as you walked from all the bone shards in your chest," she said, cocking an eyebrow.

"Hmm," he said quietly, "you sure know how to make a guy appreciate what he's got." He chuckled and then groaned in pain.

"It'll pass my love," she smiled at him.

"Your love?" he said quietly.

"I've loved you for years, Austin," she said gently. "I simply didn't know how to tell you."

"What told you now was the time?" he asked.

"You passed through hell to save me," she replied. "I figured now was as good a time as any."

"Good call," he said, grinning at her. "I love you too, Chloe. I've known since the Labyrinth. I was so caught up in my own affairs that I never paid you enough attention, but when you suffered your own worst fears to stand at my side, I knew I loved you.

"I truly didn't mean anything by that joke about marrying the Princess. I'm sorry if it hurt you," he said, gazing up at her.

"I know Austin. I'm not sure why it bothered me. I knew you weren't serious, but the thought of another woman having you just hurt me deep inside," she said, lowering her eyes.

"Well," he said, trying to catch her attention, "I want no other woman, Chloe. I want you in my life forever."

"And I want you to be in mine," she replied, bending down and kissing him gently. "But, you have to rest, and to be honest so do I," she said.

"Yes, I was wondering why the two of you looked so out of it. And why hasn't Will moved since we started speaking?" he asked, concerned.

"He's going to need a lot of rest. You were too weak to keep your body alive. So he gave you much of his energy, and some of his spirit to keep you going," she explained.

"He saved me?" Austin asked, a little taken aback.

"Yes, twice today," she said with a smile as she sat back in her chair.

"That's right. How did they get here just in time to save us, to save you?" Austin asked incredulously.

"I brought them," Chloe replied. "I have the ability to open gateways created by magic. When I saw that we were gravely overwhelmed, I simply opened a portal to wherever he was, to draw him here."

"But the army, how did you get them here?" the Half Dwarf asked.

“I don’t know,” she replied. “He must have sensed that we needed help and began to move. I never did anything to contact them, but I desperately wanted them to come. I knew with their help, you could overcome Kiamet and his troops.”

“I was a fool to turn his offer away,” Austin said with a sigh, “But he came anyway, and saved my people. We owe you Andrayans a debt of gratitude,” he said seriously.

“No Austin,” she said with a smile. “No, no debt. The Creator made us all equals, and we all deserve to be free. Free from corruption, free from intrusion into our lives, but most importantly, free to be who we were created to be. It is our job to see to it, that all around us are afforded the same rights.”

“Well, you and your countrymen have been the standard bearers of that ideal for a long time,” Austin said, looking up at the tent roof. “Now it is time for Elanders to pick up the standard and help carry it forward.”

“You will, my love,” she said with a smile. “But for now, sleep. Your body needs time to mend itself. We can discuss this more in the morning. And when I am strong enough, I’ll see what I can do to help hurry your healing along.”

He nodded his agreement and closing his eyes he nearly slipped back to sleep, when he said, “I love you, Chloe Duthain.” And hearing her gentle breathing at his side, fell asleep with her.

Several days passed with very little excitement. A couple of Kiamet’s men attempted to escape, but they were hunted down by the Dwarves who did little to ease their trip back again. Kiamet himself rarely shut up during the entire time. That is until Chief

Yorgund got tired of hearing his voice and tied a gag in his mouth. By and large everything was at peace.

It wasn't until the fourth day, when Austin could walk around again, that things began to get interesting. Etherion had returned as promised the very first night and delivered the decree from King Porthanaclies. Duke Wesset arrived with a large delegation of the aristocracy. He attempted to make a claim that he was the rightful heir to the throne, but one look at the letter from the King with his seal on it caused him to nearly choke on his own tongue.

To make matters worse for the Aristocracy, the King himself arrived with Matt to confirm the validity of the letter. And because he wasn't afraid of a coup, he stripped them of all their land and holdings, including that of his own nephew.

William too had a pleasant surprise. One day as he roamed the Andrayan/Elander camp he stumbled upon two familiar faces. The man and woman, whose cabin his forces passed on their march into Eland years ago, were a part of Austin's forces. They spent several hours that day and even ate together, telling stories and enjoying the renewed sense of hope that was taking root around them.

But finally, after a week had passed and Austin was able to move around with far fewer agonizing moments, plans for his coronation began. He attempted to remain calm, taking the poise of a general on the battlefield, but his fears began to mount. He had heard stories from William, how he got married on his coronation day, but that practice was not allowed in Eland. So he would have to face the day all on his own.

But he knew that even if he stood alone during the ceremony, he would never again be alone. His Grandfather, Ba'toth, had arrived, and Al'bet remained with their clan to help them. Lonny and Mary Ann were there with him at all times, as were his friends, Matt, Cason, Keira, Lyra and Artole.

He had never felt so full, as he did now, knowing all of these people were a part of his family. And now, on the day of his coronation, he knew they would all share in his joy at finally freeing their people.

He had discussed how to do it at length with William, and had a plan that he would implement over the next few months. He had discussed all of the details with Artole and Lyra, who had become his greatest advisors, and they assured him they would help him achieve their ultimate freedom.

But most of all, he had Chloe. She had never left his side, from the night she began healing him, and he knew he never wanted her to leave him. But he knew too, that she couldn't be cooped up in a city, and so it was that he was faced with a problem. As king, his place was in Lytton, the Eland capitol city. But he knew she would be miserable there. It was a problem he had no solution for.

His quiet moment was broken though, as the horns calling for him began to ring out. It was time to face his people. He stepped out of the tent that had been erected for this occasion and walked on a long red carpet, towards a large raised dais, where King Porthanaclies stood. He was surrounded by his friends and family on either side of the red carpet, who all smiled at him with pride.

Finally as he reached the dais, he stepped up two of the three steps and, following the command from his king, he knelt before him.

"High General Austin Ironfist," the king spoke loudly, "as the last king, born of the Porthanaclies line, it is my pleasure to stand before you today.

"Many kings come before you, young man. My family blood line has helped build this kingdom into the beacon of strength it has become. We worked hard with our subjects to move our people forward through time.

"But we were not the first royal line to rule in Eland. When the line of Benasear failed, the Porthanaclies family stepped up to rule and guide this land onward. And so it is that now, as the Porthanaclies line comes to an end, the line of Ironfist shall take its place.

"So with gladness in my heart, I pass this crown to you, my young friend," he said, as he took the crown from his own head and held it above Austin's. "Take up this mantle, a symbol of power in our kingdom, and rise." Taking his cue from his king Austin reached up and taking the crown guided it with the help of King Porthanaclies onto the top of his head. "As High King Austin Ironfist the first, rightful ruler of Eland!"

And as Austin rose, he exchanged smiles with the king, then turning he faced his subjects for the first time as king.

Austin waited for a moment to let the clapping and cheering around him to stop before he spoke. "My thanks to you, King Porthanaclies. The kingdom of Eland shall honor you, your daughter and your family for all you've done to guide us during the age of Porthanaclies," he said, bowing low. His action caused everyone in attendance to bow to their former king as a sign of respect.

"But it is a new day, and a new age for our people," Austin said turning back to those assembled. "It is time for change in our kingdom, a change that I promised all of you that I would make when I came to power. I will not break that promise. But change takes time, and we will not shift our people from the chaos of war, to the chaos of political confusion.

"Instead we shall transition Eland to the new government gradually over the next several months to a year," he explained. "To facilitate this change, our friends from Andraya have offered their experience and support. I would like to thank you, our Andrayan brethren for all your help in achieving this victory for our people. Your example shall lead us into that new life we Elanders wish to share with you.

"But I cannot accomplish the governance without the help of our own people," he said to everyone around him. "So I call upon Artole and Lyra Telaries, Cason and Keira Rolwaith and Matt Longblade." As he called their names they each stepped onto the dais and knelt before him.

"Matt, your valiant efforts on the battlefield have earned you the title of Trolls Bane," he said with a smile. "To you I give command of the new Eland Ranger Division. You shall mete out justice in the borderlands, protect our people from dangerous creatures and be the eyes and ears of the rulers of this kingdom. You shall be our protectors, hidden in clearest sight, with the solemn duty to uphold justice for our people. Do you accept this commission?"

"I do, my king," Matt said bowing low. Then whispering, "You finally found a way to conscript me, didn't you?" causing Austin to nearly break out laughing.

Composing himself he continued, "Cason and Keira Rolwaith. From the quarries of Andraya, to the plains of Tumare, you fought at my side. I make you both joint High Generals of the Eland army. May you guide our troops wisely, to protect our people and to ensure we are always prepared to defend ourselves. Do you accept this commission?"

"I do, milord," Cason replied.

"As do I, my king," Keira replied after.

"Artole and Lyra Telaries," Austin said moving before the couple still kneeling before him. "Rise my friends," he said, causing them to come to their feet. "Lyra, you are the one who started this journey for all of us. Artole, you have been my most loyal commander. When I was unable to see to our people after the battle you took command and ensured that all of our people were taken care of. I hereby make you the First Family of Eland. Artole, I ask that you retire from the field and that you and Lyra take residence in the palace with the rulers of the day. I ask that you take on the position of Prime Minister Artole, to act as Eland's council in ruling. May you and Lyra always have Eland's best at heart to ensure that no one man can ever lead her astray in the future. Do you accept this commission?"

Artole looked over at his wife at his side who nodded her agreement. "We accept, milord," Artole said proudly.

"You have my thanks, my friends, and the thanks of all Elanders for your service to our future," he said with a smile, and signaling them to step back he turned back to those assembled.

"King Al'bet of Verengrath, would you please join me?" he asked, looking at his uncle standing in the front row. The Dwarven king walked forward and stood straight and proud before his nephew. "King Al'bet, I believe it is time that the people of the Kingdom of Verengrath had a more open relationship with the people of Eland. It is to this effect that I wish for you to send a delegate to take up residence in the capitol city of Lytton, to act as the voice of the Dwarven Royal Council. Let us open trade between our people and usher in a new age of prosperity for all of us."

"I would be honored to take your request to my peers on the council, and to do our part in making that prosperity a reality," Al'bet said with a nod. Then stepping back he took his place next to his brother, Ba'toth once again.

"Finally," Austin called out, "I would respectfully ask that Chief Yorgund of the Polar tribe please come forward."

The large chief stepped away from the other chiefs that had come to the coronation at Austin's request, as thanks for their support with Kiamet and his men.

"Chief Yorgund, for far too long our people have been at war. I humbly ask that we set the old grievances aside and we work to better both Elander and Northerner lives alike. Instead of raiding our villages, let us trade with each other. Bring to us skins and other rarities of the North.

"Let us work together, rather than constantly being at each other's throats. Let us talk to our neighbors, the Andrayans, and open trade between you both as well. It's time that peace finds its way between all our peoples. Would you consider this offer?" he asked, holding his hand out to the man before him.

"I would have to speak to the other chiefs, but I believe it is time for a change in how we deal with you Southerners. I agree to try, King Ironfist," Chief Yorgund replied and, clasping Austin's forearm, the two men shook. The chief then stepped down from the dais and returned to his people.

"Ladies and gentlemen of Eland, the war is over. Let a time of peace settle amongst our people." Smiling, he then reached out for Chloe, who came to his side. "And when I take a queen, let us celebrate a new age in Eland. Let us celebrate a freedom hard fought, and dearly paid for. Let us celebrate our perseverance. But most importantly, let us celebrate our future!" And with that a loud cheer rose up from everyone, Elander or friend alike.

Everyone assembled could sense something new in the air. It was a time for change, but most importantly, it was finally a time for peace.

The End

Appendix

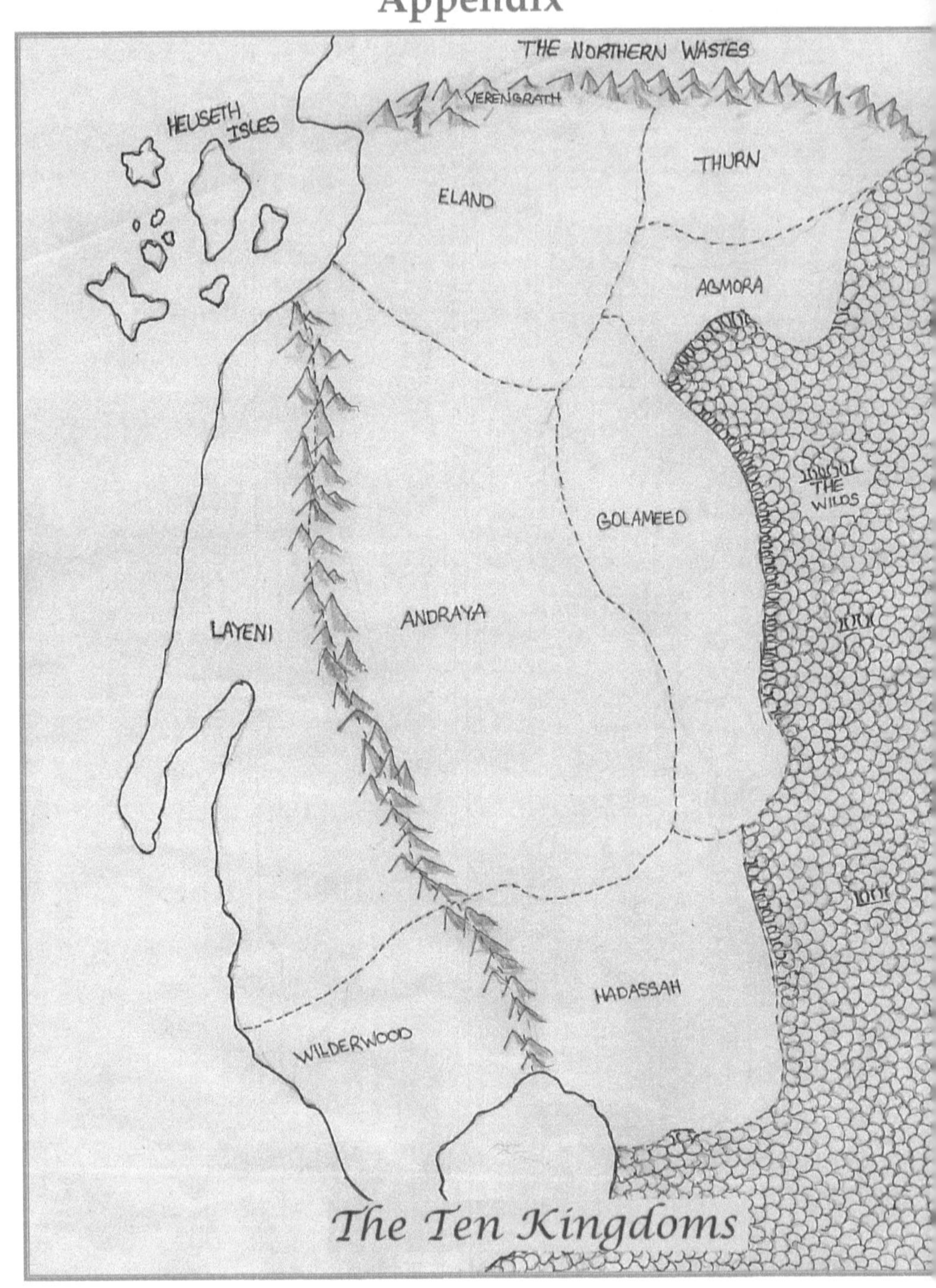

The Ten Kingdoms

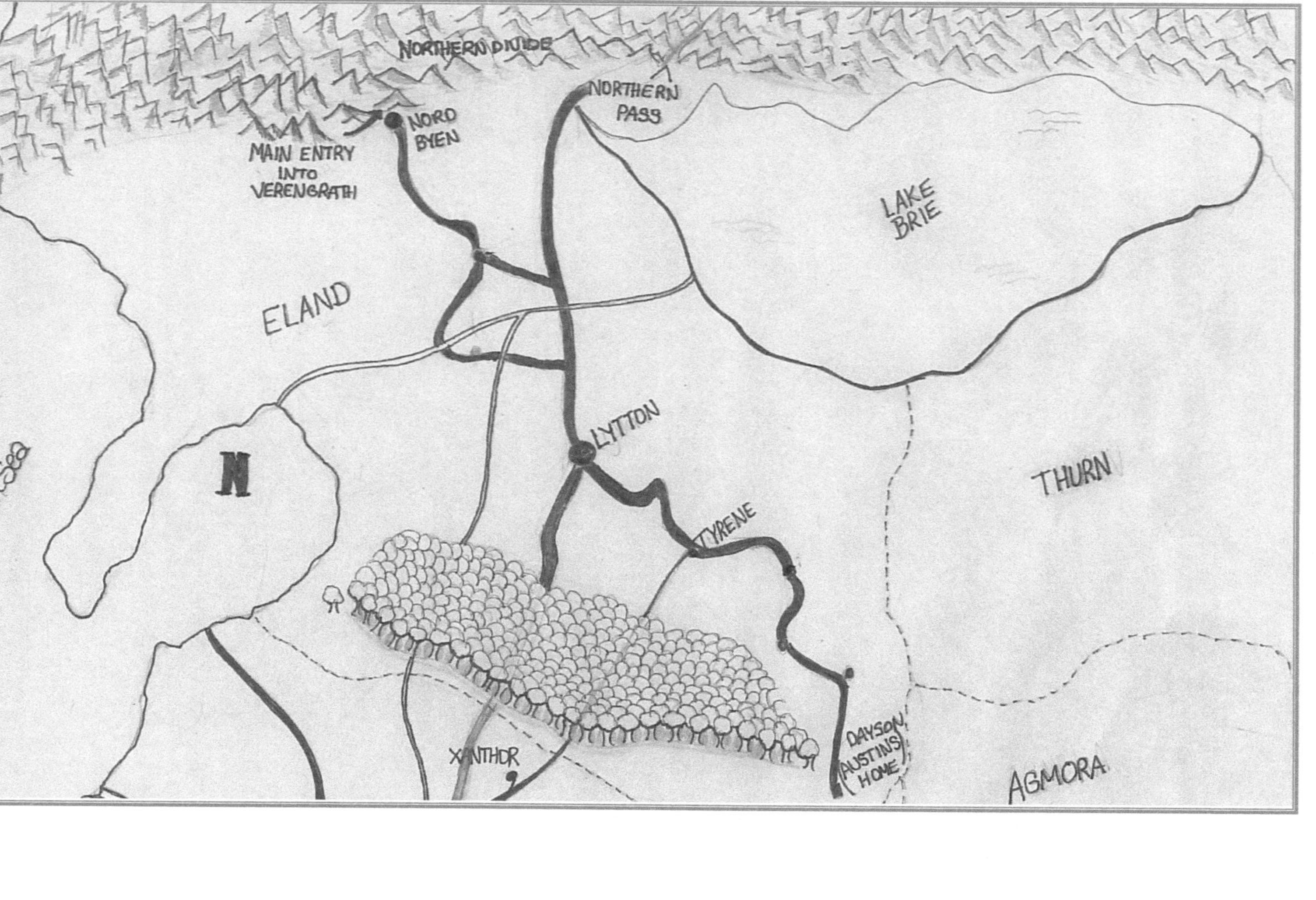
NORTHERN DIVIDE
NORTHERN PASS
NORD BYEN
MAIN ENTRY INTO VERENGRATH
LAKE BRIE
ELAND
LYTTON
N
THURN
TYRENE
XANTHOR
DAYSON AUSTIN'S HOME
AGMORA

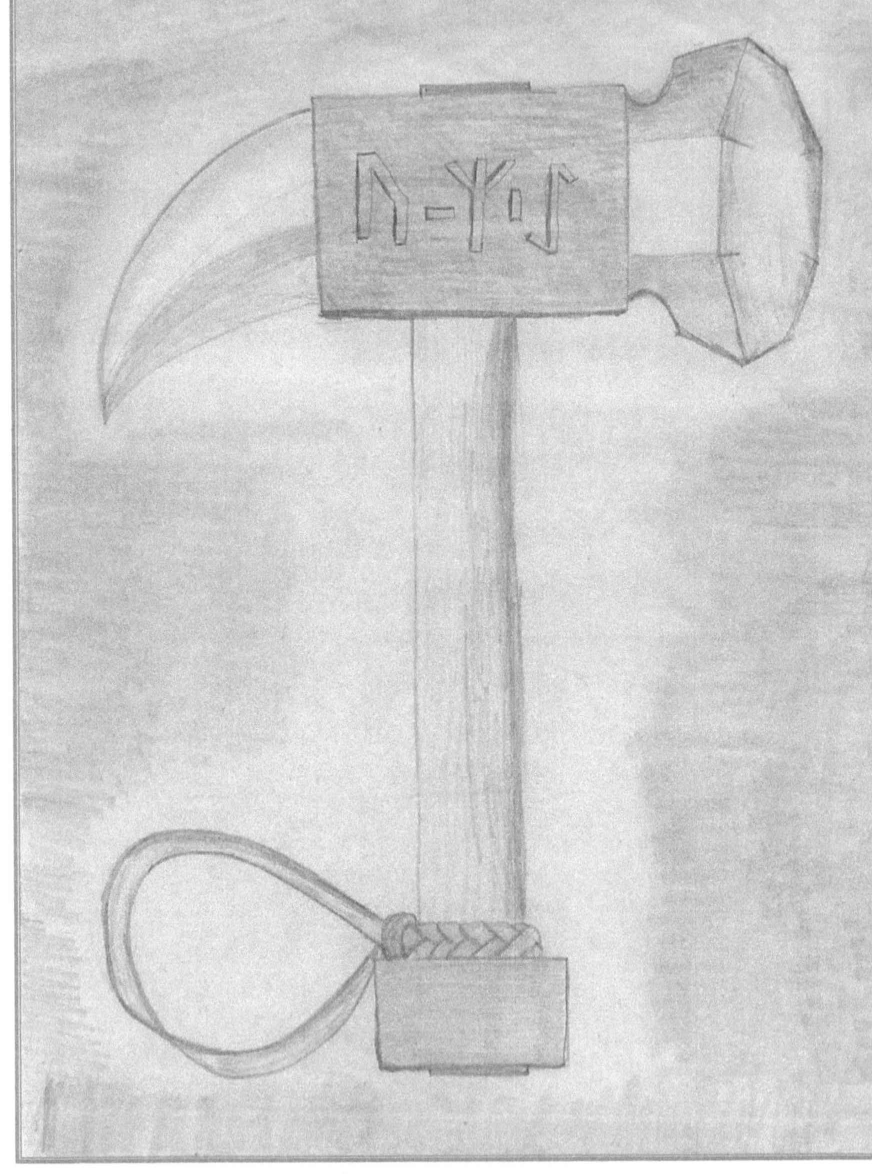
Eksils Torden

Character List

The Ironfist Family

- **Austin Ironfist –** High General of the Eland Army, leader of one of the factions vying for the throne of Eland during the age of the Eland Civil War
- **Ba'rel Ironfirst –** Dwarven Father of Austin Ironfist, son of King Ba'toth Ironfist, creator of the Natal
- **Cassidy Ironfist –** Human Mother of Austin Ironfist, owner of the Wounded Hand pub in Nord Byen
- **Ba'toth Ironfist –** Ba'rel's father, First King of Verengrath and ruler of the Emerald Throne during the age of Emperor Hou'tung
- **Ba'lain Ironfist –** Ba'rel's younger brother, ruler of the Sapphire Throne during the age of Emperor Di'an
- **Al'bet Ironfist –** Verengrath General, Ba'toth's younger brother, First King of Verengrath and ruler of the Emerald Throne during the age of Emperor Di'an, hero of the Path of Fire

The Dwarven Kingdom

- **Le'Stal Strongarm –** Ba'rel's best friend.
- **Emperor Di'an –** Emperor of Verengrath, ruler of the Jeweled Thron, chief of the Gold Clan
- **King Mar'kal –** First King of Verengrath, ruler of the Emerald Throne, chief of the Iron Clan
- **King Shar'tal –** Dwarven king of the Ruby Throne, chief of the Copper Clan
- **King La'met –** Dwarven king of the Diamond Throne, chief of the Silver Clan.

- **Mar'di Strongarm –** Le'stal's younger sister
- **Li'sa Sureswing –** Mar'di's best friend and cousin of the Ironfist family
- **Ro'tan Sureswing –** General of Verengrath

Members of the Andrayan Royal Court

- **Chloe Duthain –** Princess of Andraya, leader of the Andrayan Rangers, hero of the Path of Fire
- **William Duthain –** King of Andraya
- **Declan –** General of the Andrayan Troops, Williams cousin
- **Brody –** Prime Minister of Andraya, Williams best friend

Austin's Comrades

- **Artole Telaries –** Commander of Austin's armies
- **Lyra Telaries –** Artoles wife and commander of Austins armies
- **Keira Rolwaith –** Commander in Austin's army, twin sister of Cason Rolwaith, assassin and spy
- **Cason Rolwaith –** Commander in Austin's army, twin brother of Keira Rolwaith, master of defense
- **Matthew Longblade –** Commander in Austin's army, thief turned spy
- **Lonny Robison –** Austin's adoptive grandfather, master smith, blacksmith of the village of Dayson.
- **Mary Ann Robison –** Austin's adoptive grandmother
- **Kierra Berenhom –** Cassidy's younger sister

The Ancients

- **Etherion –** Archatect and guide within the Path of Fire, a Wind Walker

- **Graltor –** Controller of the labyrinth within the Path of Fire, a Fire Lord
- **Fire Lords –** Fire elementals
- **Water Sages –** Water elementals
- **Wind Walkers –** Air elementals
- **Rock Titans –** Earth elementals
- **Zenatha –** Silver dragon within the Path of Fire
- **Forthozan the Fallen –** A fallen Arch Angel who was tasked with being the Keeper of Knowledge, creator and holder of the Qua,drac amulet, the storage receptacle for all accumulated knowledge
- **Garatories the Fallen –** A fallen Angel of the Host, Forthozan's middle brother, who was tasked with being the Keeper of Time, creator and holder of the Harkrin the Staff of Time, which controls the flow of time
- **Unisorin the Fallen –** A fallen Angel of the Host, Forthozan's youngest brother, who was tasked with being the Keeper of Energy, creator and holder of the Esrit the Mace of Energy, which controls the flow of energy throughout the Universe

About the Author:

Growing up in rural Manitoba, Cameron's love of nature comes to the fore in a genre rich with life, hard work and a commitment to ones community. After being introduced to the genre of fantasy as a boy, his passion for reading quickly became one of writing.

The feeling of wonder and freedom that came from creating people, places and events of his own imagination quickly took seed in his heart. After years of planning and shaping he succeeded. Welcome to a Kingdom where community, justice and a desire for peace exist. Welcome to Andraya.

www.ingramcontent.com/pod-product-compliance
Lightning Source LLC
Chambersburg PA
CBHW030820310726
48980CB00006B/571/J